D0435716

Praise for the Dragonfire Novels

Whisper Kiss

"Terrific. . . . The author has Cooked another winner with the tattoo artist and the dragon shape-shifter." —The Best Reviews

"Bursting with emotions, passion . . . don't miss this sizzling addition to Deborah Cooke's Dragonfire series—it is marvelous!"
—Romance Junkies

"The sparks really fly." —The Romance Readers Connection

"Cooke introduces her most unconventional and inspiring heroine to date. . . . The sparks are instantaneous. . . . Cooke aces another one!"
—*Romantic Times* (4½ stars)

Winter Kiss

"A beautiful and emotionally gripping fourth novel, *Winter Kiss* is compelling and will keep readers riveted in their seats and breathing a happy sigh at the love shared between Delaney and Ginger. . . . Sizzling-hot love scenes and explosive emotions make *Winter Kiss* a must read!" —Romance Junkies

"A terrific novel!" —Romance Reviews Today

"All the *Pyr* and their mates from the previous three books in this exciting series are included in this final confrontation with Magnus and his evil Dragon's Blood Elixir. It's another stellar addition to this dynamic paranormal saga with the promise of more to come."
—Fresh Fiction

continued . . .

"Combustible . . . extremely fascinating. . . . Deborah Cooke has only touched the surface about these wonderful men called the *Pyr* and their battle with the evil dragons. . . . I am dying for more."

—Romance Junkies

Kiss of Fire

"Cooke, aka bestseller Claire Delacroix, dips into the paranormal realm with her sizzling new Dragonfire series. With a self-described loner as a hero, this heroine has to adjust to her new role in the supernatural and establish bonds of trust. Efficient plotting moves the story at a brisk pace and paves the way for more exciting battles to come." —*Romantic Times*

"Wow, what an innovative and dazzling world Ms. Cooke has built with this new Dragonfire series. Her smooth and precise writing quickly draws the reader in and has you believing it could almost be real. . . . I can't wait for the next two books." —Fresh Fiction

"Deborah Cooke has definitely made me a fan. I am now lying in wait for the second book in this extremely exciting series."

—Romance Junkies

"Paranormal fans with a soft spot for shape-shifting dragons will definitely enjoy *Kiss of Fire*, a story brimming with sexy heroes; evil villains threatening mayhem, death, and world domination; ancient prophecies; and an engaging love story. . . . An intriguing mythology and various unanswered plot threads set the stage for plenty more adventure to come in future Dragonfire stories." —BookLoons

THE DRAGONFIRE NOVELS

Kiss of Fire

Kiss of Fury

Kiss of Fate

Winter Kiss

Whisper Kiss

Darkfire Kiss

Flying Blind

THE
DRAGON
DIARIES

DEBORAH COOKE

NEW AMERICAN LIBRARY

NEW AMERICAN LIBRARY

Published by New American Library, a division of
Penguin Group (USA) Inc., 375 Hudson Street,
New York, New York 10014, USA
Penguin Group (Canada), 90 Eglinton Avenue East, Suite 700, Toronto,
Ontario M4P 2Y3, Canada (a division of Pearson Penguin Canada Inc.)
Penguin Books Ltd., 80 Strand, London WC2R 0RL, England
Penguin Ireland, 25 St. Stephen's Green, Dublin 2,
Ireland (a division of Penguin Books Ltd.)
Penguin Group (Australia), 250 Camberwell Road, Camberwell, Victoria 3124,
Australia (a division of Pearson Australia Group Pty. Ltd.)
Penguin Books India Pvt. Ltd., 11 Community Centre, Panchsheel Park,
New Delhi - 110 017, India
Penguin Group (NZ), 67 Apollo Drive, Rosedale, Auckland 0632,
New Zealand (a division of Pearson New Zealand Ltd.)
Penguin Books (South Africa) (Pty.) Ltd., 24 Sturdee Avenue,
Rosebank, Johannesburg 2196, South Africa

Penguin Books Ltd., Registered Offices:
80 Strand, London WC2R 0RL, England

First published by New American Library,
a division of Penguin Group (USA) Inc.

First Printing, June 2011
10 9 8 7 6 5 4 3 2 1

 REGISTERED TRADEMARK—MARCA REGISTRADA

LIBRARY OF CONGRESS CATALOGING-IN-PUBLICATION DATA:

Cooke, Deborah.
  Flying blind/Deborah Cooke.
  p. cm.—(The dragon diaries; 1)
  ISBN 978-0-451-23388-2
  1. Supernatural—Fiction. 2. Dragons—Fiction. 3. Fantasy. I. Title.
  PZ7.C774347Fly 2011
  [Fic]—dc22   2011003177

Set in Janson
Designed by Catherine Leonardo

Printed in the United States of America

PUBLISHER'S NOTE
This is a work of fiction. Names, characters, places, and incidents either are the product of
the author's imagination or are used fictitiously, and any resemblance to actual persons,
living or dead, business establishments, events, or locales is entirely coincidental.
    The publisher does not have any control over and does not assume any responsibility for
author or third-party Web sites or their content.

For my readers,

particularly Debbie, DJ, Sam, Stephanie, and Anne,

whose enthusiasm is a constant source of inspiration.

Thank you all.

ACKNOWLEDGMENTS

I could not have written this book without the assistance of a great many people. Credit must go to Kerry Donovan, my editor, who loved the idea of this series from the outset and did the footwork to make it a reality; Dominick Abel, my agent, whose counsel and support are invaluable; Kara Welsh, Claire Zion, and the entire team at NAL, whose enthusiasm and attention to detail has made this journey a pleasure; Pam Trader, friend, writer, and technical wizard, who is always up for a glass of wine, a good talk, or both; Lisa Stone Hardt, friend and editor for hire, who took an early peek at the manuscript in-process—and whose keen insight left me wondering whether she knows more about dragon shape shifters than I do. Finally, credit goes to Kon, my husband, for everything he does.

Thank you all.

Flying Blind

Chapter 1

Thursday, April 4, 2024—Chicago

*T*here was a guy in my bedroom.

It was six in the morning and I didn't know him.

I'm not much of a morning person, but that woke me up fast. I sat up and stared, my back pressed against the wall, sure my eyes had to be deceiving me. No matter how much I blinked, though, he was still there.

He seemed to think my reaction was funny.

He had dark hair and dark eyes, and he wasn't wearing a shirt, just jeans—and he had one heck of a six-pack. His arms were folded across his chest and a smile tugged at the corner of his mouth.

But he seemed insubstantial. I could see through him, right to the crowded bulletin board behind him.

Was he real?

I was going to try asking him, but he abruptly faded—faded and disappeared right before my eyes.

As if he'd been just an illusion. I jumped from the bed, then reached into that corner. My fingers passed through a chill, one cold enough to give me goose bumps. Then my hand landed on a pushpin holding a wad of drawings, and everything was perfectly normal.

Except for the hairs standing up on the back of my neck.

I took a deep breath and looked around. My room was the pit it usually was. There were some snuffed candles on my desk and bookshelves, a whiff of incense lingering in the air, and the usual mess of discarded sweaters and books all over the floor.

No sign of that guy. If I hadn't seen him, if I'd woken up two minutes later, I wouldn't have thought anything was wrong at all.

I shuddered one last time and headed for the shower. Halfway there I wondered, had Meagan's plan worked?

The visioning session had been my best friend's idea. Her mom calls herself a holistic therapist, which makes my mom roll her eyes. I was skeptical, too, but didn't have any better ideas. And Meagan, being the best friend ever, had really pulled out all the stops. She'd brought candles and mantras and incense for my room, and even though I'd felt silly, I'd followed her earnest instructions.

When the candles had burned down and she'd left—and my mom had shouted that I should open a window—I'd been pretty sure it hadn't worked. Nothing seemed to have happened.

But now I didn't know what to think. Who had that guy been? Where had he come from? And where had he gone?

Or had I just imagined him? I thought that if I was going to imagine a guy in my bedroom, it wouldn't be one who thought I was funny when I wasn't trying to be, never mind one who kind of creeped me out.

I'd have imagined Nick there.

In fact, I frequently did.

I heard my mom in the kitchen and my dad getting the newspaper and knew I had to get moving. I did my daily check in the bathroom, but nada. No boobs. No blood.

Four more zits.

At its core, then, the visioning session had failed.

I'm probably not the only fifteen-and-a-half-year-old girl who'd like to get the Puberty Show on the road. Even Meagan got her period last year, which was why she was trying to help. But my best friend didn't know the half of it.

That was because of the Covenant. I couldn't confide in Meagan because I'd had to swear to abide by the Covenant of our kind. I come from a long line of dragon shape shifters—*Pyr*, we call ourselves—and we pledge to not reveal our abilities to humans on a whim.

That would include Meagan.

The Covenant goes like this:

> I, Zoë Sorensson, do solemnly pledge not to willfully reveal the truth of my shape-shifting abilities to humans. I understand that individuals may know me in dragon form or in human form, but I swear that I shall not permit humans to know me in both forms, or to allow them to witness my shifting between forms without appropriate assessment of risk. I understand also that there will be humans who come to know me in both forms over the course of my life—I pledge not to reveal myself without due consideration, to beguile those who inadvertently witness my abilities, and to supply the names of those humans whom I have entrusted with my truth to the leader of the *Pyr*, Erik Sorensson.

Do humans know we exist? Sure. Humans always have—thus the dragon stories they tell. But knowing dragons exist, believing that there are actually dragon shape shifters, and being convinced that your neighbor is one of them are entirely different things.

That's probably a good thing.

The Covenant came about pretty recently. During the Dragon's Tail Wars, some *Pyr* decided they wanted to be more active and visible. My dad, though, remembers when we were hunted almost to extinction. The Covenant is a compromise between putting it all out there and living in secret. So humans might see Sloane on the news, appearing at the scene of natural disasters to help—he's the tourmaline dragon—or Brandt, the orange dragon, making another daring rescue, but they don't know their names or where they live in their human lives.

We teenage *Pyr* had to pledge to the Covenant after Nick tried to impress the twin girls living next door, and his dad caught him.

I still thought it was funny that they hadn't been impressed.

I, in contrast, was awed by Nick in dragon form.

The fact is that most humans don't believe they could personally know a dragon shape shifter. Those twins thought Nick had pulled some kind of illusion to make himself look cooler than he was.

So, in a way, we might as well be a myth.

Which is funny, if you think about it.

The trick is that the dragon business is all theoretical when it comes to me. I'm the daughter of a dragon shape shifter, so I should also be a dragon shape shifter. Sounds simple, doesn't it? Except it's not happening. Nothing special has happened to me. I can't do it and I don't know why—much less what I can do to hurry things along.

Dragons are by nature patient. That's what my dad says. He should know, seeing as he is about twelve hundred years old. That's supposed to reassure me, but it doesn't.

Because dragons are also passionate and inclined to anger. I know that from spending my life around all those dragon shape shifters who are my extended family. And the fact that my dragon abilities were AWOL—despite my patience—was seriously pissing me off.

The *Pyr* are all guys—men and their sons—except for me. The story is that there's only one female dragon at a time, and that she's the Wyvern and has special powers.

Yours truly—I'm supposed to be the Wyvern.

The issue with there being only one female dragon shape shifter at a time is that the last one died before I was born. And it's not like anyone has her diary. Zero references for me. Zero advice.

Zero anything.

Just an expectation from my family and friends that I'll become the font of all dragonesque knowledge and lead the next generation to wherever the heck we're going.

Sooner would be better.

No pressure, right?

My dad says I was a prodigy, that I was already showing special powers before I could walk. Then I started to talk and all the Wyvern goodness went away. *Poof.* Instead of being special and a prodigy, I was just a normal kid.

I'm still waiting for the good stuff to come back.

No sign of it yet.

Some incremental progress would be encouraging. It's one thing to be a disappointment to everyone you care about, and quite another to just sit back and accept that inadequacy. In fact, I was starting to think that those dragons who believed I wasn't really the Wyvern might have it right.

Thus Meagan's session.

An act of desperation.

Because the one thing I did know was that the other dragon

teenagers like Nick had come into their powers with puberty. Their voices cracked and bingo, they were shifting shape like old pros. So being a late bloomer has bigger repercussions for me. Meagan thought we were doing the ritual for my period to start. She didn't need to know I was after a little bit more than that.

Instead I got a guy mocking me in my own bedroom at the crack of dawn.

Like I said, it wasn't the best way to start the day.

THE DISSOLVING GUY WAS at my school.

Still shirtless.

Still mightily amused by me.

He was leaning against the brick wall, away from groups of other kids, gaze locked on me as I walked up to the school. I could still almost see through him. I felt a blush rising from my toes. Would he talk to me here? Would he tell me what the deal was?

What exactly would be the best opening question to get him talking?

Meagan caught my shoulder and I jumped. "Well?" She pushed her new glasses up her nose, almost bouncing in excitement. "Did it work?"

I glanced over at the smug half-naked dude. "Who is that? Do you know?"

"Who? Mark Smith?" Meagan rolled her eyes. "Be serious, Zoë."

"No, the other guy. The one leaning on the wall."

She gave me a stern look. "There is no other guy, Zoë." She nudged me. "Come on, tell me. Any *results*?"

"Nothing." The guy waved at me, smirked for a moment, then sauntered away. He had to be freezing without a shirt on. It was even starting to snow lightly. I watched Meagan follow my gaze, scanning the schoolyard.

She couldn't see him.

Neither, apparently, could anyone else.

Bonus. I was delusional as well as a failure and a disappointment. I'd lost my powers at the ripe age of two, and some thirteen and a half years later was losing my mind.

"Nothing?" She wrinkled her nose. "No change?"

"None."

She exhaled heavily and fell into step beside me. "Not even a cramp?"

"New pimples. Does that count?"

"It could." Meagan bumped my arm and whispered, "Did you have any dreams, at least?"

It was on the tip of my tongue. I wanted to tell her about the guy, and I would have, if she hadn't been unable to see him. When you're going crazy, I think it's better to keep the news to yourself for as long as possible.

"Nope." I shrugged and smiled.

I felt like seven kinds of a rat for lying to my best friend.

"I really thought it would work," Meagan said, so disappointed that the whole session might have been for her benefit. "Maybe we should try again."

I could do without more strangers showing up in my bedroom while I was asleep. "Maybe it just takes time." I smiled. "See you in gym?"

Meagan groaned. "Highlight of my day." She rummaged in her backpack and nearly spilled textbooks all over the floor. "Hey, draw me a dragon on my new notebook?"

Now she was trying to cheer *me* up. "Sure. Any preferences?"

"Whatever you want. Surprise me."

I took the book and tucked it in with mine. "Don't scare them with your brilliance in math class."

Meagan laughed, flashing a mouthful of hardware. She was good at math. Truly genius. Meagan's destiny was in the realm of the brainiacs.

Mine? Apparently in the land of liars and losers.

I was thinking that my day couldn't get any worse.

I HATE GYM CLASS. Nothing like ending the day with a reminder of your inadequacies. The only good thing about having it last period is that I can skulk home after the ritual humiliation. That day, I wanted to be anywhere else in the world, but cutting class isn't really an option for me.

My dad isn't just a dragon shape shifter and leader of the *Pyr.* He also has the talent of foresight. If you think your dad always guesses when you're going to do something wrong, imagine if he really did *know* it. It's not an accident that I'm a Goody Two-shoes, solid-B-student, color-within-the-lines kinda chick: I've got a dragon watching over my shoulder.

I changed and followed the others to the gymnasium, even less motivated than usual. Then I froze in shock. That guy was lounging in the bleachers.

Watching me.

He gave me a salute with two of his fingers and seemed amused.

Once again, no one else seemed to notice him. Those abs should have distracted every female in the class, even Coach O'Connor, but they were all oblivious to his presence.

"*Unktehila,*" he whispered, and I heard it clear across the gym. I had no idea what that meant, but no one else even heard him. I turned to stare at him and he grinned.

Then the basketball hit me in the shoulder.

And I remembered: not getting injured in gym—or doing injury to anyone else—requires all of my concentration.

Suzanne taunted me and I focused on the game. I'm tall, but being tall is not an advantage in basketball when you're a complete klutz. Artistic skill gets you nada on the court. Basketball is for the coordinated girls.

Like Suzanne.

Suzanne scored a three-pointer immediately. We had ended up on the same team, her and me and Meagan. Suzanne complained about having to carry the whole team, getting louder when Coach O'Connor wasn't looking.

(I suspect, actually, that O'Connor looks away on purpose.)

I was thinking Meagan and I would just mark time, get out of there relatively unscathed, if humiliated.

As usual.

But when the seconds were counting down, Meagan actually caught the ball.

Meagan would prefer to *never* get the ball. We're in sync on that. This time, though, it was passed to her so hard that she couldn't help but catch it.

And then she didn't know what to do with it.

That would be the hazard of never having caught the ball before. The fact that our side was behind by two points and the game was in the final minute didn't help.

I knew it would go badly. I saw Meagan's shock change to terror. I saw her hands shake, and if she had tried to say anything, she would have stammered. That's what always happens when the focus of attention is on her.

Unless she's calculating a hypotenuse or the area of an ellipse, right in her head. She is a human computer.

"Shoot already!" Suzanne shouted.

The second hand swept past the six.

Meagan's lips set and I knew she was going to try. Okay. I was with her. I managed to block one guard, Anna. Meagan defended her possession of the ball from another guard; then she eyed the net.

Calculating. I dared to hope geometry could help. Something had to go right on this day.

Meagan stepped back, her form perfect, and threw. The ball

sailed through the air. Perfect! My heart pounded. The trajectory looked good.

Really good.

Oh, my God. We all stared.

The ball sank toward the net and I crossed my fingers. I heard Meagan catch her breath. O'Connor lifted her whistle to her lips.

The ball bounced off the backboard not six inches above the net, rebounded, and missed.

The whistle blew as our entire team groaned in unison.

Game over.

I hazarded a glance at the bleachers but the mystery guy was gone.

Just as well.

"Twenty-eight to twenty-six for Team Blue," O'Connor shouted. "Good game, girls! Five minutes to shower."

"Nice try," Fiona said to Meagan, and Meagan had time to blush a bit before Suzanne turned on her with a snarl.

I knew we had big trouble on our hands.

I HATE THE SHOWERS ALMOST as much as gym class itself, but Suzanne's expression had me dreading it. Everyone crams into the tiled space together, checking one another out, comparing bra cup sizes. That's bad enough without the most popular girl in our class looking to get even. Meagan and I stuck together instinctively.

"Gonna need a bra anytime soon, Sorensson?" Trish sneered at me when I pulled off my shirt.

"At least mine won't be sagging before I'm thirty." Like I knew anything about it. My mom gave me that comeback. She's a teacher and knows how girls are.

"Hurry up, girls." O'Connor made her ritual stroll past the shower area.

"Jameson will be blind by the time she's thirty," Suzanne mocked.

It was a cue and I saw it too late.

"She's blind now." Yvonne, one of Suzanne's pack of cool friends, snatched Meagan's glasses off her face.

"Hey!" Meagan protested.

She was defenseless and we all knew it.

Yvonne tossed the glasses across the shower room to Suzanne, who put them on and made a face. The lenses made her eyes look small and beady. "Seriously defective eyeballs." She pulled off the glasses, then tossed them into the air. "Oops!"

Suzanne snatched them out of the air in the nick of time, laughing. Her followers gathered closer, Yvonne and Anna and Trish. All the other girls stepped back, avoiding the confrontation as they showered quickly and disappeared.

Meagan had found the wall and was feeling her way toward Suzanne with a determination I'd seen before. "Give me my g-g-g-glasses back, please."

"G-g-g-glasses," Trish mimicked. That made me mad. It wasn't as if they were perfect.

"Puh-leeeeeeeeeeese," Yvonne said.

"Or what?" Suzanne taunted. She leaned closer to Meagan. "Whatcha going to do to me, Four Eyes? You can't even find me." She backed away suddenly as Meagan snatched in the direction of her voice, and they all giggled when Meagan missed. Meagan flushed but she kept after Suzanne.

"Give them back to her," I said, knowing they'd turn on me.

They did. "You gonna make me, Sorensson?" Suzanne spun the glasses by the ear wire as she taunted me. She pivoted to face me, bouncing a bit on the balls of her feet.

Ready to fight.

Confident that she could win. But she wasn't bargaining on my anger. I was mad enough to take her dare.

Maybe mad enough to win.

"You can only win if you don't fight fair," I challenged, and saw her surprise. "Give her the glasses."

"So, you want to fight, Sorensson?" Suzanne took a step toward me. Her team laughed and circled behind me.

Meagan took advantage of their distraction. She lunged for Suzanne, but Trish body-checked her. Meagan slipped on the wet tiles. She slammed her back into the wall and caught her breath, blinking rapidly. I knew that had hurt.

They laughed.

And I saw red.

A shimmering heat began to boil inside of me, feeding on my anger and becoming stronger. I knew what it was, what it had to be, even though I'd never felt it before.

If I'd been thinking, I would have shoved it back in its jar.

I wasn't thinking: I was mad.

"As if *you* could take me," Suzanne whispered to me. Her eyes were dancing. She was so sure she'd win.

For once, I didn't step back. For once, I didn't back away. For once, I was ready to challenge expectations.

The red tide of fury seethed, and I let it.

"Maybe I *will* take you." I took a step closer, noting how her gaze flicked. I had a new sense of power. Dangerous power. "Maybe you'll be surprised."

"Oh, I'm so scared!" Suzanne said in a falsetto, and her team giggled.

"Leave it, Zoë." Meagan had the resolve that got her perfect scores on math tests every time. "I'll g-g-g-get them myself."

Suzanne pitched her voice higher. "Oh, so brave! Come on and g-g-g-get your glasses *all by yourself* then. Look! Here they are!" She waved them in front of Meagan, who lunged toward the shiny lure.

I knew what would happen right before it did.

"No!" I shouted, and snatched for Meagan. Yvonne was faster. Trish blocked me with an elbow in my ribs. Yvonne hooked Meagan's ankle with one foot, jerking it hard. Meagan fell quickly, cracking her jaw on the tile floor.

She didn't move.

And there was blood running toward the drain.

I was right there beside her, on my hands and knees.

"All those expensive toothies getting smashed," Suzanne said in her fake baby talk. "But I thought she was the smart one."

"Meagan?" I put my hand on her shoulder. I felt her shaking.

"I'm okay," she whispered, but I knew better.

She wasn't okay.

And it was Suzanne's fault.

I felt the strange crimson strength growing inside me. I knew it was my dragon finally awakening, but I didn't imagine for a moment that it would take shape.

And let's be honest—if I had, I wouldn't have cared.

"Better make your shot next time, Jameson," Suzanne hissed. "I don't *like* losing." She tossed Meagan's glasses carelessly toward her, probably hoping they'd break when they hit the tiles.

I snatched them out of the air, surprising both of us by how quickly I moved.

"Bitch!" I snarled. I had Suzanne cornered in a heartbeat, moving faster than I ever had before. It shocked both of us. I thought I was just finally mad enough, but soon learned different.

Because when I raised my hand to slap her, I saw that my thumbnail had become a talon.

A long, sharp white claw.

A dragon talon.

Holy frick. It's finally happening.

Suzanne turned as white as a ghost, her eyes wide and her pupils tiny as she backed away from me. She even hit her head on the tiled corner; she was that eager to put space between us.

"Your eye," she whispered. "What happened to your eye?"

I wished I had a mirror. I knew what she had to be seeing. Maybe Meagan's session hadn't been a bust after all. I didn't actually care. I smiled at Suzanne, awed by my own body's power, and she cringed.

Before *me*. Zitty Zoë.

This was the good stuff. Suzanne was hyperventilating, staring at me in horror. I felt powerful and huge, an avenger against bullies and bitches—for exactly four seconds.

"O'Connor," murmured one of Suzanne's friends, and they melted out of the shower like wraiths.

"Meagan slipped," Trish said with feigned concern, and O'Connor's footsteps became louder.

"What a klutz," Yvonne added as she headed to the dressing room.

That was when I realized what I'd done.

I'd broken the Covenant.

Uh-oh.

"Just what's going on here, girls?" O'Connor demanded from behind us. "Meagan! When are you going to be more careful?"

There was a flurry of activity, commands that Suzanne and I get dressed, first aid for Meagan, and bunches of fast lies from Suzanne's troop. O'Connor decided that I was wanted in the principal's office.

But Suzanne was freaked. She remained pale and she kept her distance from me. It would have been funny if I hadn't been so worried.

I wasn't afraid of the principal. Whatever happened in her office wouldn't be fun and it wouldn't be the truth, but I had bigger problems.

My dad, you see, is the one who created the Covenant. He's the one who made all the other dragon shifters swear to the Covenant.

And he was the one who enforced it.

That would be the Covenant that I had just broken, even though I should have known better.

Even though I *did* know better.

Actually, I had time to realize while waiting for the principal that I'd broken the Covenant twice: once by revealing myself, and the second time by not beguiling her into forgetting what she'd seen.

Oops.

I had bigger worries than what the principal might say.

Maybe the fact that I had let loose in defense of someone else, someone weaker, someone human, would persuade my dad to cut me some slack.

Or maybe not.

Chapter 2

My mom picked me up from the principal's office. Her face was expressionless, which was not a good sign.

"*Suspended.*" The word crossed her lips in a low hiss of fury, one that made me wonder whether I'd been afraid of the wrong parent.

I knew better than to argue my case.

My mom never drives well—it doesn't hold her interest enough—but that day we used up a good half dozen lives getting home. She cut off a tractor-trailer, went the wrong way on a one-way street, ran a crapload of red lights. I couldn't believe we made it home alive. Her knuckles were white on the steering wheel the whole time, and my nails were dug into the upholstery beneath my butt.

There was no way I was going to distract her with a plea for mercy.

She hit the fender on the wall when she parked the electric Toyota in the garage beside my dad's beloved Lamborghini, then got out of the car without saying anything. She slammed the door so hard that my teeth rattled. She headed for the entry to our building, not even stopping to look at the damage. She rattled her keys as she walked, as if she couldn't remember which one unlocked the door.

I'd never seen her this angry.

This was so not good.

I followed, trying not to attract attention to myself. It was admittedly a bit late for that.

My mom held open the door and glared at me.

"When did you learn?" she asked when I was right beside her.

I shrugged, startled by the question. "I didn't know I could. She was picking on Meagan and I just . . . reacted."

My mom wasn't buying it. "Bullshit." I froze and blinked— my mom never swears. None of us do. House rules. "Even if you never did it before, you had to know what you were feeling. You had to know what it was."

I couldn't hold her gaze. I wasn't going to make this worse by lying to my mom.

Because she was right.

"You chose to let it go," she added.

I stared at my shoes, no confession necessary. The worst part was that I knew I'd do it again, exactly the same.

No, the worst part was that I was still excited about it.

My dragon powers were *back*.

She knew it, too. I could tell by the way she sighed.

"Well, your father will be pleased, at least."

Really?

I might live to tell about this, after all. I glanced up in time to see her turn away in disgust.

"I thought it was my destiny," I dared to say.

My mom was impatient with the idea. "Well, you can't blame me for hoping that destiny might pass you by, that you might just be a normal teenager."

"But you're the one who studies stories. . . ."

"Not every story has to come true, Zoë." She pinched the bridge of her nose briefly, then shook her head. "Here's another one for you. You know all those medieval stories about Saint George conquering the dragon? Do you know why they were so popular?"

I shook my head, knowing she was going into lecture mode and that there was no escape until she was finished.

"Because the dragon was a metaphor. The story was about overcoming a challenge. There are some scholars who believe that paganism was the force being defeated by Christianity in those stories, but I think it was even simpler than that." She put her hand on my shoulder and her voice dropped low. "I think that in conquering the dragon, Saint George was overcoming his own base instincts."

"The dragon within," I murmured.

"Or the anger that feeds the dragon. You can react in anger, or you can think before you act. Everyone has that choice. There are just bigger repercussions for you now."

But my fingernail had shifted shape only because I'd been angry. Did she mean that I should ignore what I could do, or control it, for the greater good?

Locking my dragon in the closet sounded like a losing proposition to me. I liked the idea of becoming a dragon—and yes, maybe roasting people once in a while.

When they deserved it. I could compile an Incinerate Now list on the spot, with Suzanne in the number one ranking. What was not to love about the ability to mete out justice?

My mom squeezed my shoulder. "I thought it might be easier for you if your father was wrong."

I wasn't sure what to say to that.

"Homework, *now*. I don't care how much you have—you'll find more to do until your father has time to speak with you." Her eyes got that glint, the tough look of a woman who had survived as the partner of a dragon shape shifter for more than sixteen years, and her voice hardened. "Move."

I ran to my room.

Two disciplinary intervals down, one to go.

IF NOTHING ELSE, MY DAD knew how to pick his moment. You might think your parents know how to play mind games, but trust me: they've got nothing on my dad.

My dad made me sweat.

He left me to worry.

He gave me lots of time to imagine dire scenarios, each in glorious detail, each of which ended badly for yours truly. He has more patience than anyone I've ever known.

He's definitely got more patience than I do. I didn't dare pick up my pencils, even though it would have settled my nerves—drawing dragons clearly was not homework and would have only gotten me in more trouble.

But there's only so long that nineteenth-century English literature can hold my undivided attention. There's only so much I can read about the wind on the moors even on a good day, before my thoughts wander.

On this particular night, they wandered in several (very predictable) directions.

1. Could I shift without getting pissed off? I tried, in the privacy of my room, without success.
2. What color would I be in dragon form? Mine had been a nice pointy talon, but I was disappointed that it had been white. I mean, really, if you're going to be a dragon, what color would you want to be?

I'd always thought I'd be a flaming orange dragon, maybe with red and gold details. Like Smaug there, framed on my wall, immortalized by both J. R. R. and the Brothers Hildebrandt.

I could even go with black. Maybe a nice zingy lime green. My wardrobe is what my mom calls "oil on water," so any of those colors would work for me. Purple. Electric blue. Lime. One of ten zillion shades of gray.

My dad is an onyx and silver dragon, very impressive-looking. Big and dangerous. It works. Or Donovan—my friend Nick's dad—is the blue of lapis lazuli in his dragon form, with gold edging his scales.

Nick is a yellow so bright that it's as blinding as the sun. It turns to shades of gold on his back. Yum. It works for him.

But my talon had been so white that it was almost clear. I was pretty sure it hadn't even had any glittery bits in it.

I wanted more flash.

Nick's eyes went all amber and radiant when he shifted, for example. Very hot. Just thinking about them made another flame light inside me.

A different one.

3. I thought about Nick. This was a habit of mine. Not only had Nick razzed me since forever about my inability to shift, but he was *Nick*. All that almost-big-brother stuff went out the window when he'd gotten those broad shoulders, that deep voice, those hot amber eyes.

He's the guy I've always known, my best friend since forever, but now with way better packaging.

The other thing is that there's this story, one no one will really tell me, about Nick and the Wyvern having a destiny together. Now that it looked like I was actually going to be the Wyvern, I desperately wanted to see Nick and show him what I could do.

Maybe, just maybe, he'd stop acting like a big brother toward me when I was a real live dragon girl.

His *destined* dragon girl.

I switched to my history homework, but all the battles of the Civil War pretty much bled together in the face of such interesting questions. I didn't even care whether Meagan's visioning session had been the trigger, whether patience had finally won out, or who that shadowy guy was. Not having caught a glimpse of him for a few hours made it easier to forget him.

Everything had begun, and I couldn't regret a thing.

I just wanted more.

MY DAD ENSURED THAT THERE was enough time to get my homework done—the homework for this week and the next month—and I would have, if I hadn't been playing around.

As it was, I nearly jumped out of my skin when he finally confronted me.

Maybe because he challenged me in old-speak.

"*Why?*" he demanded, the single word cracking like a whip within my own thoughts. I sat up, halfway thinking it was my dragon again, and spun from my desk to face him.

He looked grim.

That was so not good.

So much for American history.

Maybe *I* was history.

My dad was leaning in the doorway of my room, arms folded across his chest. His eyes were vividly green—not a good sign— and he was shimmering blue a bit around the edges.

That's a warning sign. Dragon shape shifters on the cusp of change shimmer a bit. It's always a blue shimmer and I usually love how it looks. But I was thinking we'd have a more reasonable discussion if he stuck with human form. Things tend to get dramatic when anyone breathes fire.

I tried to think of something clever to say.

In old-speak.

Uh-huh.

It's spooky, old-speak. It throws me off my game. It's the way dragons have communicated for millennia. It's like human speech, but lower, slower, deeper, at a frequency well below the range of human hearing. Although technically it's just like any other speech—but lower—you feel it more than you hear it. It's guttural and primal, and when you've mastered it, like my dad has, you can merge your words with the thoughts of the person you're addressing. You can make your words sound like their thoughts.

Like he'd just done to me.

I hate old-speak.

And yes—big surprise—I'm terrible at it.

But it would have been rude—if not asking for major trouble—to not answer my father in kind. It's not that hard to believe that dragons have protocol, is it? And I could do without pissing him off even more.

He was plenty mad already.

"She was making fun of Meagan."

Probably the longest string of old-speak I'd ever uttered. No, it definitely was. It exhausted me.

My dad was impressed. He tried to hide it, and he was fast about that, but we are of a kind. Dragons are all superobservant. We hear things that humans don't, see things that humans don't.

Actually, I thought it was pretty cool that I'd noticed my dad's reaction.

The longer he stood and considered me, though, not moving, not blinking, the more I began to doubt myself—or how likely it was that I could persuade him to go easy on me. I had still broken the Covenant.

I didn't know how long he stood there, just thinking, before he unfolded himself and stepped into the room.

"How much did you reveal?"

"I don't know." I frowned, concentrated on forming the words. *"She said something about my eye."* I swallowed, feeling myself break a sweat from the effort. *"I saw my talon."*

He studied me. The room felt full of his presence, full of his strength and intensity, as if there weren't even room left to breathe. I realized the magnitude of my mistake.

And there was nowhere to run.

Big, big screwup, Zoë. Epic.

Would I live to tell about it?

Would I even have a chance to show Nick?

"Have you done it before?"

I shook my head.

"Since?"

I looked down, not wanting to admit that I'd been less than racked with guilt since being confined to barracks. I hadn't had any success, anyhow. I shook my head.

His old-speak slid into my mind again in a dare. *"Do it now."*

You'd better believe that I tried.

I threw everything into it, sensing that this could save the day. I tried to change just my nail, but no luck.

In fact, I couldn't find one speck of dragon awesomeness in my guts. Maybe my dragon had bailed on me—again.

I even tried to get pissed off to invoke the change.

Zip.

My dad gave me time. There was no pressure beyond his bright unblinking stare and his presence—okay, that wasn't an insignificant force, but he is my dad. I should be used to him.

He watched and he waited, and I'm sure he was aware of the sweat trickling down my back. He could probably smell my anxiety rising when my nail stubbornly stayed as it had been for fifteen and a half years.

Human.

My dad's hand landed on my shoulder, the contact making me jump. "You can't force it," he said softly, speaking aloud. "Remember the hurdles?"

Oh, I remembered. I'd been signed up for a track-and-field event in sixth grade. (You know that a gym event like that wouldn't have been my choice to join, and it wasn't. And my performance had been predictably pathetic.) I hadn't been able to jump the hurdles at first, even the low ones, instead always knocking them over. It had been mortifying, and yet more proof that I'd never, ever be an all-star.

"You said I was thinking about them too much," I said. "You told me to think about running and jumping, not about the hurdle."

"To look at the goal instead of the obstacle," he agreed.

I'd been able to do it about every third time after that, when I'd managed to follow his advice.

He crouched down beside me. "Within you, there's a trigger to the change. It's in some corner of your mind. You found it once in anger, and you will find it again. You can't force it, but you do need to learn how it feels to find the trigger and touch it—when you *aren't* angry."

"What happens if I try to change when I am?"

"No control." It was clear he disapproved of that.

My dad stretched out his hand and I saw the blue shimmer dance over his flesh. I watched it with awe.

And yearning.

"I know where to find this light," he said very quietly. "And when I need it, I summon it. I let it grow. I encourage and coax it." While he was saying this, the shimmer got brighter and brighter. "Until it claims me completely. I *choose* to invoke it. I choose when to let it run its full course. It doesn't run me."

"I saw red."

He smiled at me and tapped the tip of my nose with one fingertip. "It was running you. You have to change the balance of power so the shift is your choice."

"Otherwise I'll never be able to do it again?"

His intensity doubled. Maybe tripled. There are times when I catch glimpses of his dragon, even when he's in human form. This was one of them. "Otherwise, you won't have control of your abilities. You'll only be able to retaliate. You also won't be able to manage the timing, to ensure that you have the chance to hide your clothes."

I nodded, and proved that I'd done my dragon homework. "So no perceptive human can snatch them up and refuse to give them back to me unless I fulfill three wishes."

My dad smiled a very reptilian smile. "Three wishes would be the least of your worries. They might ask for more than that."

My dad, in case I haven't mentioned as much, is Mr. Super Logic. Sometimes he seems like an android, completely lacking in feelings. My mom says he actually feels too much, but keeps it all contained. I think she likes shaking that emotion loose, kind of like tickling the dragon's belly, but I understood his point. Acting in passion wasn't a good plan.

My mom had said pretty much the same thing, in a different way.

"What does your mom say about things worth having?"

"That they're worth working for?"

My dad smiled a little. I have to say that he didn't seem overly concerned about the whole thing, as if he wasn't taking me seriously.

Or maybe he knew something I didn't.

I would have asked him more but he was already turning away.

"I'll talk to Donovan tonight," he said.

I sat up, instantly intrigued by whatever my dad's plan might be. He kept his gaze averted, watching his own hand slide down the doorframe.

I felt a sudden certainty that he was going to announce something big. Huge. My heart skipped.

"I want you to go to boot camp this year, with the younger *Pyr*. The competition might be just what you need." My father spoke so quietly that I didn't dare shout with joy. "All I have to do is persuade your mother that I'm right."

He smiled, quick, conspiratorial.

And then he was gone.

I flung myself on my bed with a hoot of glee.

Boot camp! Yes!

BOOT CAMP IS AN ANNUAL competition for the younger *Pyr*, one week of trials and tests, with prizes. It's run by Donovan, who is huge on training, and so far only Garrett, Nick, and Liam had been allowed to go. It's top secret, although there's always a kick-ass prize.

In short, boot camp is gym to the thousandth degree.

It should have been my worst nightmare. The other dragon guys would eat my liver with their experience and power and just raw knowledge of their capabilities. I would lose on every conceivable level.

But I still bounced on the bed. I wanted to squeal, even though that's not my style. Because Nick would be there, and we would be forced to spend a whole week together, being dragons.

Wrestling, maybe. The prospect made me dizzy.

I would get to see Nick's fab new packaging up close and personal.

Maybe *really* personal.

I'd learn more about my abilities as Wyvern and my secret destiny with Nick. It was a score on every possible level, and I couldn't wait to go.

And that was when I realized something astonishing. I had broken the Covenant. Twice. I had ditched my usual Goody Two-shoes game plan, broken the rules, yet I *was being rewarded*.

Just as I'd always suspected, the return of my dragon powers was changing everything.

Chapter 3

I woke up suddenly in the middle of the night, as if someone had tapped me on the shoulder. It was cold in my room, colder than it should have been, and the hair was prickling on the back of my neck. I had the feeling that I wasn't alone.

You know who I was expecting to find watching me.

I rolled over, keeping my eyes squeezed shut, telling myself that I'd find everything just as it should be when I looked.

Except it wasn't.

The walls and floor of my bedroom were gone. Sort of. But if I squinted, I could still see them. I could see the framed posters of dragons—drawn by me and others—and my crowded bulletin board. The bare-chested guy wasn't there.

But there was a large tree. It grew where the doorway normally was, one big root snaking across the floor to disappear beneath my bed.

Plus I could see the sky through my ceiling—but it was filled with stars, as if I were far out in the country. It certainly wasn't the sky over Chicago, the stars dimmed by the ambient light of the city. That's what should have been on the other side of my ceiling.

But that wasn't even the weirdest bit.

The weirdest bit was the old woman sitting in the corner of my room—well, the corner of my room that looked more like it was under a huge tree. She was knitting.

The hairs on my neck had it right—I wasn't alone.

She didn't seem to be aware of me, so I had a good long look. She was more substantial than Buff Boy had been, which was a reassuring sign of sanity on my part. (All things being relative.) She was old, but not in a creepy way. Think Mrs. Claus. She had white curly hair and little round silver glasses. Her cheeks were rosy and her lips were pursed. She was soft and plump, as if she'd been sampling cookies she made daily from scratch.

She could have been the grandmother I'd never had.

My mom knits, but with my mom, knitting is an Olympic event. My mom knits with furious speed, needles and elbows flying. She's usually talking at the same time—no, lecturing—and she's not above making her point with, well, a needle point. She knits as if she's got something against the yarn. Or she's on a deadline.

This woman knit quietly. She was almost motionless, only her right index finger dancing back and forth, moving so fast that it was a blur. Like a hummingbird. Instead of the ferocious clack of steel on steel that accompanies my mom's knitting, Granny's knitting made only a faint clicking sound. Like the ticking of an old clock. She was knitting something white, something that seemed to grow faster even than she was knitting.

I was going to ask her a question—whether she was real, why she was in my bedroom, where the tree had come from, just how crazy a person had to be to have these kinds of visions—but no sooner had I opened my mouth than she shot me a look. There was something dangerous about her expression, something not quite as fluffy as the rest of her, and I shut up fast.

She smiled a bit. *Good choice.*

Then she held my gaze and shut her left eye.

She opened it again, then shut her right eye instead.

With both eyes open, she smiled at me again. She returned to her knitting, concentrating on it as if I weren't there. As if I were the imaginary friend. Ha.

Message received.

I shut my left eye and Granny disappeared. My room looked exactly as it usually did, right down to my dirty clothes that I'd tossed in the corner by the door the night before.

I opened my left eye and she was back. Sort of. She looked ghostly, as did the tree, and so did the walls of my room. I had the same dizzy sense of things overlaying each other in irrational ways.

I shut my right eye and Granny was as clear as could be. I was in the same place as her and the tree, and there was no sign of my room. I was lying in the snow, and when I looked back where the wall and window should be behind me, all I could see was endless tundra.

It was a bit spooky. I opened my right eye again and I could see both realities.

Of course I had to play with that. I shut my right eye over and over again, getting a good look at this snowy place. It was like a 3-D dream.

Was that what I should have done with the mystery dude? I wondered what I would have seen if I'd known to play the eye game.

It was almost—but not quite—enough for me to wish him back.

Meanwhile Granny kept knitting. Steadily. It—a blanket? a shawl?—spilled over her lap and piled around her feet like a snowdrift. It grew deeper and wider and it even glittered a little. That made me think of the diamonds that the sun picks out in the snow.

But it was April and there was no real snow left in Chicago. Just those flurries during the day.

The dream made no sense. I started to sit up, determined to talk to her, but she gave me that hard look again. It might not have stopped me, but she lifted one hand, dropping her knitting into her lap. The needles disappeared as if they'd fallen into deep snow.

She blew something off her palm toward me.

It looked like a stone, which made no sense. I caught it instinctively and closed my hand firmly around it—proof positive that this was a dream and not gym class.

An instant later, I was surrounded by swirling snowflakes. I couldn't see anything else—there had to be thousands of them, and they were huge. They landed on me and around me. I could have been inside one of those paperweights, the kind you shake to create a snowstorm.

I opened my hand to look at what I'd caught. It *was* a stone, maybe two inches across, irregularly shaped, and red. There was a circle on one side, etched into the surface, although the marks looked old. I wondered whether the circle was part of the natural shape of the stone.

When I turned the stone over, there was a symbol scratched into the other side. Like an *F*. Or a tree with two branches to the right. I ran my thumb over it: these cuts were ground deeply into the stone. Fresh and raw.

What did it mean?

I looked to Granny for more information, but she was gone, gone as surely as if she'd never been.

The snow was gone, too, and so was the tree.

No matter which eye I used to look around.

It was just my room, as messy as ever.

The weirdest thing was not that I went right back to sleep, but that I woke up with the red stone still in my hand.

Was I gathering Wyvern accessories? Nothing happened when I looked through one eye—the view didn't change at all—but I had the stone.

I decided to pack it for boot camp.

Just in case Granny had given it to me for a reason.

EVEN BETTER, WHEN I DID my routine bathroom check, there it was.

Yes! After I'd waited so long, it didn't seem to be real, but there was honest-to-goodness blood. Meagan's flaky visioning session was a success! I couldn't wait to tell her. I ran for my mom, who matter-of-factly pulled out supplies and set me up.

As if it were no big deal.

As if it weren't the beginning of *everything*. Boys. Bras. Dragon powers and destiny.

Not necessarily in that order.

"When do I get breasts?" I asked, cupping my hands where they should be. I was tired of looking like a tall twelve-year-old, with guys treating me as if I were a kid. A kid sister. I could imagine myself with torpedo boobs, Nick checking me out. . . .

She was amused. "Maybe never."

"No, seriously."

"No, seriously."

"When do I get Wyvern powers?"

My mom shrugged and gave me a hug. "Maybe I'm not in that much of a hurry for you to grow up," she whispered into my hair, then kissed me. Her eyes were all sparkly when she pulled away, as if she was going to cry.

But my mom pretty much never cries.

Even so, I gave her a hug back. "It's okay, Mom. I promise I won't get suspended again."

She smiled, although she still looked a bit sad. "No matter how big you get or what you learn to do, I still get to worry about you. Deal?"

"Deal."

I took a chance, since we were having this mushy chick moment of confidences. "Will you tell me what Wyvern things I used to be able to do?"

My mom glanced toward the living room, where my dad was already working on his computer, then looked back at me. I knew that she knew he could hear whatever she said.

"Not my responsibility," she said lightly.

"What about the story of the Wyvern and Nick having a destiny together?" No one would ever tell me this one, although I'd heard snippets over the years from the adults before they caught me listening.

My mom shook her head. "Ditto. But I'll make you another deal. If you still want to know when you get home from boot camp, I'll tell you a story about a Wyvern named Sophie."

So . . . the last Wyvern had been Sophie.

And my mom thought I would learn more at boot camp. I was excited enough to dance, but I'd take the insurance where I could get it.

"Deal." We hugged again and I was glad she wasn't mad at me anymore. "You tell the best stories, so maybe I'll ask you anyway."

She smiled then but her eyes stayed serious. "Be careful, Zoë. None of this is a gimme."

I smiled at her, because she was just worrying about me again, exactly as she'd said she would.

Everything was starting!

I had to send Meagan a message. I might not be able to tell my best friend all of the truth, but sharing some of it was better than nothing. I retreated to my room before my mom could confiscate my messenger and render me incommunicado.

MEAGAN CAME BY WITH MY homework after lunch. My mom had decided to work at home because of yours truly getting suspended, and my dad was off in meetings for some big upcoming fireworks display. (That's what he does—coordinate big pyrotechnics shows, which is cool, but not as cool as being a dragon shape shifter. Call me biased.)

It was the last day before spring break and I truly couldn't believe that there was anything important for me to do for school.

Nothing more important than packing for boot camp, that was for sure. I couldn't decide what to wear for a week of Supergym with the guys.

I was glad to see Meagan. We sat on the stools at the kitchen counter and she spun on one, the way she always did. My mom was on the other side of the living room, focused on her computer screen, tapping on the keyboard.

Meagan had a killer bruise on her jaw, which tempered my excitement. She showed me the additional chunks of plastic and metal that the orthodontist had installed in her mouth the night before.

"Ow," I said with sympathy.

"And then some," she agreed.

"Frankenstein city." I felt bad that she'd taken such a hit. It just didn't seem fair.

She was trying to be upbeat, but I wasn't fooled. "So much for losing the hardware before senior prom."

"No!"

"Yes. He said I might have added a year to the treatment protocol with my *carelessness*." Meagan avoided my gaze, picking through my trig homework as if it were interesting. I knew she could have done it in two minutes, blindfolded with one hand tied behind her back. It would take me a while longer. A lot longer.

She sighed. "No point arguing with my mom about contacts now."

The thing is that Meagan is pretty as well as smart. She's got it all going on—the braces and the glasses just obstruct the view. She's getting really curvy, too. If it had been anyone else getting those boobs, I would have been beyond jealous. As it was, I wanted to cheer for my best friend. She was going to be *hot* when the equipment came off, and we had schemed together over her making a big entrance at senior prom.

To lose that moment because of Suzanne was just wrong.

"But you weren't careless! Suzanne started it."

Meagan shrugged. "Doesn't matter much in the end, does it?" For the first time ever, I heard bitterness in Meagan's tone. "She didn't even get detention."

It was so unfair.

We spun on the stools in silence. I couldn't think of one thing to say to cheer Meagan up. She had her old glasses on, the ugly Coke bottles, and it was just sad.

"What did you say to Suzanne?" Meagan asked finally.

"What do you mean?"

"In the corner. You must have said something, even though I didn't hear it. She's telling everyone that you're a freak."

My heart skipped a beat. I could feel my mom glancing over from the computer. "Nothing I remember," I lied, then decided to check my sanity again. "Maybe she didn't want to lose, with that guy watching."

"What guy?"

"The one in the bleachers."

"There was no guy in the bleachers, Zoë. I would have noticed that. I would have *missed*."

I opened my mouth to say that she had missed, then shut it again. Meagan laughed, liking that she'd almost faked me out.

I liked a whole lot less that I'd just lied to my best friend. Again. But I couldn't tell Meagan about my dawning abilities. I couldn't break the Covenant a third time in just a day.

My messenger chimed suddenly. Mine is a combination phone and digital notepad. Like all the others, it gets text messages and e-mails. It's so painfully antique, though, that I can store only a half dozen books in its memory, and its outdated drawing features are enough to make me weep. And it's huge—almost as big as my hand and as thick as my finger. I try not to yearn for any of the fabulous fast-featured new models, and I pretty much fail. Meagan and I are the only two girls in school to still be toting such ancient hardware.

At least when we're alone together, I don't mind tugging mine out of my pocket.

"Who's that?" Meagan asked, which was fair. She was the one person in the world most likely to send me a message at any point in time, and she was sitting right beside me.

We're not *that* dorky.

I scanned the message, surprised and skeptical. So skeptical that I read it twice.

"What is it? Phone spam?" Meagan said.

"It's from Trevor Wilson."

"*The* Trevor Wilson?" Meagan nearly leapt across the counter. "As in Suzanne's Trevor?"

I nodded. This was one of the great mysteries of our time, that Suzanne would take up with Trevor Wilson. We had spent many nights trying to figure out this relationship. Meagan and I agreed that Trevor was hot, because he could play the sax so incredibly that it gave you shivers, but Suzanne was usually more for the football-captain type.

Meagan leaned closer. "So he wants to beat you up for scaring his girlfriend?"

I shook my head. "He wants me to go out with him."

"No!" Meagan grabbed my messenger and read the display, just as shocked as I was.

"It's a trick." She handed it back to me. It says a great deal for my social life and general level of popularity that neither of us could take this seriously, even for a moment. "He's trying to lull you into complacency so he can get even for Suzanne."

Only Meagan could say "lull you into complacency" and not sound like she was putting it on.

She was right. It had to be a joke.

Although it didn't do much for my ego that the conclusion was inevitable.

"Well, I'm not that stupid." I deleted the message.

"He should know that." Meagan spun on her chair. "But then again, he's the one who needs tutoring in math."

I stared at her. "No."

"Oh, yeah." She acted casual, but she was blushing. Big-time. I remembered that it was Meagan who had talked so much about Trevor's musical skill. Was it possible that we both had secrets? She couldn't even look me in the eye. "Order of operations completely blows his circuits."

"You *tutored* Trevor Wilson and you never told me? I thought we were friends!"

Meagan's face was so red, and she started to stammer a bit. "It was only . . . only the once, at the math clinic." She tried to shrug it off. "Not like I made a difference to his skill set. I'm sure he doesn't even remember me."

She was right. He'd pinged me, Meagan's best friend, instead of her. I'd never even talked to him. I certainly hadn't spent hours working through equations with him.

Ouch. I developed sudden and complete confusion over my homework. Needing to be smart always perks Meagan up.

It worked like a charm. We poked through the homework for a few minutes while she explained things to me. Being arty, you know, means that everyone is ready to believe I don't get much else. In this case, I was glad.

She complimented the dragon I'd drawn on her new notebook, and I felt like we had our own mutual admiration society. "What are you doing next week, anyway?" she asked, spinning on the chair. "Want to do our homework together?"

"I thought you were going to California."

Meagan shook her head. "Dad says I blew the budget."

More injustice. I knew Meagan was dying to go to San Francisco. She'd been talking about it since Christmas. The plan had been to check out Silicon Valley and the AI labs at Carnegie, as that was likely where Meagan would end up after high school.

I'd always thought it must be nice to have a destiny that had some chance of coming true. Me, I was okay at a lot of things, but not brilliant at any one subject. I got good grades but had to work for them. Nothing, but nothing, came easily—well, drawing did. Drawing dragons. I hadn't yet found a career option that fit that.

Even this dragon stuff, which Nick and the other *Pyr* guys made look so easy, wasn't effortless for me. They had just gotten it overnight, along with hair on their chests.

I'd tried the nail trick again this morning, with no luck. And I couldn't help feeling betrayed—shape shifting was *supposed* to be in my blood.

"The thing is," Meagan said, spinning her stool, "it was kind of my fault."

"What do you mean? They tripped you!"

Meagan grimaced. "Suzanne came to the math lab, you know. Last month."

This was news. "With Trevor?"

Meagan shook her head. "Alone." She traced a pattern on the counter and I knew she was going to tell me something important. "She acted like we could be friends, but she only wanted me to help her cheat."

"So you said no," I guessed.

Meagan nodded. "She was pretty mad." She pushed up her glasses. "I guess I had it coming."

"No!" I said. "No, you did the right thing. . . ."

"Doesn't feel like it."

And there was nothing I could say to that.

Meagan sighed. "Want to hang out next week?"

"I can't. I'm going to Minnesota."

Her face fell even further. "I thought you were staying home."

"So did I. I found out last night."

"Minnesota? What for?"

I shrugged, pretending to be less excited than I was. "Friends of my parents." I left out the bit about their hunky son and our entwined destinies.

Meagan grimaced. "Let me guess. They have kids and you're all supposed to get along together."

"Got it in one." I stuck out my tongue as if the whole idea were hideous. We laughed and joked around then, but I felt bad. It just wasn't right. My best friend was seriously on the wrong end of every deal, *and* I'd lied to her.

More than once.

Was this the price of my dragon's return? That I lose my best friend? It felt like a catch, and one I hadn't anticipated. I felt trapped between what I had been and what I might become, without the advantages of either dragon or human.

That just made me more impatient for the future to happen.

For boot camp.

Bring it on.

Chapter 4

I got a message really late, and to make it worse, my messenger chimed loudly. I had to jam it under my pillow to muffle its perky sound. House rules: no socializing after ten. But the message was from Nick, so there was no chance of my waiting until the morning. Had he heard? Was he as excited as me? I had to know.

My fingers shook as I—one more time—broke the rules.

As messages went, this one was disappointing. Nick hadn't written anything. Not one word. There was just an attachment.

It looked like a song file.

Bracing myself for some kind of joke—he'd sent me a version of "Happy Birthday" woofed by dogs just last year, which had been too lame to even be funny—I loaded it up and listened.

He must have heard. This was sexy music.

I didn't recognize the song. I was sure I'd never heard it before. It was instrumental, but haunting.

Romantic.

Wow. Things were looking up.

I put in my earbuds and listened to it again. It made me feel alive and alert in a different way, the way I'd felt in the showers at school. I could imagine slow dancing to this music, unaware of anyone but Nick, our bodies bumping together. It made me tingle.

Maybe it was some kind of *Pyr* music. I felt as if my dragon were uncoiling like a cobra, dangerous in the dark. That felt good, forbidden, a peek into the darkness ahead.

I listened to it thirty-nine times in a row.

I stopped only because I fell asleep.

IF WE WERE GOING TO Minneapolis, odds were that we'd fly. And given the choice between commercial airlines and dragon power, Dragon Air is the only way to go. I love it when my dad flies us somewhere, when he shifts shape and carries my mom and me to our destination. There's something amazing about flying with a dragon and feeling the wind in your hair. I don't even care if it rains.

Theoretically, I should be able to fly myself. Of course, I'd need to be able to shift more than my thumbnail, and be able to do it by choice.

I'd work on that at boot camp.

In the meantime, I was seriously excited about having my dad fly me to Minneapolis, so excited that I was ready early.

But there was an airline ticket at my place at the breakfast table.

I couldn't even try to hide my disappointment. "I thought you were flying me."

My dad gave me a grim look. "How much did you pack?"

Okay, there were two bulging duffel bags by the door. I hadn't been able to whittle it down. I looked at the pile, knowing he was following my gaze.

"I don't do checked baggage." He snapped his newspaper. My dad is the only person left in the world who reads the news on paper. I'm sure of it. He says dragons are never in a hurry to change.

"But . . ."

"And you broke the Covenant," my mom added from the kitchen. My dad looked at me and I understood.

This was my punishment.

"I am hoping no one believes this Suzanne," my dad said, speaking with precision, the way he did when he was annoyed. His British accent gets stronger then.

"I could beguile her after break."

I got a look for that, and then he returned to his paper. End of discussion.

I fingered the airline ticket as I ate. I didn't have to like the plan, even if I knew it wasn't unfair and that I wouldn't be able to negotiate my way out of it.

It was true that my dad always traveled with a black messenger bag slung over one shoulder, nothing more and nothing less. My mom, too, packed light. I guess she'd learned.

Maybe she'd been given airline tickets once, too.

But worse than not having the dragon flight—which completely would have started the trip off right—was the lost opportunity to interrogate my dad.

I felt a dire need for more information of the dragon variety. I quickly formulated plan B—I'd ask him questions on the way to the airport. Maybe I'd manage to get in two or three. They'd better be good ones.

But my dad got a call right then and left for work before I even finished eating.

My mom took me to the airport.

At least she didn't ding the car again.

I CHECKED IN AND GOT to the gate before they started to board. I tried a human strategy and sent a message to my dad, but after five minutes, it was clear he wasn't going to reply.

I could guess why. He was testing me. I took a deep breath and tried a dragon trick. I closed my eyes tightly and tried to send him a question in old-speak.

Over distance.

Graduate work in old-speak.

I'd never managed it before, but maybe things had changed. It couldn't hurt to try.

I thought about where my dad would be—at the warehouse, where they stored and rigged the fireworks. He'd be on his messenger, directing his foreman at the same time that he talked to the client, rummaging through a delivery. Supermultitasker, that's my dad.

I concentrated on the warehouse's precise location, how exactly I'd get there from the airport, and tried my best.

"*I have questions,*" I said, hoping it would work.

I sensed my father's surprise, but it didn't slow him down. I was pretty much stunned that I could feel his reaction.

"*Then you'll have to find the answers.*" He was as curt in old-speak as he could be in real life.

He was busy.

"*But . . .*"

"*Work it out, Zoë.*" His old-speak softened. "*That's part of the challenge. Everyone's different, so you'll have to find your own way.*"

The *Pyr*, you know, could have used instruction manuals.

On the other hand, I was the only one who seemed to need one. Which said nothing good about my being a runaway success as a dragon. Was it possible that the talents I'd lost when I'd started to talk were gone forever? Had I blown the chance to become the Wyvern before I could even read the job description?

And what did that mean I would become instead?

I've always liked riddles and puzzles. When it seems as if a riddle has no solution, it pays to review the clues. I pulled out my messenger and began to type out what I did know, in the hope of finding a clue to what I didn't know.

I had some time to fill anyhow.

The first thing I wrote down was the most obvious.

In the beginning, there was the fire, and the fire burned hot because it was cradled by the earth. The fire burned bright because it was nurtured by the air. The fire burned lower only when it was quenched by the water. And these were the four elements of divine design, of which all would be built and with which all would be destroyed. And the elements were placed at the cornerstones of the material world and it was good.

But the elements were alone and undefended, incapable of communicating with one another, snared within the matter that was theirs to control.

And so out of the endless void was created a race of guardians whose appointed task was to protect and defend the integrity of the four sacred elements. They were given powers, the better to fulfill their responsibilities; they were given strength and cunning and longevity to safeguard the treasures surrendered to their stewardship. To them alone would the elements respond. These guardians were—and are—the *Pyr*.

That was the first thing I ever learned about dragons. My mom calls it a creation story. My dad made me memorize it when I was about four, and now I knew it as well as my own name.

It calmed me down to write it out again, reminded me of the good bits of being a dragon shape shifter.

But it gave me no answers.

Onward.

FIVE THINGS THE *PYR* CAN DO IN DRAGON FORM

1. Breathe fire. (Duh.)
2. Breathe smoke. Dragonsmoke is a protective barrier that only other dragons can perceive. Any *Pyr* who crosses another *Pyr*'s dragonsmoke without permission gets burned. Literally.
3. Communicate in old-speak.
4. Beguile. Beguiling is a kind of hypnosis, which can be used to persuade humans of things—like, for example, that they haven't seen dragons flying through the air over Chicago.
5. Fly. I said it before, but it bears repeating. It's that cool.

Pyr power that I want the most badly: number five.
Duh.

SO, OUT OF FIVE, I could do two. With varying levels of success. I had a ways to go this week to score even a B on any *Pyr* final exam.

But it got worse:

FIVE THINGS ABOUT THE WYVERN

1. She's the only female *Pyr* in existence. One Wyvern has to die for the next one to be conceived.

2. She can dispatch dreams, both to *Pyr* and to humans.
3. She can take other forms than dragon and girl, including salamander.
4. She's a prophetess, one who can see past, present, and future simultaneously.
5. She can travel instantly to other locations. This means that dragonsmoke, for example, is not a barrier to her. She just appears on the other side of it.

Number of these things I could do with any level of expertise: zero.

Okay, I was depressed enough. I saved my files and listened to Nick's music instead.

At least it made me feel better.

IT WAS SNOWING IN MINNEAPOLIS.

Not the way it does in Christmas movies, with harmless fluffy flakes. No, no, no. There was an honest-to-goodness blizzard going on. I could have left April behind in Chicago, and landed in January instead.

I hadn't thought Minneapolis was that far away.

The other passengers complained about the unseasonal weather, and I hoped I'd brought enough warm gear. We descended until I could see the airport, shrouded in white. The snowdrifts on the roof looked like giant marshmallows. There were snowplows driving up and down everywhere, their blue lights flashing.

The airplane landed with a thump, then skidded, tipping in a crosswind. Then we slid sideways. It was a crappy moment to be traveling alone, with no one's hand to hold.

Everyone cheered when the plane came to a halt. The pilot announced that we had been the last flight allowed to land, that they were closing the airport until the blizzard stopped.

The rough landing had shaken me up a bit. But now I was

closer to Nick! And maybe he would have some answers for me about the whole dragon thing. Some tips. After all, he was in full control of his dragon.

My dad had gone through the change so long ago, he probably didn't even remember what it was like. Maybe it had been different in the olden days, when avenging knights had to be barbecued and damsels plucked from danger.

By the time I hefted both of my bags from the carousel, I had to consider the merit of packing more lightly. I was panting as I left the baggage claim area. Superkiller gym class had evidently started early.

Bonus that my aching shoulders were my own fault.

But it didn't matter. I was here and so was Nick and it was destiny time. The doors opened to the arrivals area and my heart began to thump. I scanned the crowd. I saw Donovan immediately, head and shoulders above the rest.

Sure enough, Nick was right beside his dad.

"Nick!" I shouted, and jumped up and down. This was a feat with two loaded duffel bags, but I was motivated. Nobody heard me, even with their keen *Pyr* hearing, which should have warned me.

But I refused to care. What would I say first? What would I do first? How much did he already know? I galloped toward Nick, the weight of my junk forgotten.

As I got closer, my heart squeezed so tightly that I could barely breathe. Nick must have grown another six inches taller since I'd seen him last, and he'd been working out. *Oh, yes.* His shoulders were really broad and there couldn't have been an ounce of fat on him. His hair brushed his collar and it was the same russet as his dad's—straight instead of wavy.

Yum.

He was facing the other way, surrounded by the others.

"Nick!" I yelled, and this time he glanced my way.

He smiled.

He nodded.

Then he turned away again.

What?

I was expecting at least a hug. Especially after he'd sent that music.

I rushed forward, unable to believe that anything could be more interesting than seeing me—especially as I didn't think there was anything more interesting than seeing him. I realized that I was last to arrive, and that even Rafferty was here.

Rafferty?

All the way from England?

But why? He didn't even have a son.

Maybe Rafferty was going to teach us something special. Rafferty could communicate with the earth, after all.

Then the group parted and I saw who held Nick's undivided attention.

Crap. My sucker heart ripped itself in half, then went splat on the tile floor.

Because Nick was talking to Isabelle.

Isabelle. Rafferty's adopted daughter.

Older than any of us.

Gorgeous.

Curvy.

She had a thick chestnut ponytail, which bounced as she walked. That should tell you everything you need to know. Gorgeous girls with ponytails are a painful amount of trouble.

Worst of all, she had a British accent.

The guys were already starting to drool.

And Nick was first in line.

As I stood there looking on, I thought my knees would give out. That would have made me look even more stupid than I did with my mouth hanging open in dismay. I shouldered my stuff, forced a smile, and joined the group.

Rafferty and his mate couldn't have kids, so Isabelle was adopted. Her presence explained his, but I couldn't figure out why she had come. Was she attending boot camp?

Please, Great Wyvern, make it not be so.

No one else had any issues, though. In fact, I was thinking the airport would have to call in an extra shift of janitors to mop up all the slobber from the three guys. They were interrupting one another, trying so hard to get Isabelle's attention that I barely recognized them.

Nick gave me a punch in the shoulder as a kind of greeting, which absolutely did not meet my expectations—especially not after he'd sent that song. (Which, yes, I had been listening to all day, and which, yes, had raised my expectations somewhat.) Liam gave me a hug—he's like that—and Garrett shook my hand. They were all taller than me, and I'm not exactly short.

I hauled my own bag to the car, while the guys fought (*fought!*) over the chance to carry Isabelle's pretty suitcases.

So much for my exciting vacation.

So much for my great extended bonding time with Nick.

Crap.

WE ALL PILED INTO DONOVAN'S hybrid four-wheel-drive and Nick's electric sports car, and you can guess who sat where. Me, I won the backseat of the four-wheel-drive, Donovan driving and Rafferty in front.

Isabelle—queen of all she surveyed—was in the front seat of Nick's car, with the other guys piled in the back and leaning over the seats, desperate for her attention. Most of the baggage was with me.

Enough said.

My only consolation was that Nick would have to clean up the drool in his car.

It wasn't nearly good enough.

Just so you know.

Donovan and Rafferty talked in old-speak the whole way to the house.

Fascinating.

Not.

Donovan was telling Rafferty about a Mage sending him a ransom letter, and how easily he'd gotten rid of him. Rafferty was having a good laugh over the idea of Mages casting spells to ensnare the *Pyr*. Rafferty said he hadn't even caught scent of a Mage in two hundred years.

Yawn. For the lack of anything better to do, I added to my list of Known Facts. It occurred to me that although there wasn't a guidebook to the *Pyr*—much less to becoming one—I was kind of building my own.

A DIY dragon survival guide. How sad is that?

FIVE THINGS ABOUT MAGES

1. They are humans who do magic, and first were noticed by *Pyr* during the Renaissance. Their magic must be pretty lame, though. I'd seen the *Pyr* Lorenzo do *his* magic, and that smoked anything else around. His stage show was awesome. And what he did offstage was even more incredible. Dragon magic rocks.

2. The *Pyr* have never lost a battle to the Mages.

3. None of the *Pyr* have seen a Mage in recent memory.

4. None of the *Pyr* are worried about the Mages.

5. The only reason they were even talking about this was that warriors of all kinds get bored in peacetime. With the *Slayers* defeated and eliminated, we dragons were

fresh out of enemies, and the old guard were making up spooky ghosts. Now, that is sad.

RAFFERTY'S RING GLINTED IN the light as he talked. He'd worn that black and white ring for as long as I'd known him. My parents told me that, as a kid, I always went to Rafferty to touch his ring. When the light was right—as it was now—the ring looked as if it had a light deep inside it. It looked as if it were made of glass, black and white glass swirled together.

When there was a lull in their old-speak, I leaned forward and spoke out loud. "Rafferty? Can I ask you a question?"

"You just did." He smiled at me, teasing.

"When I was little, my dad said I could do some Wyvern stuff. Do you know what it was?"

Rafferty took a deep breath and frowned into the snow swirling against the windshield. One thing about Rafferty—he takes his time, even for a dragon. (Which is saying something.) "You used to send us dreams."

"Really?"

He turned to smile at me. "You gave me a vision, one that saved the day."

"Really?" I squeaked a bit. This was unbelievably cool.

Even though I'd lost that power.

"Why can't I do it anymore?"

Rafferty looked down and I thought he wouldn't answer me. *"Maybe the time isn't right,"* he said in old-speak. *"There's a solar eclipse on Monday. See what happens then."*

The motion of the sun was linked to my becoming a Wyvern? I couldn't believe it.

I thought Rafferty must be putting me on. He smiled, and I decided that if he was going to razz me—or not take this Wyvern stuff seriously—then there wasn't much more to say. I tucked in my earbuds and listened to Nick's music.

And that just put everything in perspective. Nick had sent me this provocative song. Even if he was putting on a good show of being polite to Isabelle, this song said it all.

I wasn't giving up on Nick and our entwined destiny yet.

After all, I hadn't had a chance to show him what I could do.

Chapter 5

It was snowing like crazy, drifts piling up white against the windows, but I felt cozy once we were inside Donovan's house. And dinner was good. I didn't eat the barbecued ribs—no meat for me—but the guys ate as if they'd never see another meal again. Donovan's partner, Alex, made a joke about being glad they didn't all live at her house. Two dragon sons were enough, I guess. Nick's kid brother, Darcy, was staying with a friend for the night.

Isabelle also abstained from eating meat, explaining in her posh accent to Alex that she was vegetarian. Like me. I felt that she was trying to be friends, but I knew better.

The ponytail said it all.

We were crowded around the dining room table, more tightly squeezed in than the last time I'd been with the guys. They were all getting broader in the shoulders.

Garrett is the oldest of the guys—sixteen and the son of the

Pyr's blacksmith, Quinn. He looks like Quinn—black hair, blue eyes, and a powerful build—and he's quiet like his dad.

You could think of him as being like smoldering coals—they could burn slowly forever or flare up with the right impetus. A breath of wind. New fuel.

Whenever the guys arm wrestle, Garrett wins. Period. His shoulder muscles are something else and he earned them the hard way—hammering hot iron.

Nick is next-oldest, also sixteen. He's the classic, popular, captain-of-the-football-team, every-cheerleader's-dream kind of guy.

He's like a bonfire that everyone wants to gather around. Sociable. Attractive. Girls are drawn to him like, well, moths to the flame.

Including me.

And, apparently, Isabelle.

I'm next-oldest; then there's Liam. He's always been called Carrots because of his hair. He's about as freckled and wholesome as a farm kid can be, but he's easy to talk to. I like that he has no ability to lie. At all. It's quite sweet, really.

I'd compare Liam to a roaring blaze on the hearth. Comforting. Reliable. Predictable in a way. Liam is someone I'd want to have at my back in a dragon fight.

These three had done boot camp together for two years now.

I usually find it easy to be with the guys, probably because we've known one another so long. Like finding your fave jeans at the bottom of the drawer in the fall—you pull them on and they're still perfect. But even though we joked around like usual, I felt off.

Maybe this was PMS.

Except I wasn't pre- anything.

"You okay, Zoë?" Alex asked when I passed on dessert. "I thought chocolate cake was your favorite."

"It is, Alex. I'm sorry. I'm just tired."

"Rough flight?" Liam asked, bumping my arm in a companionable way. "Our plane was all over the fricking sky."

"You came on a plane, too?" Nick teased.

"Sure." Liam smiled at me. "Me and Zoë were keeping our cover, just like the Covenant says." See? Liam knows how to make me feel better.

"We also came by commercial carrier," Rafferty said smoothly, and got up. "I'll head out now, on my own."

"*You sure, in this weather?*" Donovan asked, and the two adult *Pyr* changed to old-speak. They kept talking as we carried on with regular conversation. It's kind of protocol—when your elders switch to old-speak, you're supposed to pretend you can't hear. Like human parents spelling out words.

"I can see the rough flight put you off dinner," Nick said to Liam.

"Good thing, or we wouldn't have gotten anything," Garrett teased. "I flew in yesterday, and I'm still starving." He accepted another piece of cake from Alex.

"By yourself?" I had to ask.

"Under my own steam," Garrett said with satisfaction.

I was impressed and probably didn't hide it well. It wasn't that far to Traverse City—at least not compared to Rafferty flying home to England—but still, he'd flown alone. Liam looked impressed, too.

"He's just showing off," Nick said, trying to make light of it.

"Or lobbying for extra points," Liam suggested.

"Too early for that," Alex said. Rafferty kissed Isabelle and waved to all of us. I got up to give him a hug and to thank him again. He winked at me, then strode out of the house. I wanted to see him shift shape and take flight, but he walked down the street until the flying snow obscured his figure.

I remembered the Covenant. He'd find somewhere deserted before he changed forms.

"Which reminds me." Donovan went into the living room and returned with a box, which he placed on the table. It was the perfect distraction. We all stared in shock and delight at it, every one of us knowing what it contained.

We were literate, after all.

"It's the boot camp grand prize," he added, although we'd all done that math.

No way.

"Awesome," Garrett breathed.

The box was for the newest messenger, the hottest piece of hardware available in the civilized world. It was smaller than any messenger ever made before and yet more powerful. Maybe three inches by three inches. It was supposed to be wafer-thin and supple, so you could just jam it into your pocket.

We all gaped at the pictures on the box, raging with simultaneous, overwhelming gadget lust.

"It's not supposed to ship until Christmas." Nick's awe was almost tangible.

Donovan smiled. "Alex has connections." He flicked a look at his partner, who smiled.

"You can text the moon with this," Garrett said, excitement in his voice. "It's got that much range."

"Chat simultaneously with twelve friends." Liam's eyes were round.

"Store forty-five million songs," Nick contributed. "And play them in stereo."

"Carry fifty thousand books," Isabelle added.

"And draw in forty million colors," I concluded. "Look. It's even the metallic anthracite version."

My fave color option.

We sighed as one, lost in complete admiration, then snatched for the box in unison. Nick—bigger and faster than any of us—got it and ripped off the lid. The protective foam that should have been cradling the eighth wonder of the world was . . .

Empty.

"Gone," Garrett whispered.

"Who stole it?" Nick demanded.

"Oops." Donovan's eyes glinted with humor.

Alex laughed. "Vanished." She snapped her fingers and chuckled. Their laughter told me everything I needed to know to solve that riddle.

"Hidden!" I leapt to my feet. I knew the first challenge and I knew who was going to win.

I love puzzles.

Donovan quickly summarized the clues. "It's somewhere in the house. Alex has pulled the drapes in case you need to shift. Whoever finds it and manages to bring it to me gets today's point. Whoever has the most points at the end of the week takes it home." He put out his left hand, palm up, and his eyes gleamed. "Go."

We lunged from the table.

WHERE WOULD DONOVAN HIDE the messenger? Their house was huge, which left tons of possibilities. Dragons tend to vacation together, so we all knew one another's houses really well, as well as our own. A person could search for a lifetime in Donovan's house and lair but not find every trinket in his hoard.

But Donovan didn't want us to find his hoard. He wouldn't want us to even see it.

No. The messenger was somewhere else.

Garrett and Liam raced toward the garage, which housed Donovan's motorcycle collection. Their thinking was probably that he'd hide it with his most precious treasures.

I thought otherwise.

But where?

Isabelle started to look between books on the shelf in the library. I thought that was too obvious, even though it would have easily slipped between two books and disappeared.

Nick streaked toward the basement stairs and I figured he knew something I didn't know. I went after him, heart aflutter.

Being in the dark with Nick could be a good enough door prize for me.

Was that why he headed down there? So I'd follow? So we could really talk? I dared to hope.

There were two staircases to Donovan's basement, because it was that big. Nick took the one closest to the kitchen, but I ran down the hall to the other one.

I opened the door just a crack, seeing instantly that the lights were off downstairs. This was promising. My mouth went dry and my pulse leapt.

I stepped onto the top step and closed the door behind myself, letting the darkness surround me.

That seductive music played in my thoughts, persuading me that Nick had a different agenda.

Destiny.

One kiss to start a future.

The prospect made me tingle.

Even with my keen *Pyr* senses, I couldn't hear or see anything. But I knew that Nick was down there. I could smell the cool dampness of the basement and feel the weight of the earth pressing against the walls. I thought I could hear the snow falling outside.

And I heard someone breathing.

Not too far away.

I inhaled and caught his clean scent. Yup. He was there.

Waiting for me.

It was almost too good to be true.

I eased down a step, moving in silence. I felt sharp and observant, aware of every detail. My *Pyr* senses were on full alert.

As I took another step and another, the cool air closed around me. I could smell the tile floor and plaster walls, the wooden shelves in the wine cellar, and the stones in the foundation.

And Nick.

He caught his breath. He was close. He was listening.

To me.

I shivered. He had to know it was me. His senses were probably even more developed than mine.

He was waiting for me to get closer.

He'd probably been listening to that music, too.

I swallowed, my heart leaping with anticipation. I moved down the last half dozen steps, wondering whether he could hear my heartbeat. Smell my excitement. Feel the hairs standing up on my nape. It's said that when the *Pyr* mate, their pulses synchronize. They breathe as one. The *Pyr* essentially becomes one with his destined human partner.

What would it be like when two *Pyr* paired off? Would it double the reaction?

Or square it?

My palms were damp just at my thinking about the possibilities.

I reached the bottom step and waited, one hand on the banister. Nick was close, closer than he had been, maybe four steps to my right. I could almost discern his silhouette, dark against the shadows, and I could see the gleam of his eyes.

Amber.

He began to shimmer blue, the sight electrifying me.

I could live with Nick being protective of me.

"You won't beat me," he taunted in old-speak. Hearing his low voice in my thoughts was unspeakably sexy. It made me shiver, but made me hot at the same time.

Then I realized what he'd said. Right. Theoretically, we were looking for the messenger.

Maybe his plan was that we'd wrestle for it.

I'd play along. I peered into the darkness and saw a glimmer of anthracite on the far side of the basement.

"*Dream on,*" I retorted, and dashed forward.

Nick leapt for the messenger's shine, just slightly ahead of me. I hip-checked him by accident and he stumbled.

He was agile, though—he turned a somersault in midair and landed on his feet. I was impressed, but he didn't need to know that.

He really didn't need to know that I would have been sprawled across the floor.

I took advantage of the moment and snatched up the messenger. "Ha!" I shouted, victorious.

I felt rather than saw that brilliant shimmer of blue. Nick was shifting. I pivoted to run back toward the stairs but wasn't fast enough.

Brilliant orange light flashed through the basement as Nick breathed dragonfire. I had to figure that Donovan had planned for this kind of hazard in the house's construction.

Then Nick pounced.

Oh. Yes.

For one precious moment, Nick was wrapped around me, his strength against my back. A golden dragon held me in his grasp and there was nowhere else I wanted to be. This was exactly what I had wanted to happen.

Maybe I even swooned a little. I certainly stumbled and lost my balance. I fell to the floor, and Nick didn't exactly cradle my fall. When I hit, the wind was taken right out of my lungs. The messenger bounced out of my hand and danced across the tiles, sliding into the wine cellar. I didn't care.

Because Nick was still wrapped around me. On top of me. All muscled golden power. I felt dizzy with the prospect of a kiss.

Finally.

But there was no kiss. One second Nick was on top of me, warm hard scales against my back; the next he was gone.

He went after the messenger, his eyes gleaming amber.

So much for romance.

So much for *me*.

What?

He grabbed the messenger and held it up, triumphant. "Got it!"

"No!" This time the tide of lava inside me moved so fast that it took me off guard. I lunged after Nick and snatched at his ankle. The dragon's heat ripped through my body like nothing I'd felt before. It roared through me, raging, hungry, incredibly powerful.

But something was wrong. It felt mean and angry and not like me at all. Where was the blue shimmer that my dad had told me about? Where was my ability to control the shift? I had none and I knew it.

This wasn't right.

But there were two talons on my hand. I could see my third nail shimmering on the cusp of change and fought to contain the urge to shift.

Without a lot of success.

Holy shit.

House rules had nothing on this. My eyes widened in terror as the bloodlust seized me. How could anything in me make me want to hurt Nick?

I thought, oddly enough, about the guy who had turned up in my bedroom. What had he said?

Nick meanwhile spun to fight me, easily breathing a spout of fire that missed me completely.

Probably on purpose. He had his dragon in check.

Not mine. His dragonfire made me let go of his ankle, but that crimson tide welled higher and stronger within me. Nick backed away and beckoned to me, spoiling for a fight, as I fought against the force within me.

What if I lost?

Nick's old-speak slid into my thoughts. *"C'mon, Zoë. Shift already. Let's see what you've got."*

His dare only fed the fire, I can tell you. I panicked as I fought for supremacy. I don't know what gave me the edge—terror, maybe—but I finally felt the tide turn. I shoved and I pushed and I fought with every scrap of strength I had.

I was panting by the time I shoved the dragon back in the jar. I was shaking so hard that I didn't truly give a crap what color my dragon was. One thing was for sure: I never wanted to let the dragon loose again.

But if I didn't ever shift shape, could I manage to be the Wyvern?

Was it all or nothing?

THE LIGHTS CAME ON AND I found myself on the tile floor of the basement, shaking so hard I thought I might puke.

"What's the matter with you?" Nick asked, serious now. As if he was concerned. He was back in human form, and knelt beside me. Of course he had the messenger in his hand. "I thought you'd shift." He sounded disappointed.

"Joke's on you." I wasn't quite ready to talk about what had just happened.

"I thought we were finally going to wrestle." Nick looked mischievous.

"You could have shifted back to wrestle."

He grinned. "It's better dragon-style."

"You only want to wrestle with Isabelle."

"Jealous?" Nick was unrepentant. He bent to tickle me, just like he always did. Just like I was his baby sister. I wished he didn't know all my spots. "Is your dragon green, Zoë?"

I swung at him and missed, noting as I did that one nail was still a dragon talon. Nick saw it, too, and he mocked me as only a big brother can do.

I didn't want him to act like my brother.

"Come on, Zoë, let's wrestle for the messenger." Nick tossed it into the air, then caught it, waggling it in front of me. "Show me what you've got."

I stood up and folded my arms across my chest. It seemed like a good way to hold myself together. There was no way I was even going to think about shifting again.

Not without knowing more about what would happen.

"I don't want to hurt you."

He laughed, which was fair but insulting. "I'm not too worried," he teased, but I couldn't smile. He considered me for a moment, then shrugged. "Well, if you don't want to wrestle, let's score some more cake."

He turned to the stairs and I knew he'd take them three at a time. Much as I was looking forward to a view of his butt, some information of the dragon variety would be more useful.

"Hey, Nick."

He paused, glanced back.

I could only wish for his confidence. I hoped my question didn't sound stupid. "Your dragon . . . Does it want you to do things you wouldn't do otherwise?"

"What do you mean?"

"Is it like you? Under your control?"

"Well, yeah."

"Is it mean?"

He chuckled again. "Not any more than I am."

I stared across the tiled floor. Was it different for girls? Or was there something wrong with my dragon? Was it a Wyvern issue or a failure?

When I didn't say anything more, Nick shook his head. "Zoë,

this vegetarian thing is screwing with your head. The dragon is part of us, not something else inside us. It's not like we're possessed or anything." He shrugged, at ease in his own skin. I was wicked jealous of that. "We just have more abilities than most people."

Right.

Nick came back down the stairs, his voice softer. "Is that why you didn't shift? Because you're afraid of it?"

"No, no, of course not." I saw that he thought I was lying. I wasn't. I hadn't shifted because I wasn't sure I could shift.

Back.

And yeah, that did spook me.

Nick gave me a quick hug, too quick a hug. "You can do it, Zoë. We all did. Just go with it. Don't think about it too much."

"I didn't want to hurt you."

"Be serious. You think I can't win a fight with a girl?" He laughed as if I were a comedian or something. Okay, he was a foot taller than me and a lot more muscled, but still. "Don't stay awake nights worrying about that." He tried to tickle me again, but I didn't want to play.

Why had he sent me that song anyway?

Before I could ask, he strode to the stairs. "C'mon. I've got to give this to my dad, prove I won."

I watched him go, and even the view of his butt didn't help much. As romantic fantasies went, this one had really fallen short.

And I had a feeling it was my own fault.

Maybe I would have some chocolate cake.

Chapter 6

We were leaving early in the morning for some rural property Donovan had rented, so after some cake, I made excuses to the group and bailed. I had to think. I was going to draw. Maybe work on my list of clues. Alex pointed me to the spare room.

When I saw the two single beds, I knew I'd get to share the spare room with Isabelle.

Yippee.

Maybe I could be in a coma by the time she came to bed.

I pulled out the red stone and checked it out. I played the eye game Granny had taught me and got a surprise again.

I saw a face within the circle on the one side of the stone. It was like catching a glimpse of a passing car, gone almost before I saw it. It was a guy's face, with dark hair and dark eyes. And a knowing smile.

I slammed the stone down onto the mattress, truly spooked.

It was the guy who had been in my room, the one I'd seen at school and again on the bleachers. How did he get there?

Where had he gone?

What did he want? I took a deep breath and turned the stone over. It was just a rock now. I played the eye game over and over, trying to catch sight of him again.

No luck.

"Hey, Zoë." I jumped when Garrett spoke. He stood in the doorway with his hands shoved in his pockets, watching me peer at a rock as if it held the secrets of the universe. Nice to have witnesses when you lose your mind. He looked uncomfortable, as Garrett just about never does, almost as uncomfortable as I felt.

"I wondered if I could ask you something."

"Sure."

He glanced back to the kitchen, then to me again. "My dad said that the last Wyvern opened a conduit between himself and his dad. He learned the secrets of being the Smith from his father that way."

I didn't have to be a whiz kid to guess what Garrett wanted from me—or to recognize that I had absolutely no idea how I might deliver.

"So my dad says he can't teach me more, not until I master the connection with fire." His gaze was searching—interrogation blue—and I knew he'd see if I lied. "Can you help me?"

I stalled. "What's it like?"

"My dad can talk to the fire." Garrett raised his hands, molding invisible flames in the air. His awe was clear. "He can coax a fire to burn higher or lower, hotter or colder. He can bend the flames, extinguish them, direct them, light them."

I was surprised. "Quinn can light a fire out of nothing?"

Garrett nodded. "He refuses to tell me how to do it. He says I need to find the way myself."

Didn't that sound familiar?

"I figure I need the new Wyvern to make that connection for me." Garrett eyed me. "Would you?"

"I'm not sure . . ."

He stepped into the room, eyes bright, and sat on the bed beside me. "Zoë, I want to be the next Smith." His intensity made my mouth go dry. "I want to be able to heal our scales, so that none of us have to head out there without our armor intact. I have to nail this! This isn't a joke. I need your help."

His request made sense, except that I had no clue how to fulfill it. "Do you know what happens if we mess up?"

He shook his head, surprised by the notion. Here was another confident dragon to whom all dragon feats had come easily. I would have been irritated with the guys if they hadn't been my best pals in the world.

"Then we'd better be right the first time," I said with a confidence I didn't feel. "Planning, you know."

"Maybe we can try this week."

I forced a smile. "Give me a few days."

Garrett's eyes narrowed and I knew he'd heard something in my tone. "Do you have your powers yet?"

I ducked the question. "I just don't want to mess up. Wyvern stuff isn't exactly cut-and-dried. Let me think about it."

Garrett stared at me for a long moment, long enough that my cheeks started to heat. "Sleep well, then. Tomorrow will be killer."

"Right."

I fell back on the bed when he was gone, perching the stone on my chest. So all I had to do was figure out how to foster Garrett's missing connection with fire. Uh-huh. While I managed to figure out my own powers, both as *Pyr* and as Wyvern, and win the boot camp challenge on the side.

No pressure, Zoë. No pressure.

Sleep well. Ha.

I felt like a failure to the nth degree, so I sent Meagan a

message. If nothing else, my having a crap vacation would make her feel better about her canceled vacation.

She didn't answer me, which fit the day's pattern perfectly.

I tried to sleep, but I couldn't stop the questions that kept running through my mind.

Why had Granny given me a rock?

Why had Nick sent me a love song?

Had I finally found some riddles I couldn't solve?

Impossible. I added to my list.

FIVE TRADITIONAL ROLES ASSUMED BY THE *PYR*

1. Leader. He calls the shots. That's my dad.
2. Apothecary. He heals our wounds, mostly with herbal remedies. That's Sloane, who lives in California.
3. Warrior. He commands the four elements as weapons to be used in battle. That's Donovan, Nick's dad.
4. Smith. He uses a hammer and forge to fix our scales. A missing scale is a point of vulnerability for a dragon. That's Quinn, Garrett's dad.
5. Wyvern. Prophetess chick, who typically remains apart from dragon society—maybe because other dragons ask her for stuff she can't do. That would be yours truly.

Theoretically.

As I've said.

I WOKE UP IN DARKNESS. All I could hear was the sound of someone breathing.

And the tinkle of icy snow against the windows.

I still had the stone in my hand.

Isabelle was asleep in the other bed, her hair spilling over the pillow. She even looked pretty when she slept. She could have been an enchanted princess.

I was tempted to chuck the rock at her head.

Temptation from my badass dragon was exactly what I didn't need. I burrowed lower in my blankets, intending to go back to sleep. That was when I noticed that there was snow drifting across the carpet.

I sat up and stared, then realized it wasn't really there. The eye game revealed that it was only half there.

Like Granny in my room at home.

And the tree root.

And *him*.

Okay, so this was a dream. Good. I was better with screwy dreams than screwy reality, mostly because there were fewer witnesses. I opened my hand and looked at my stone. It had the same tree *F* on it, no matter which eye I used, but with my left eye, the tree *F* was red.

Dark red.

As if it were dipped in blood.

Nice. I caught my breath, then glanced at Isabelle. She looked ethereal, half there and half not.

What was my dream trying to tell me? There had to be a message here.

Like a puzzle.

I was on that like ketchup on fries.

I stared at Isabelle and shut my left eye. There was the Isabelle I knew and did not love, the perfect fairy princess lost in her enchanted sleep. I was *not* going to get Nick to come kiss her awake. (For all I knew, that was what *he* was dreaming about. Ugh.)

When I shut my right eye, she changed. She wasn't Isabelle at all. She was an entirely different woman. An adult. This woman was blond, very fair, and petite. She looked fragile.

And her eyes were wide-open. She was watching me, as if she'd expected me to look at her. She held my gaze without blinking, and soon she was outlined in that familiar blue shimmer.

Wait. I was the only girl dragon.

My mouth had time to fall open in shock before she shifted shape. A slender white and silver dragon filled the bedroom, its eyes filled with the same knowingness as those of the other woman. She bared her teeth—smiling at me? defying me to believe?—then shimmered again.

This time she became a white salamander, a small glittering lizard on the carpet.

The salamander flicked its tongue, then changed back to a dragon again.

By this point, I was gaping. A woman becoming a dragon? That could mean only one thing in the world of the *Pyr*, but my brain stalled on the inescapable conclusion.

This was supposed to be *my* trick.

Was it a vision of my future?

But I would never be blond in this lifetime, not without the aid of many nasty chemicals.

I shouldn't have been surprised that this dream dragon spoke in old-speak, but when she did, I nearly fell out of bed.

"The present is where the past shakes hands with the future," she said, her voice melodious and deep. It resonated in my mind, the way my dad's old-speak does, merging with my thoughts. In a moment I wasn't sure whether she'd said the words, I'd thought them, or I'd dreamed them.

Except that she was still there.

Watching me.

She extended one dragon claw toward me. Her talons glimmered like they were made of stardust.

I reached out to shake her claw. Just before we made contact, I blinked.

And she was gone.

So was the snow.

No matter which eye I used, the room looked normal, Isabelle asleep in the other bed.

I threw myself back in my bed, worrying at the stone as I frowned at the ceiling. Okay, the only female *Pyr* was the Wyvern. I was (theoretically) the Wyvern. So who had this woman been?

The present is where the past shakes hands with the future.

I blinked. I, as the future Wyvern, had been visited by the dead (i.e., past) Wyvern.

That had been *Sophie*.

I sat up straight. Wow.

And I hadn't even thought to ask her any good questions. Would she come back? Would she mentor me? Could she tell me how to help Garrett manipulate fire? How could I find her again?

Figuring out the puzzle only gave me more questions.

Plus one biggie. I looked across the room, watching Isabelle sleep. What did Sophie have to do with Isabelle?

I didn't know.

I couldn't think of a single person who might tell me.

Except my dad.

And he was in Chicago.

Plus, odds were very long that he wouldn't have told me, even if he did know. *Figure it out*, he'd say.

Well, I would.

Somehow.

IT'S ALWAYS ABOUT CLOTHES, isn't it?

Never mind dragons having armor; people do, too. "Clothes make the man" is a saying my mom likes a lot, but even without being a man, I couldn't help giving serious consideration to wardrobe choices.

I woke up early, rummaged in my duffel bags, eyed Isabelle,

and chose my outfit. I was in competition for Nick's attention; that much was clear. I had to show that I had the right stuff.

At the same time, I had to be ready for boot camp. Wildly romantic girly things would not be a good choice. Plus, I needed two zippered pockets to carry my stone and my messenger with me.

Ha. Two treasures. I already had a hoard.

I liked that.

I went with my charcoal skinny jeans and a cabled alpaca turtleneck my mom had knit for me in the same dark gray. Silver earrings with malachite, because my dad said they highlighted my eyes and I liked the swirly green of the stones. Black boots with low heels and thick soles that laced up the front.

It was a bit of an austere look, even for me, so I added a swoosh of green eyeliner, a heart-shaped black beauty mark on my right cheek, and a lace shawl in acid green. My mom had made that, too, on request, and it had iridescent copper beads in it. It was one of my fave things because I could wear it so many ways.

For the moment, I wrapped it over my shoulders and knotted it around my waist, making an impromptu cardigan. I had gloves in coppery fake leather, too. My usual array of silver rings, my messenger, and my rune stone in my pockets, and I was ready to go.

I knew I looked good. That had to count for something.

Queen Bee was still asleep. Double bonus.

The day was starting off right.

"SLEEP WELL, ZOË?" NICK'S MOM asked when I turned up in the kitchen, looking for breakfast.

"Yes, thanks." I smiled. I like Alex—she's a scientist, which is really cool. Puzzle solving in a big way. She doesn't nag or hassle anyone, either. When Alex throws out advice, which isn't very often, I listen.

I thought she looked a bit tense, but I wasn't sure how to ask her about it.

And she probably wouldn't want me to ask.

"Yogurt and fruit, I'll bet." Alex put a bowl in front of me. There were fresh strawberries and peaches on top of the yogurt and it looked delicious.

Of course, I was starving.

"Local greenhouse," she added, indicating the strawberries. "Picked when ripe, so they're really good."

"Thanks." I felt spoiled.

"You might want to have some toast, too." She was pulling a ton of food out of the fridge, but then, there were three teenage boys on their way. "Seeing as boot camp is on."

"Isn't there an official announcement or anything?"

Alex smiled, a fast and thin smile, gone almost before it appeared. "That test last night with the messenger was the opening ceremony."

"Did I miss anything during the night?"

"Only Donovan setting his plans in motion." She shook her head. "I'm not sure who has more fun." She held two pieces of whole-wheat bread above the toaster and gave me a look.

I nodded. "Toast would be great, then. Thanks. Is Donovan coming?"

She frowned and her lips tightened. "No, he's gone." She turned back to the counter, fast.

Was it that Alex didn't like boot camp?

Or had she and Donovan had an argument?

"Hey, Zoë." Liam was yawning and stretching in the kitchen doorway. "Leave some for me."

"Hey, Carrots. Pull up a chair and tell me the rules."

Liam grinned as he poured himself a massive bowl of cereal. "There are no rules. Donovan sets challenges left, right, and center, and we deal with them as best we can."

"What kind of challenges?"

"All kinds. Physical tests, riddles, teamwork." He shrugged and dug in. "Changes every year," he added, mumbling around a mouthful of cereal and milk. "Depends what he thinks we need to know. Last year the theme was fire. We had to focus on breathing dragonfire, fighting, and shifting fast." He grinned, looking like a kid on Christmas morning. "It's more fun than it should be."

"Is there a clue?" Garrett tugged on his T-shirt as he came into the kitchen. He looked rumpled and sleepy, which made me wonder how late they'd all stayed up. Garrett is a morning person, not a party animal, which said a lot about Isabelle's allure. "Sometimes Donovan leaves us a hint."

"Sometimes not." Nick was already wearing a heavy fisherman's knit sweater and his jeans, ready to go. He looked good enough to eat.

"He did say we were going into the country," I said.

"Pick a direction," Liam muttered.

"Still thinking?" Garrett asked me quietly, and I nodded.

Alex handed me a plate with my toast. I acted cool, but my heart started to thump when Nick sat down beside me.

If Isabelle weren't coming along, things at boot camp could radically improve.

Starting now.

Nick's leg bumped against mine and I had a hard time catching my breath. I thought of that music he'd sent me and was filled with a yearning so strong it made my knees go weak. Good thing I was sitting down.

"You okay?" He leaned closer to look into my eyes. "I thought maybe you were sick last night."

"Just tired," I lied.

"Sore loser?" he teased, and I elbowed him.

"Haven't lost yet." We grinned at each other.

Nick bumped my arm and the contact had my heart thumping. "Good. We don't want to have to leave you behind."

"Or have to carry you," Garrett added.

"Ah, Zoë's so skinny that she'd be light," Liam said.

I gave him a look. "Thanks a lot, Carrots."

"Why are you here, anyway?" Liam asked. "Did you get your Wyvern powers?"

"That would be awesome," Nick said, and leaned closer. I could smell his soap and liked it a lot. "We could use someone with psychic powers at boot camp."

I stared into his eyes. It was entirely possible that this week could be saved. I had time to hope. . . .

Then *she* came into the kitchen.

The guys pivoted as one, me and everything else forgotten.

So much for that.

Chapter 7

"*P*sychic powers? That's my gift." Even early in the morning, Isabelle was all bright and perky and British. As a non–morning person, I found this offensive. "Is there room for me?"

The guys stumbled to their feet. "Take my chair," Liam offered.

"No, there's room here." Garrett moved over.

"I can stand," Nick insisted, and the warm press of his leg against mine was gone before I could get used to it.

I realized a bit late that Liam was watching me closely. By the time I glanced at him, he decided to be fascinated with his cereal.

"Why, thank you." Isabelle smiled and slid into Nick's chair, smelling like spring flowers. She wore riding pants and caramel leather riding boots worn to a soft patina.

I felt boot lust, big-time. I love boots and shoes. Hers were gorgeous. Life-of-the-gentry, lady-of-the-manse, fantasy riding boots. Perfectly worn in.

Isabelle was wearing a white cotton shirt, but it was pleated and tucked to make her look like a curvy goddess, and her chestnut hair fell in shiny loose waves over her shoulders. She wore no discernible makeup, although maybe a bit of pink lip gloss. She was as wholesome as a shampoo commercial.

Actually, her look reminded me of a bunch of ads Meagan and I had torn out of vintage magazines for an art project, ads for some designer named Ralph Lauren. Everything in those ads was carefully composed and evocative of a British-country-life ideal. I loved them, but it was a bit disconcerting to find Isabelle channeling that vision.

And doing it so well.

She sat beside me and I could see down the front of that shirt to the white lace of her bra.

My camisole—which was really just an undershirt with aspirations—suddenly seemed impossibly juvenile.

Her bra almost certainly had underwires.

I took that as a warning. Nick was gaping at her like he'd been hit with a brick. I bit into my toast with ferocity. It was appropriate that I'd worn acid green—I felt as if there were a green monster on my shoulder.

Nick had never, ever looked at me like that.

"Seriously? You're psychic?" Nick asked Isabelle.

"But Zoë's supposed to be the Wyvern," Garrett argued.

I heard the implication. "I'm not psychic," I said into my toast, but no one cared.

Maybe my dream had meant that Isabelle was going to steal the whole role from me. Maybe I'd lost my destiny due to incompetence.

The guys started to pester Isabelle with questions about her powers, Isabelle laughing in all the right places.

I might as well have been invisible. Nick was completely fixated on Isabelle. I didn't doubt that he'd seen the lace on her bra, too. He smiled at her warmly and she smiled back. I could practically feel the little zing of sexual awareness between them.

Even Liam made kissy noises toward Nick and Isabelle. Garrett laughed. Nick was too besotted to even notice.

Ugh.

When I couldn't stand it anymore, I tried to remind everyone why we were here. "Shouldn't we talk about boot camp? What happens next?" I asked.

Liam looked at Isabelle. "I guess you're not here for that."

"Oh, but I am. I don't really get it, but Donovan insisted that I had to come along."

"Maybe it's because you're psychic," Nick suggested.

"But you're not *Pyr*," I argued, knowing as soon as I said it that I should have shut up.

"Zoë!" Nick hissed. "Don't be rude!"

"She's just jealous," Liam contributed.

Nick looked between Liam and me, and a blush started to creep up my neck.

"Don't be ridiculous," Isabelle said easily. *She* was defending me? "I'm not *Pyr*, so Zoë's absolutely right to wonder why I'm here." I realized at that moment that I could have liked her—if circumstances had been different.

If I hadn't known about pretty, popular girls already. I reminded myself about Suzanne and Meagan, and kept my guard up.

Isabelle shrugged. "Rafferty said that my attendance wasn't optional. So here I am, goddess only knows why, and my internship canceled." She looked a bit annoyed.

"Internship?" I blinked, astounded that Isabelle could be less than thrilled to be at boot camp.

Her face lit up as she turned to me. "I met this amazing woman who reads tarot cards and casts astrological charts. Her interpretations are incredibly accurate. She says you just have to know how to look at the evidence. She was going to tutor me this month because she saw my psychic abilities. I already know how to cast charts, but can you imagine being able to see people's futures with clarity?"

"It would be pretty awesome," I had to admit.

"Can't you do it after you get home?" Garrett asked.

"No. She's leaving. It was now or never." Isabelle pushed her bowl of fruit away. "Never is what it will be." She forced a smile. "So I'm hoping I *am* here for a reason."

I started to feel bad for her then, at least until she smiled at Nick and he sat taller.

She leaned toward him, earnest and wide-eyed. "It's important, don't you think, to learn about destiny? The reason you were born?" She spread her hands. "If we know why we're here, we can make the choices to fulfill our fate. . . ."

"Never thought about it," Nick said. "Hey, can you pass the peanut butter?"

Isabelle watched him for a moment, visibly disappointed.

What *was* her deal?

Nick was supposed to have some destiny thing with the Wyvern. That would be *me*.

"Maybe your being here is one of the riddles we need to solve," Liam suggested to her. "Maybe you're here for a different reason."

Isabelle granted him a thin smile, clearly unconvinced. "I wondered." She watched Nick covertly.

Kind of the way I did.

Nick ate breakfast, confident, hunky, and oblivious.

"Maybe you should all eat up," Alex said, just as there was a knock at the door.

The guy standing there made a mock salute when Alex opened

the door. "Reporting for duty," he said, then swaggered into the kitchen.

I stared. I couldn't help it.

IT WAS POSSIBLE THAT MY previous experience hadn't prepared me for extremely hot guys. This guy had to be at least twenty, with long dark blond hair hanging over his shoulders. It was wavy and thick, the sort of hair I'd always wished for. His eyes were green, and he was tall, too, probably taller than me. He was dressed all in black and shook the snow off the shoulders of his leather jacket. He moved like an athlete. Or a dancer. All muscle and ease.

He had a tattoo on his arm, although I could glimpse only the end of it beneath the hem of his cuff. He had a dangerous smile, and held two black motorcycle helmets. He was slapping a pair of black gloves against his thigh.

He had long legs covered in tight jeans and leather chaps.

And a silver stud in his left ear.

A renegade.

An impatient one. He looked like the kind of person you'd meet downtown in a big city, maybe in the middle of the night, outside a bar—not someone who'd come knocking at the door of a nice suburban Minneapolis house in a snowstorm.

He kept looking at me, hard. I glanced behind myself, wondering what the deal was, and his smile flashed at that.

But he kept staring.

My mouth went dry.

My heart went thumpity-bump.

"Hey, Jared." Nick waved. "My cousin," he informed us.

Jared wasn't *Pyr*; I'd known that instantly. Dragon boys have a definite scent. His was yummy, but not dragon.

Human.

Other side of the family. Alex's side.

"Right on time, too," Jared added, as if he expected to be challenged.

"For once." Alex exuded disapproval. "What duty is that?"

"The one Donovan made me swear to complete." Jared flicked the door shut with his fingertips and grabbed a piece of toast. He gave Alex a wolfish smile, as if he knew he could get away with anything, and she tightened her lips.

He leaned against the counter, ate dry toast, and considered me. Thoroughly. "Not what I expected." He finished his toast in one great bite. "Not at all."

I was having a full-body blush, just so you know. It's one thing to find a guy incredibly hot, another for him to tell the world that you don't measure up to his expectations.

Whatever they might have been.

Although they probably involved underwire bras.

"Are you *Pyr*?" Isabelle smiled at Jared. Nick frowned, glancing between the two of them.

So, now *he* had some competition.

Jared laughed. He had a great laugh, a hearty, deep one, which surprised me. In fact, it made him look like a different person. I liked how his eyes twinkled when he laughed, but he still looked wicked.

"No. But that doesn't mean I can't get roped into Donovan's plans."

So, Mr. Urban Pirate knew something about the *Pyr*.

Interesting.

"You could say no," Garrett suggested.

"Not a chance. Not to Donovan." Jared slapped his gloves again and eyed me. "Let's go. I haven't got all day."

"What are you supposed to do?" Liam asked.

"Give someone named Zoë a ride." Jared pointed at me. My heart leapt to my throat, right on cue. "That must be you."

My face burned. "Wild guess?"

He wasn't daunted by my tone. If anything, his grin got wider. He had a dimple on the left side, a deep one.

"Well, Zoë is a girl's name." He indicated Isabelle, his gesture almost dismissive. "And she's not *Pyr*. I know I'm giving the Wyvern a ride, so that leaves you."

I nearly choked. How could this human guy know about my destined role? It was against the Covenant. . . .

"Forget it," Alex protested.

"Donovan's orders." Jared watched me. There was a dare in his eyes and I understood that it was up to me.

He didn't think I had the nerve.

That made me decide instantly that I was going to do it.

I stood up. He *was* taller than me, but I refused to be daunted. "First you have to tell me something. You can't know anything about Wyverns. It's against the rules."

He shrugged, unapologetic. "Well, I do. Screw rules." He winked at me as Alex glared at him. Then he proved that he knew some Wyvern lore. "Send me a dream, Zoë. Or maybe you already have."

The guys hooted and Nick gave a wolf whistle. But Jared just smiled at me, smiled in a way that made me get even warmer and more flustered.

"On the other hand, you might be right. Maybe I don't know nearly enough about this particular Wyvern." His voice dropped low. "Yet."

I was blushing furiously and the guys were laughing. I felt awkward as the center of attention, and slightly confused that the one person on the planet convinced that I was the Wyvern was this hot guy.

"Well, I can't do all the stuff I should be able to do," I said quickly, wishing he'd just look away, wishing he'd give me a minute to catch my breath.

Wishing I were cooler than I was.

Jared leaned closer, dead sober. "Maybe you're just not trying hard enough, Zoë."

My mouth fell open in shock, and even the guys looked between us in surprise.

Jared, absolutely untroubled, offered me a helmet. "Come on; we'll be late."

I didn't take it. "A motorcycle? In this weather?" My mother would have a fit if she knew. "Nobody rides a motorcycle in a blizzard."

Jared was dismissive of such concern. "Blizzard's over. Streets are plowed." He smiled at me, that daredevil light in his eyes again. "Don't tell me you're scared? A dragon girl, scared of snow?"

I glared at him. "I'm not scared—not of you and not of motorcycles. Let's go. Where are we going anyway?"

Mr. Trouble grinned. "You'll see."

"Wait a minute." Alex stopped Jared and me. "Donovan really told you to do this?"

Jared nodded. "Gave me a schedule, too. Don't make me piss him off."

"He never mentioned it to me," Alex said.

"It could be the clue, Mom." Nick got to his feet. "After all, Dad sold Jared his bike, and he wouldn't trust the Ducati to just anyone."

Alex looked unconvinced.

"Come on, you guys; we'll follow Jared." Nick inhaled the rest of his breakfast.

"Good luck," Jared said, reckless and confident. "You'll be eating my dust in five."

You know, I described the other guys in terms of flames. Let's go with that. Jared was like darkfire. That's a special kind of fire known to the *Pyr*. It burns blue-green. It's erratic and unpredict-able, flares up suddenly, and can burn you to a crisp.

But it's exciting, too.

That was Jared. Dangerous but impossible to resist. I sensed that the destination wasn't important to him. Getting there would be a heck of a ride. Surviving the journey was optional.

But I had a feeling the adventure would be worth it.

"I'll get my stuff," I said.

"No stuff," Jared insisted. "Unless it fits in your pockets."

"Let me at least lend Zoë a leather jacket," Alex said. "Other-wise she'll freeze."

Jared flashed that killer grin when Alex left the kitchen. "Maybe you'll just have to breathe a little dragonfire, Wyvern, to keep us both warm." He dropped his voice to a sexy whisper that made my heart stop—then race. "Or light my fire." His eyes were dancing and they seemed to promise magic and unpredict-ability.

For the second time in minutes, I didn't know what to say.

THE ONLY THINGS I TOOK were the stone, my ID (at least my body would be identifiable in case of a fatal accident), my messenger (shoved in my pocket), and supplies for my period. The shawl was bunched around my neck, since most of it didn't fit into the leather jacket, but I figured I'd need the insulation.

Even though I didn't take long to put on Alex's jacket and grab my boots, Jared was already waiting on me outside, stamping his feet.

The cold air slapped me hard as soon as I opened the door. I didn't even want to breathe, in case my lungs froze into big ici-cles. The sky was such a bright, clear blue that it looked fake, like the skies Photoshopped into postcards. The snow was crunchy enough to squeak under my awesome black thick-tread boots. The roads were clear, just as he'd said.

Jared had his helmet on and the bike idling. It was still on the kickstand, making puffs of exhaust. I did like its throaty rumble. It looked pampered and polished.

Okay, so he took care of the bike.

That didn't necessarily mean he'd take care of me.

He handed me the other helmet, and this time I took it. I tugged it on, but fumbled with the strap. I was juggling the stone in one gloved hand, which didn't help, and couldn't find the catch.

"Let me." Jared leaned in close, really close, close enough that I could see all the shades of green in his eyes. His fingers were warm on my chin as he fastened the strap, and I got all shivery at his touch. I had to close my eyes as he checked it. "Okay?"

I nodded.

It was hard to say anything with my heart lunging around my chest as if it were trying to break free.

He tapped the helmet where it wrapped around his chin, and I heard his next words right in my ear. "Speaker okay?" His voice was strangely close, almost like old-speak but not quite.

It was intimate to hear his voice this way.

What kind of moron was I to find this guy attractive? He'd be in jail before I finished high school. Maybe he'd already been there. Alex didn't like him—that should have been good enough for me.

I nodded, but Jared arched one brow. "It's good."

"Good, I can hear you, too." He got back on the bike, swinging one long leg over the seat. He braced his boots on the ground, then offered me one hand.

Unexpected gallantry, but I liked it. I passed the rune stone to the other hand, then grabbed his hand to get on the bike behind him. His grip was strong.

Wow. It was a tight fit on the bike. My legs were wrapped right around his hips, and there was no way to wiggle away or leave a gap between us. I was glad to be a skinny chick. His shoulders were broad and he was quite a bit taller than me—he blocked a lot of my view.

On the other hand, he'd block the wind, as well. It'd be warmer than if I were in front. He showed me where to put my feet, and it was kind of surprising how careful he was. That built up my confidence about the prospects of my survival.

"What's that in your hand, anyway?"

"Just a stone." I hid it from view.

"It looks like a rune stone." He revved the bike and kicked off the stand.

"What's that?" I stole another peek at it.

"Kind of like tarot cards for Vikings. They carved symbols on small stones, then used them to tell the future."

Interesting. "How do you know that?"

He shrugged. "I know lots of things. Does it have a symbol on it?"

I opened my hand and showed him one side. "It looks like an *F*."

"That's a rune, all right. You'd have to look up the symbol and its meaning. I don't remember them."

"How many are there?"

"Don't you know?" He didn't seem to expect an answer, because he just continued talking. "The Elder Futhark, which is the oldest part of the rune alphabet, has twenty-four characters. There were more runes added in other places afterward. Where'd you get it?"

"Someone gave it to me."

"And you just carry it around without knowing what it is?" He scoffed. "Guess I'm right about you not trying."

"You don't know anything about me!"

"Just making conclusions from the available evidence. You're coasting, Zoë, and that's not going to cut it if you really want to be the Wyvern. In fact, it doesn't cut it for pretty much anything."

I bristled. "And I should take advice from you? What do you do, anyway?"

He laughed. I wished I could have seen his eyes. "I do what makes me happy. I call that success." He revved the bike. "Put the stone in your zippered pocket, pull down your visor, and let's go."

I did as he instructed, because it made sense. He closed his own visor and drove the bike slowly toward the road. His heels were still on the ground, as if he were walking it. The motor thrummed beneath me and it was kind of exciting. I'd never been on a motorcycle before, but it occurred to me that it might be like riding a dragon.

"Now hang on to me."

"I can hang on to the back."

"You can, but it's not as safe."

"But—"

He interrupted me with impatience. "Zoë, I promise not to bite, at least not today. That's supposed to be a dragon's tendency, anyway."

"You sound skeptical."

"I'm not the one who doubts that you're the Wyvern."

What was I supposed to say to that? I put my arms around his waist. He was hard, all muscle, and felt strong.

Male.

Something heated deep inside of me. I felt something new, something strange and quivery.

Something good.

But that was nothing compared to when he let the bike loose. I hung on for dear life as the bike rocketed down the street.

No, I clutched Jared, and yes, I screamed.

It seemed as if there were nothing but frosty air between us and disaster, and I knew that if we hit anything, we'd be smeared from Minneapolis to Santa Fe in the blink of an eye.

And Jared was loving it.

Oh.

My.

God.

Chapter 8

"Zoë, you've got to let me breathe," Jared said a minute later. I guess he'd been giving me time to adjust, but was now moving on to plan B. "What are you going to do when we get on the highway?"

"Have heart failure."

"Some Wyvern! You should be bold!" He took a turn with more verve than I felt it deserved. I clenched my teeth, positive that he was trying to scare me.

He didn't need to know how well it was working.

Maybe he already did. My gloved fingers were digging into him in a big way. I tried to relax.

Talking would be good. A distraction.

I asked the first question that popped into my thoughts. "How do you know anything about the Wyvern, anyhow? How can you know anything about the *Pyr*? There's a Covenant. . . ."

"Which forbids *Pyr* to willingly reveal themselves in both forms to humans without serious advance planning, and was established by your father, Erik Sorensson, leader of the *Pyr*, after the events of the Dragon's Tail." He sounded as if he were reading from a textbook, although his knowledge made my eyes widen. "And you are the new Wyvern, although you're only coming into your powers, because there's only one female *Pyr* at any given time, and you're the daughter of Erik, conceived during his firestorm, so you *must* be the Wyvern."

I was shocked. "You shouldn't know all this."

"I told you. I know lots of stuff." He passed a sedan, the bike engine roaring. "Call it a hobby."

"But the rules . . ."

"Fuck rules."

Right. "Did Donovan tell you about the *Pyr*?"

"No way. He'd have been breaking the Covenant."

"Then how did you find out?"

Jared hesitated a beat before he answered me. "There's this book called *The Habits and Habitats of Dragons: A Compleat Guide for Slayers.* I've read it through a bunch of times. I think I might have it memorized."

My heart was in my throat. I knew about this book. I'd heard about it from my dad. It was the only compilation of *Pyr* lore, and even though it was incomplete, my dad had been pretty annoyed when the only known copy had vanished years ago.

How could Jared even have seen this book?

He must have taken my silence for disbelief—which it was, in a way—and added more information. "It was written by a guy named Sigmund Guthrie. Nineteenth-century stuff."

"That book is lost," I said in a whisper.

"Not so lost as that. I have a copy."

Maybe the copy I knew about had been stolen.

I wondered whether I had my arms around the best suspect.

I tried to sound cool. "Where'd you get it?"

"I found a copy in a used bookstore, about ten years ago."

No, that couldn't be the same copy. The copy I'd heard about had been in the possession of Sara, Garrett's mom. She'd had it until five or six years ago, when it had disappeared from her bookshop. I was relieved.

Although Jared could have been lying about the timing.

Of course, it was a book. There had probably been more than one printed in the first place.

Who had the other copies? I'd never thought of that before.

Maybe I just wasn't trying as hard as I should be. I ground my teeth.

"It talks about everything. Firestorms, dragonsmoke, the Wyvern—"

I interrupted him. "But where is it?"

"Safe." Jared shut up so fast that I knew he wasn't going to tell me where it was.

"You could loan it to me."

"Why?"

"So I could read it."

"Don't you know what you are?" he asked, laughter in his voice.

"Not all the lore."

"Forget it. I'm not lending it to anyone."

"Don't you think it should be kept by the *Pyr*? We have a personal interest in its contents."

"Don't you think it should be kept by the person who bought it? That's the definition of personal property."

Okay, he wasn't going to give it up.

"So, that book is what made you interested in the *Pyr*?"

"Oh, no. I've been interested in dragons for a long time. Since I was a little kid, actually." He paused, as if debating what to tell me. His voice dropped lower. "Since I saw one for the first time."

"A dragon or a *Pyr*?"

"Guess." He took the ramp onto the highway, merged with the traffic, and accelerated beyond my worst fears.

I bit back a scream.

This thing could *move*.

I had to be squeezing the life out of him in my terror, but he didn't complain. My teeth were clenched so hard that I thought they might crack.

Then he said something that changed everything.

"I've always thought riding a bike must be like flying," he murmured, his deep voice as soft as a whisper. It sent shivers over my skin. "Or as close to flying as I'll ever get. What is it like to fly, Zoë?"

"I've never done it myself."

"Why not? You afraid of that, too?" I heard him *tut-tut*. "You're some kind of lame Wyvern; that's for sure."

And that made me angry. "Look, I can't shift shape, so I can't fly. It's that simple." It was easy to admit it when I couldn't see his eyes. I thought of how incredible it was to fly with my dad. Even as a passenger, it was wonderful.

I really wanted to be able to do it.

He was right. Riding the bike was similar. That helped me to ease up and enjoy it.

"You can't shift shape at all?"

"I did a bit. When I got mad." I heaved a sigh, not sure why I was telling him anything. Maybe it was because I thought I was going to die soon, when the bike skidded into a minivan and we were both crushed to oblivion under transport trucks.

"What made you mad?"

I was reluctant to tell him the story, as it would sound so high-school. Juvenile.

"Well?"

"These girls were picking on my friend."

I heard the smile in his voice. "You know that it's a defensive posture, right? Seems reasonable to me that you'd shift the first time to protect a friend."

I blinked. I hadn't seen it quite that way—just hoped for leniency, since I'd defended a human—but it made perfect sense. On the other hand, it was kind of annoying to have Jared be the one to explain my own nature to me.

"So why haven't you done it again?"

I leaned my forehead on his shoulder. "It scares me." I spoke quietly, but he heard me.

"What?"

"The dragon. I'm scared to let it loose."

"In case you can't get the genie back in the jar." He wasn't making fun of me, which was nice.

I nodded, then realized he couldn't see it. "Yeah, pretty much."

"Is that typical?"

"Nick doesn't know what I'm talking about."

"So what are you going to do about it?"

He was right. I needed a plan. It would be better if I could test-drive the shift first, gain a little confidence in my ability to control it before I went the whole way.

I reviewed the available clues.

"Is there anything in that book about controlling the shift?"

Jared shook his head. "No. I'm sure of it. Won't the others tell you?"

"Nick says his is easy to control. No biggie."

"Maybe it's different for Wyverns."

Maybe. I realized then that I did have one clue. Maybe there was a reason Granny had given me the rune stone.

"Is there a library on the way to wherever we're going?"

"Why?"

"I could look up the meaning of the rune."

"Didn't you look it up already?"

I ground my teeth. "No. And I can't exactly use my messenger here."

Jared nodded slightly, clearly reviewing the route we were going to take. "Yeah. I think there is. I don't think there's time, though."

"But I need to find out. It could be important."

"I don't want to let Donovan down."

"I don't want to let my friends down, either. Boot camp is about tests."

"Point taken." Jared was silent for a moment, calculating; then he nodded. "I think I can make up the time."

He was going to ride *faster*? I bit back a protest. He was trying to accommodate my request, right?

"Maybe if we stop at the library, we'll give the guys a fighting chance to catch up." I heard the laughter in his voice. "How about a trade?"

"What kind of trade?" No surprise that I was suspicious. Who knew what this guy would ask of me?

"Take me for a ride when you do learn to fly?"

His question made me smile. "That depends."

"Depends on what?"

"Whether I survive this ride."

Jared laughed then, that great laugh that made me want to laugh, too. "I think I can guarantee that," he said, all breezy confidence one more time. "Come on—let's move. I hate being late." Then he leaned lower over the bike and I leaned with him.

It was easier this time to curve myself against him. I closed my eyes and dared to enjoy the feeling of speed and power.

Flying.

Donovan had entrusted me to Jared's escort. That must mean that Mr. Urban Pirate had good intentions. And nothing bad had happened.

Yet.

Maybe I could even get that book for the *Pyr*.

WE'D BEEN GOING FOR LESS than two hours when Jared took an exit from the highway. He turned into a small town, one that he evidently knew, and headed downtown. He parked the bike and once again offered me his hand for balance as I got off.

I was stiff and cold, and it felt good to stretch. The town was pretty, a main street lined with old buildings and shops. A post office. A corner store. Town hall. A couple of restaurants and a coffee place. Snow all over everything, like a Christmas card.

We were standing at the bottom of a set of steps. At the top was a red sandstone building.

The public library.

He turned to march up the steps, swinging his helmet by the strap. It would be so easy to follow him, to play along, to do the research together.

But then, that was just what he expected, wasn't it?

I had a moment of doubt there, something prickling at the back of my thoughts. He had kind of set me up for this detour by chiding me for not doing any research. Anyone could have bet that a schoolgirl would want to go to a library, and he had chosen this particular library. I wasn't sure where I was, much less where he was taking me.

I should just stop right on the steps and use my messenger to get some answers.

But Jared was already on the move and I wanted to go with him.

Was it stupid to be so cooperative?

It was weird that Jared had found that book, when the *Pyr* had been looking for copies for so long. Humans shouldn't know much about our identities, even though they now know that we exist. Could there be another reason for his interest in me?

Did the *Pyr* have stalkers?

Fans? I had heard rumors of it happening before.

Donovan wouldn't have put my welfare at risk, would he?

No. My dad would have had his liver for that.

But what if Donovan was wrong about Jared?

My gut insisted I should trust Jared, but my mind was full of doubts.

On the other hand, if ever there had been someone who would know things he shouldn't know—maybe just for the principle of it—I already understood it would be Jared. Plus, what harm could come to me at a public library? I had asked him to modify his travel plan and he'd agreed.

That could, however, have been a trick to win my trust.

I might find out something other than what the rune meant.

I hate riddles with no clear solution. I had a feeling that Jared was just that—and it wouldn't change anytime soon.

He turned, realizing I wasn't immediately behind him. "Chickening out?" The glint in his eye had me moving.

"Maybe it's foresight."

He laughed, then opened the door for me. There was an appreciative gleam in his eye, one that flustered me even more. "Oh, I hope so."

It's so hard to be cool when you can't stop blushing.

THE LIBRARIANS WERE NOT PLEASED to see Jared saunter into their refuge. And it wasn't my imagination—he did saunter. He was perfectly polite but he moved in a loose-limbed way.

A suggestive way.

The sight made my mouth go dry.

"He's helping me with my homework," I said to one disgruntled librarian, and she sniffed.

"Careful what you learn," she muttered.

"Let's check the catalog." Jared was typing quickly on the

keypad of the library's computer. If he was going to be a super-student, then I could go one better. I memorized the call number of the most promising title, and headed into the stacks. He strode right behind me, and I glanced back to find him smiling slightly.

Okay, so maybe I wasn't hiding my awareness of him that well.

Or at all.

There were three books on runes. I grabbed two and he took the third. I chose a big table in full view of the circulation desk. He glanced between me and the librarian—who was practically swallowing her lips in disapproval—then put the helmets beside me. I was already deep into one book.

"It's called Fehu." I liked the sound of the word. It felt familiar in a way, and I said it again, softly.

He sat down beside me. Close. Really close. I pretended to be indifferent and pretty much failed. He wouldn't have had to be *Pyr* to hear my heart pounding.

"First rune of the first aett of the Elder Futhark." Jared bumped his shoulder against mine as he read.

He had to be deliberately messing with me, so I didn't respond. Like I hadn't noticed how close he was sitting. (I'd have noticed even if I'd been dead—and he knew it as well as I did.)

I kept reading. "What does that mean?"

"It's like they divided their alphabet into chunks. The Elder Futhark is one alphabet, maybe the oldest one."

"And the first aett is the first group of runes. Okay."

I turned back to the book.

"It means *cattle*!" I wrinkled my nose. "I don't even eat meat. Last thing I need is a cow."

"No." Jared tapped the book with an emphatic finger. "Wealth, which was cattle in ancient times." He dropped his voice to a pitch that gave me shivers. "Look beyond the metaphor, Zoë. We're talking symbols."

"Money and credit." I read further but still didn't understand why Granny had given me this stone.

"Don't skip the story," he chided.

"Okay." I read aloud in a muted voice. " 'The symbol is associated with cattle and their life-giving powers. In the Norse creation myth, the primal cow, Audhumla, licked a block of salt until the first man emerged. That was Buri, father of humans.' "

"Beginnings." Jared leaned back in the chair, balancing it on its back two legs, folding his arms behind his head. I stared. You know you would have, too. His black T-shirt was tight enough to show his six-pack to advantage. "It means something is beginning." He lifted one brow, inviting . . . something.

How did a person manage to have such green eyes?

Could he see right through to my heart? My deepest secrets? My thoughts? I had a feeling he could, and as soon as I thought that, he smiled.

I looked away. I forced myself to think straight. (It was tougher than it should have been.)

Something *had* started after Granny gave me the rune stone. My period had turned up. Just the day before—which technically could have been the same day—I'd been able to make a partial shift into dragon form.

And then there was that guy.

I had an easier time believing that Granny and the rune stone had kick-started everything than that it had been Meagan's visioning session. Maybe she and I had just prodded the change.

Jared tipped forward, chair legs landing with a thump. He flipped through the second book, his arm against mine. His eyes gleamed as he pushed it toward me and tapped a single word.

Right after *beginnings*, this book listed *fire* as a meaning for my rune.

Our gazes locked. "In the beginning, there was the fire," Jared said quietly, and I caught my breath that he was voicing my thoughts. I knew the phrase well enough to finish the paragraph. It was typed into my file of clues on my messenger.

You already know that it's from the foundation myth of the *Pyr*.

JARED WAS WATCHING ME AS I rolled through this verse in my mind. "So, what powers do you have already, baby Wyvern?" he asked.

I shrugged and looked away, not really wanting to itemize my incompetence.

"Come on, you can tell me. I've got the book, remember?" Jared leaned closer and counted off on his fingers, his expectation persuasive. "Communicating in old-speak?"

"I'm getting better."

"Shifting shape?"

"Not fully."

"Breathing fire?"

I shook my head.

"Dispatching dreams?"

I bit my lip and dared to meet his gaze. "I have them."

Jared was unimpressed. "Everyone does. Foresight?"

"That's my dad's power."

"No, the Wyvern sees past and present and future. If you can see the future, that's a kind of foresight, but the Wyvern gets the whole enchilada simultaneously."

I frowned, thinking about my dreams. I worried the rune stone in one hand. Had I invoked those dreams? Or invited them? It was a possibility. "Maybe. I'm not sure."

"I'll guess that taking alternate forms and spontaneous manifestation are part of the advanced class." He drummed his fingers on the table and I sensed that I'd disappointed him. It was not a good feeling. "Can you feel the earth? Take its mood?"

I shook my head.

"Control any of the elements?"

Nyet. I was feeling as suave as a toddler.

The fact that I had been more on my game as a toddler was pretty depressing.

Jared leaned even closer, his nose almost touching mine. "Well, here's the thing, Zoë. I think the problem is that you doubt that you're the Wyvern, and until you believe it yourself, you're not going to be able to do any of this."

I was insulted. "What do you know about it?"

"More than you do, from the sound of it."

I hated that his argument made so much sense, so I disagreed. "I don't think so!"

"Can you sense the location of the other *Pyr*?"

"No!"

"Be serious. You could at least try." His shoulder pressed against mine; I could feel his breath in my ear. "I *dare* you to try," he murmured. His eyes shone brightly, as brightly as a cat's, and I understood that he was pushing me.

In fact, that was his point.

I wanted to deck him. I wasn't a loser and I wasn't a sloth. What did he—a human!—know about the challenges I faced? He could never understand. I wanted to wipe that half smile off his mouth and eliminate that daring glint from his eyes.

There was only one way to do that.

I had to try.

Chapter 9

"You're on." I shut my eyes before Jared could look triumphant.

I felt with all my senses for the *Pyr*. I was sure it wouldn't work, so I wasn't surprised that I didn't feel a thing. "Satisfied? Or are you just trying to embarrass me?"

"I'm trying to get you to claim your legacy," he replied. "Nothing worth having comes for free, Zoë."

"Well, I tried!"

"But you need to believe."

"I believe."

"Bullshit."

I closed my eyes. I willed myself to believe. I was the Wyvern, the only female *Pyr*, our prophetess, the one born to lead us into the future with my innate powers.

I am the Wyvern.

I will shift shape and I will cast dreams and I will be everything that I am forecast to be.

I.

Am.

The.

Wyvern.

And I will claim my birthright, right here and now.

I felt a prickle of awareness then. A hum like the current on an electrical line. The sound a motor makes just before it starts to turn.

Jared's hand closed over mine. "Chase it," he whispered.

How did he know? I'd worry about that later.

I listened to the hum, and it developed into a vague sense that Nick and the others were behind us. I felt them on the same road we'd taken, saw the point where they were, then lost it.

Jared squeezed my hand, as if to encourage me.

"I felt them," I whispered. "I saw them! They're at that turn by the gas station four, maybe five exits back." I met Jared's gaze, unable to hide my astonishment.

"And now?"

I frowned, seeking that sense, and found nothing. "I lost them."

"Can you send them old-speak? Maybe you could pinpoint their location by the sound of their reply?" Jared leaned closer.

Great Wyvern, but he was hot. Having him so near made bits of me tingle that I hadn't even known I had. I had to nail this, but Jared was seriously distracting.

He started to slide his thumb across the back of my hand, rhythmic and sexy, until I couldn't think of one other thing but his touch.

"The book says something about ley lines," he murmured. "They used to be called dragonlines, and are lines of force that somehow encircle the Earth. The description is pretty vague, but maybe you can feel them."

It made enough sense that I wanted to try.

It couldn't have been all bad that I wanted to impress him, either. Actually, I realized that his caress—which he was doing only to mess with me—seemed to be awakening my senses. Or taking them to a sharper pitch.

I sensed that I could work with that. "Maybe I can try both together."

Jared nodded, anticipation lighting his eyes.

I'd check on my dad first. I closed my eyes and listened. Nothing beyond the library and the town pressed around us. I felt, stretching my mind out into the world, tentative, listening.

Suddenly I sensed a glimmer, like a gold line, one that flashed in the periphery of my vision. It hummed, just as it had before. I could see it vibrating, like a piano wire that had been struck.

It gleamed, then disappeared.

I looked but couldn't find it again.

"Stay calm." Jared's voice was low and soothing. His fingers slid up and down my forearm, and even through the leather jacket, he gave me tingles. "Agitation never helps this kind of stuff."

I took a deep breath, then tried Jared's other idea.

"Dad?" I asked in old-speak.

"Very good," my dad replied immediately, his praise sliding into my mind as if he were sitting beside me and murmuring into my ear. I probably bounced a bit as I heard him.

I definitely gripped Jared's hand.

"Go for it," Jared murmured.

The thing is that I heard pride in Jared's words, a pride that echoed my own. That was exciting.

I stretched my thoughts again and found that place in my mind more readily. I realized I could sense my father's presence.

It was at the terminus of a line of heat in my thoughts. I could see a ribbon of fire, one that hummed a little, one that led directly to my dad. A copper conduit. He was miles away, and even though I couldn't see him, I knew that he was in dragon form.

I could feel the wind beneath his wings and the sizzle of snow landing on his scales. I could hear the beat of his heart and could have dropped a finger onto a map to indicate his location.

He was on the roof of our loft in Chicago.

My dad was with me, too, though. His attention was upon me and his senses mingled with my thoughts, even though he was hundreds of miles away. I understood suddenly how he played superdad, how he kept track of all the *Pyr*, regardless of where they were.

Wow.

"*Yes. But you should be able to do it better than me*," my dad confided. "*Now you know how it feels. Reach for more. Stretch.*"

I did, and it was easy, now that I knew the trick. I found the guys more easily this time: Nick's car was some forty miles behind us. I could have been sitting on the top of the rearview mirror and could see the highway around them. I could hear them joking around, vying for Isabelle's attention, and thought the car was too warm.

Too much testosterone.

"You're doing it," Jared murmured, his hands locked over mine. His fingers were warm and strong, the way his thumb caressed my pinkie ring distracting me. My mouth went dry and I nearly lost the coppery glimmer.

Then I realized this ability could be used to tell me exactly what I wanted to know.

I stretched out and found Donovan. He was far ahead, waiting in a rustic cabin. It was a single room, no amenities. There was a fire burning on the hearth and a map spread on the table as he waited for us. The light of the fire painted the simple interior in shades of gold, making it look like a haven.

Could he hear me, too? Or could I speak at distance only with my dad? Was the blood link part of it?

"Donovan?" I asked in old-speak, daring to hope.

Donovan started. *"Zoë?"* He lifted his head and looked toward me, as if he sensed my being there. But I knew by the way his gaze danced over the room that he couldn't see me.

"Did you really send Jared to pick me up?" I asked.

Donovan smiled. *"Yes."*

"But can I trust him?"

He bent his attention on his map again. *"I sold him my old Ducati, Zoë. He'll do what I asked. No more and no less. Okay?"*

"Okay." I smiled then; I couldn't help it.

You can't lie in old-speak, you know. It comes right from the heart.

Donovan spun around all of a sudden, looking past me. I wondered what he saw. He frowned. He folded up the map quickly and stuffed it into his pocket. I saw him shimmer blue; then he strode out of the cabin into the snow, slamming the door behind himself.

What was going on?

Maybe it was cheating to check up on him this way. Maybe I wasn't supposed to peek on boot camp doings in advance.

I took a deep breath, followed the gleam in my thoughts, and sought Rafferty.

He was at our loft in Chicago, in the spare room. He started in his sleep when I followed the line of fire to him, but he looked straight at me. He sat up with care, as if he feared I would slip away.

Then he smiled and nodded approval. *"Hail, Wyvern,"* he murmured, raising one hand in salute, and his ring reflected the light.

I had done it! I *was* the Wyvern!

———

MY EYES FLEW OPEN AND the library looked strange—as if the world in my thoughts were more real than this one. I played the eye game, and Rafferty was still in front of me when I looked through my left eye. Then he faded from sight, the view from both eyes becoming the library.

I glanced down to find my hand locked within Jared's, and I was uncertain how long I had been hunting the *Pyr* in my thoughts. I was trembling a little.

I had done Wyvern stuff!

The librarian was watching from the circulation desk, her expression dour.

Jared squeezed my fingers. "That was old-speak, wasn't it? The book says that old-speak sounds like thunder to humans, and I heard thunder."

I nodded, sensing his excitement. "You were right. Once I could hear them, I could find them."

"Excellent!" His eyes gleamed as he leaned closer. "Score one for the new Wyvern."

His arm slipped around my shoulders, and I could feel his muscles even through the leather. I felt his heartbeat and my eyes widened as mine adjusted its beat to synchronize with his. The sensation made me dizzy, but it could just have been his proximity. Jared's gaze dropped to my lips, and his eyes were bright, a little wild. Daring. I was sure he was going to kiss me.

And you know, I thought it would be okay.

No, I thought it would be exciting, awesome, and totally the right thing to happen.

Celebratory.

That was why I was determined to kiss him back.

I'd show him that this Wyvern *was* bold.

It was time I surprised Jared, maybe shook *his* tree.

I leaned closer, saw him start to smile. . . .

AND THE LIBRARIAN CLEARED HER throat. Loudly. She was right behind us, peering down at us, her lips so tight they nearly disappeared.

"Did you find what you were looking for?" She reached between us for the books.

"Yes, thank you," I said.

"You'd better believe it," Jared agreed. The librarian gave him a full-octane glare.

When I looked down at the table again, my rune stone was gone. Jared was on his feet, heading to the door, and I could see something in his hand.

My rune stone.

"Hey! That's mine!"

"Not if you don't take care of it," he taunted. He tossed it into the air, caught it, and headed out the door. I grabbed the second helmet and bolted after him, almost knocking over the chair in my hurry to catch up.

I jumped down the stairs, running faster than I ever had before. Even so, Jared was already on the bike when I got down the steps, his helmet on and the engine running. I thought he would leave me behind, wherever the heck we were, and that made me livid.

"I thought you couldn't say no to Donovan? How does stealing my stuff and leaving me here mesh with that?"

Jared grinned and opened his hand. The rune stone was on his palm. "I'm just giving you some motivation. I told you I hate being late."

I snatched the stone from him, compulsively checking it over, ignoring his astonishment. I was shaken by the prospect of losing it, more shaken than I would have expected. It suddenly felt like the key to everything, and I'd nearly lost it.

Because I'd trusted him. I heard that song again, playing in my thoughts, the one Nick had sent me, and my doubts about Jared seemed to feed one another. My suspicion grew and I took a step away from him.

Jared watched me, his expression inscrutable. "Has anyone ever told you that you have trust issues?"

"I'm glad I didn't kiss you," I blurted. "Only a jerk would try to steal my rune stone." I shoved the stone into my pocket, feeling hostile and jangled.

Jared's smile faded. "You're welcome, Zoë," he said, frost dripping from his words. "I was happy to give you some suggestions on following ley lines so that you could get your powers without having to figure anything out yourself."

Then he flicked down his visor and turned on the bike.

That was all it took to eliminate my anger.

As soon as it faded, I could see that my reaction had been fear.

Fear that I nearly lost the stone.

Fear that this one promising sign was the only bit of Wyvernness I'd experienced so far, and might be all there would be.

But Jared had been the one to give me a hint, to help me get closer than I'd been yet.

I was the jerk.

I scuffed my toe in the snow. "I'm sorry, Jared. I really am. Thank you for helping me."

Jared ignored me.

But he waited, fingers tapping on the handles.

I put on my helmet and got on the bike. I hesitated a moment before putting my arms around him again. Jared held himself stiff this time, as if he didn't want to touch me, either.

"Like I said," he said softly, his words coming through the speaker to my ear, "your problem is that you expect everyone to believe in you, but you don't believe in yourself. Never mind that you're too proud to accept any help."

There was nothing I could say to that.

Then we were off, the roar of the bike filling any conversational gap. I felt like I'd just taken a final exam and failed it completely.

Smooth, Zoë, really smooth.

ANOTHER TWO HOURS OF RAW speed and wind left my fingers numb on Jared's chest. My enthusiasm for the motorcycle as winter transport was waning, exactly proportionate to the amount of ice in my hands. I was relieved when he left the highway. He turned south, taking a series of turns until all I could see on either side of the narrow road was bush.

And snow.

He slowed the bike and idled beside a driveway that I would have missed completely if it hadn't had a silver mailbox. It wasn't even shoveled. A single set of tracks led down the drive, the tires having made deep grooves in the snow.

"Jeep." Jared opened his visor to eye the tracks. "Donovan's four-wheel drive." He stayed on the bike, apparently indecisive.

"Too deep for the Ducati?" I opened my visor, too.

He shrugged. "I'm supposed to drop you off here anyway." I got off the bike, but he caught my elbow with one hand. "I don't want to leave you here alone."

"Why not?"

"There is that." His smile turned rueful, and I was ashamed of my outburst all over again. He watched me, those bright eyes seeming not to miss a thing.

"I'm sorry. . . ."

"Listen." Jared turned off the engine and there was only the sound of the wind. It was still overcast, still snowing, the wind rustling through the pines.

There was no other sound around us.

I shivered. I could hear the beat of Jared's heart, courtesy of my *Pyr* hearing, and the rate of his pulse confirmed that he wasn't thrilled with the situation. I fought against letting my own heart-beat match his, guessing that that wouldn't help me remain detached and logical. Had that been my mistake earlier?

Our breath made white clouds, and the cold air stung my cheeks. I thought of Granny and wondered whether I had moved from my world to hers.

The thing was that I really didn't want to be left alone in the middle of nowhere, either.

"It's not safe, Zoë. Not smart."

It was odd to hear Jared be so cautious. "I thought risk was your style."

"Maybe. But it's not yours."

"You could stay."

He smiled. "Uninvited, at boot camp? I think not. Besides, I've got a gig in Sioux Falls on Monday, and practice tonight. The guys took my gear down."

"What guys?"

"The other guys in the band."

"You have a band?" I sounded like a moron but couldn't help it. Why else would he have a gig? Duh.

He smiled. "Didn't you know?"

I shook my head. I wanted to ask what kind of music they played, the name of the band, lots of stuff, but didn't want to push my luck. Too often when I opened my mouth in Jared's presence, something stupid fell out. Maybe I should just shut up.

It was nice to have him be a bit worried about me.

That, in fact, made me want to prove to him that I was just as independent as he was. This was not a guy who would be inter-ested in a clingy chick. (And yes, it was a long shot that he'd be interested in me anyway, but I didn't want to think that far ahead.)

"Then I shouldn't hold you up. Thanks for the ride. Hope the gig goes well." I handed him the extra helmet.

He fastened it on the back of the bike. "I still don't like this."

"But you said those are the treads from Donovan's truck," I argued, trying to stay in the spirit of boot camp and self-sufficiency and confident girls. "And the guys aren't far behind."

Jared shook his head. "You don't have any gear, Zoë, and you don't know the way. It would be irresponsible for me to leave you here alone." He gave me a quick glance. "Can you sense Donovan? Is he here?"

"I just saw him when I was tracking the *Pyr* at the library."

"I thought someone else would be here to meet you." I heard him make a little growl of frustration, which was really neat. "But I can't *not* do what Donovan asks of me."

His concern warmed me right to my toes. "Why not?"

"He's pretty much the only person in the world who trusts me." Jared tossed me a grin. "Who would want to mess with that?"

"But this has got to be one of the tests of boot camp. That's the point—to find out what we can do and maybe learn to do some new things." I had a feeling Jared could teach me some other things, some things that might have been fun to learn. "You were the one who said the Wyvern should be bold."

"That was different." He looked annoyed. "My gut tells me that this is a bad idea, and I have a policy of following my instincts."

"Even if Donovan made you promise otherwise?"

"Even if." He gave me a hot look, one that was filled with protectiveness.

Oh. I could have fallen right into his eyes and stayed there forever.

I'm supposed to be a smart kid, so I forced myself to look away from Jared, temptation, and things my mother thinks I'm too young to know. He was all about living in the moment.

I'd always wanted forever.

I was pretty sure his band had a posse of fan girls, gorgeous, sexy babes who would give him anything in exchange for five seconds of his attention.

Maybe five minutes.

They'd all have perfect boobs; you just know it.

Chapter 10

When I looked away from Jared, I noticed that the little red flag on the mailbox was up.

I opened it, intending to take Donovan his mail. I was making the walk anyway. But there were five envelopes in the mailbox, and none of them was addressed to Donovan.

Boot camp. Only the top one was addressed to me. The next three were for Garrett, Liam, and Nick. The last was for someone named Adrian.

I waved my envelope at Jared in excitement. "It's a clue! And it's for me." I left the other messages as a test for the guys. Some of the snow had fallen off the top of the mailbox, and I hoped that I hadn't left them a hint of what they should do.

It was possible that I just might survive boot camp.

"You decide, Zoë. You want me to leave?"

I nodded, even though I didn't want him to go. Maybe this

was another test. I would be bold. A Wyvern in the making. I would be confident in my powers and identity.

A real live dragon girl.

It was worth a shot.

"I'll follow the tracks to the cabin. I can follow the ley lines if I get lost." I held up the envelope. "Besides, I've got to figure out the clue before I get there."

I heard something then, the engine of a car.

No, two cars.

"The others are almost here," I said. "See? All good."

"That's a relative term." Jared was surprisingly sour.

I didn't have time to ask him what he meant, because a four-wheel drive I didn't recognize pulled onto the shoulder behind us. Jared eyed the driver with suspicion. I thought he even inhaled sharply, which was weird.

This guy was dark-haired and he wore sunglasses. He was cute, in a big-brother kind of way, and maybe five years older than me.

Cute, but not hot.

Nice, maybe.

He was also *Pyr*.

I caught a whiff of something else, too, something unfamiliar. I couldn't place it.

"You must be Zoë." The guy got out of his vehicle, leaving it running. As soon as he spoke, my doubts evaporated. He had the most beautiful voice. I just wanted to listen to it all day.

And that scent was gone.

Maybe I'd imagined it.

"You must be Adrian," I guessed.

He grinned, his gaze dancing over me. His appreciation was clear. "I'm honored to meet the Wyvern." He made a little bow. "Is that foresight or just intelligence?"

Wow. He was flirting with *me*.

Things were looking up. That he was cute but not stupendously gorgeous made it easier to flirt back. That Jared was scowling at us didn't hurt, either.

"Puzzle solving," I said. "My best trick."

He took off his sunglasses and I had an overwhelming sense of what a normal, trustworthy *Pyr* he was. It was impossible not to like him.

"We'll probably all learn some new ones this week." Adrian spared a glance toward Jared.

"I know when I'm not welcome." Jared gave me a sizzling look. I knew he wanted me to come to his side, but I didn't move.

If Jared was trying to warn me about the perils of flirting with easygoing guys, that they were a lot less trouble than extremely hot guys who wanted more and more, then I considered myself warned. If he was jealous, that wasn't all bad, either.

Jared started the bike, his gestures a little more savage than necessary. "Remember, Zoë: just as you're more than you seem to be, so is everyone else."

Before I could answer, he closed his visor, gunned the bike hard, and headed back toward the highway.

Without one backward glance.

I watched him go, feeling like I'd made a big mistake.

Another one.

I SWALLOWED MY DISAPPOINTMENT as the bike disappeared.

I'd probably never see Jared again. I wasn't going to think about the fact that I'd missed my chance for a kiss from him. I certainly didn't want to think about him surrounded by squealing fan girls, because I was pretty sure he wasn't going to think about me.

Adrian came to stand beside me. "Friend of yours? He seems a bit prickly."

"Part of his charm," I said. "Or maybe not."

Adrian laughed. "You want a ride? I'm not sure how far we'll get down this road before we have to walk, but it can't hurt to try the easy way first. You look cold."

"Freezing." I got into the four-wheel drive, which was nice and warm. The seats were even heated, with fuzzy covers on them. I could have curled up like a cat and gone to sleep.

Adrian took one look at me and turned up the heat. "You're out of your mind to be on a bike in this weather."

"Donovan set it up. I had no choice."

"So, did Attitude Boy know something you needed to know, then?"

I was startled by the question, but Adrian was concentrating on turning into the driveway. The tires sank into the snow and he changed gears, taking it slow. He handed me his sunglasses, locking both hands on the wheel.

For some reason, I wanted to lie.

I went with it. "I don't know. Mostly I just got cold."

Adrian's gaze was fixed on the road. "I can believe it."

I then wondered, had Donovan known Jared would challenge me? Had the plan been that I'd learn about the ley lines?

Had Jared been *told* to challenge me?

Or did Donovan just know what kind of guy he was?

What had Donovan seen when he'd left the cabin?

"So, why haven't we met before?" I asked.

"My dad." Adrian rolled his eyes. "You probably know him, or know of him. Felix."

I knew no *Pyr* named Felix. I knew that with complete certainty, until Adrian continued talking in those deep masculine tones. I forgot about wondering who Felix was and leaned back to luxuriate in the rich sound of his voice.

It kind of reminded me of that music from Nick.

Maybe there was a different side of me waking up, along with my newfound Wyvern powers.

Adrian kept talking. "He's a cousin of Sloane's, but they had a big argument a long time ago and stopped speaking. Something to do with my mother, who was a bit, um, troubled."

"Troubled?" This story suddenly sounded familiar. I must have heard the story, but forgotten about it.

Until now.

Adrian winced. "Crazy, more like. Dragon-crazy."

"My dad's said some *Pyr* have firestorms with complete dragon fans."

"Well, my dad was the original. At first he thought it could work out." Adrian grimaced. "But it got nasty once she got pregnant. She even tried to disappear and hide me. My dad got fed up with the *Pyr* and their advice—he'd say their meddling—so he bailed on them."

"But he found you." I could understand that a *Pyr* wouldn't handle it very well if his mate fled with his son. They're really protective dads.

Adrian nodded.

"What happened to your mom?"

"She lost it completely." His expression was strained, and I knew that something awful had happened to his mom. I reached out and touched his hand.

He cleared his throat, his fingers brushing mine quickly. "It wasn't easy growing up without anyone knowing what I was, or having any friends who were *Pyr*." I could totally relate to that—even with *Pyr* friends and my dad, I found the secrecy tough. "But I finally talked my dad into breaking his silence, and he came to Donovan to ask about having me invited to boot camp." He forced a smile, obviously trying to be more upbeat. "I'm really looking forward to the chance to learn more."

"I wonder whether he had a hard time convincing Donovan."

Adrian laughed. "Do the *Pyr* ever kiss and make up without fireworks?"

I laughed at that, because he was right. We are stubborn, proud, and passionate. It was nice to talk to someone I hadn't known before, and to tell the truth, I felt a bit sorry for Adrian. It couldn't have been easy to grow up not only without the *Pyr*, but without his mom around.

Even if she was nuts.

I hugged myself, missing my own mom a bit.

Adrian and I didn't say anything for a while, him just driving and me holding his sunglasses. I could feel the weight of the rune stone in my pocket. I didn't want to draw his attention to it by pulling it out for a look.

It seemed heavier somehow.

Beginnings.

I thought of Jared and the way he seemed to know what I was thinking, and how he laughed and he needled me to try harder, and wished we had parted differently.

Because I wanted to see him again someday.

"You've got to be careful with humans, Zoë," Adrian said. "Some of them are just into the dragon thing so much that they don't care what they have to do to get close to us."

"Or what happens to us." I thought of his story.

"Watch out for that guy. Whoever he was. There's something about him that I don't trust."

"I doubt I'll ever see him again, anyway."

"That's probably for the best."

We didn't talk any more about Jared, because the tracks from Donovan's truck abruptly stopped. There was nothing but snow and forest all around us. He must have backed out. I could see where the road must be for about another twenty feet ahead of us.

Then nothing but a lot of snow.

"I'm hoping our future looks better than our present," Adrian joked, but he didn't wait for me to do any prophesying. He just got out of the truck to look around.

I liked that. I was a little more reluctant to leave the warmth of that seat, but I got out, too.

IT SEEMED COLDER IN THE forest. The snow fell around us in fat flakes. The quiet was soothing in a way, but in another, it felt disorienting. I'm a city girl, used to the hum of traffic.

This was Granny's turf.

Maybe just as unpredictable and attractive as Jared.

A girl could get hurt. Either way. I shivered.

"I wish I had an idea where we're supposed to be going," Adrian said.

"There's a cabin."

He turned to me with interest. "Do you have any idea how far it is? Or in which direction?"

I could have told him about the ley lines, and about seeing Donovan in a cabin, but it would take longer to explain it than to do it again. And he was watching me in an expectant way.

I closed my eyes, letting my mind slide along the same paths it had taken in the library. I felt the sparky hum, like electrical current, the one that shone like a line of copper in my thoughts. I followed it, more quickly now that I trusted it.

I found the guys behind us almost immediately. They were close, close enough that they must be beside the mailbox.

Ahead of me, though, I sensed nothing.

I tried to follow the ley lines again, but I couldn't sense Donovan. I couldn't find him. I couldn't perceive him at all. Where had he gone? It was as if the current had gone dead.

Or been shut off.

I felt a bit of dread then.

No, maybe Donovan was hiding from me. A test. I'd tipped my hand too early.

I sought the others, just to confirm that. My father seemed

more distant than he had, a dim shimmer in the distance. As if the wire were losing current.

At least he was there. I felt Rafferty, but my sense of him was fainter than before. I couldn't see him at all. There was just the slow vibration of his presence.

But I couldn't pinpoint his location.

Then the hum cut out.

Completely. I frowned and tried old-speak with my dad again, but that brought zero results. It was as if the older *Pyr* had melted out of the world.

Impossible!

I opened my eyes to find Adrian still intent upon me. "I'm sorry. I can't feel the cabin's location anymore."

"Maybe you're not supposed to." He touched my shoulder with one gloved hand, as if to encourage me.

It was nice to be with someone who cut me some slack, instead of criticizing all the time.

Then I guessed what was going on. The *Pyr* were deliberately hiding themselves from me. Donovan had seen me and ensured that I didn't have an unauthorized advantage. It was part of the boot camp test.

It was also reassuring that Adrian came to the same conclusion. I explained it to him and he nodded.

"Maybe finding the cabin is the first part of what we have to solve together. Donovan didn't want you to have an edge over the rest of us." He grinned. "Thank the Great Wyvern for that!"

I smiled at him. I heard Nick's car behind us, moving slowly. We both turned at the sound of the car revving more and more loudly.

"Nick must be stuck." He'd be embarrassed in front of Isabelle, especially as Liam and Garrett would razz him. I had to like that, and wished I'd been there to see it.

Adrian winked at me. "Which gives us a minute to solve this ourselves and be the winners of the day. Isn't that how it works?"

"The prize is the new messenger, the one that doesn't ship until the end of the year. Donovan showed us last night." I didn't have to pretend to be excited.

Adrian shared my enthusiasm. "Wow! Let's go look for the cabin now."

I wondered for a second why Adrian hadn't been at Donovan's house the night before, but then he shimmered, his broad shoulders outlined in vivid blue light. I was completely distracted by the prospect of his change. In the blink of an eye, he had shifted shape, becoming a powerful dragon.

In my fave colors.

It was funny because the dragon form didn't look quite right to me for a moment. He seemed to waver a bit, more like a reflection in an old mirror than anything real. An illusion, maybe.

Then I was distracted by the magnificence of his dragon power. Now, that was *wow*. Adrian was pewter and purple with silver accents. I stared. Maybe he had hot-guy potential after all.

Adrian watched me, probably expecting me to shift. I blushed, then gestured back toward the others as if I'd decided to wait on them.

He nodded once, so regal that he took my breath away. Then he leapt into the air, two beats of his powerful wings taking him over the canopy of trees. He soared into the snow-filled sky, a vision of majestic *Pyr* power. Just the sight made me ache with longing.

Jared was right about one thing: I really, really, *really* wanted to fly. I shoved my hands into my pockets and felt the crinkle of paper.

My envelope.

Maybe I could solve something, too.

THERE WAS A SINGLE SHEET of paper inside the envelope, with one line of type on it.

It was a riddle.

Or maybe just part of one.

I slide before the sun, but make no shadow.

I stood and thought about it, the snow falling all around me, then shoved the note back into my pocket. It wasn't as if I couldn't memorize it.

What didn't make a shadow?

Hydrogen molecules. Thoughts. Fog. I needed another clue to narrow it down. Was that what the guys' messages included?

I realized that Adrian hadn't picked up his envelope.

I had no chance to tell him, because a second dragon ripped through the sky in pursuit of Adrian.

A gleaming gold one.

Breathing fire.

Nick.

Looking for a fight.

Oh, no.

"Behind you!" I called to Adrian. I had to warn him, even though I knew that Nick would hear me, too.

"What are you doing?" Nick demanded in old-speak. *"I'm defending you!"*

From what? Or who? I didn't need defending.

Although it was kind of nice that he even had the inclination.

Two more dragons flew overhead, ripping through the air like fighter jets. Garnet with gold—that was Garrett. A green as vivid as my malachite earrings, tipped in silver—that was Liam.

They were at Nick's back.

"Hey! Where is everyone?" a woman with a British accent shouted from behind me.

Isabelle.

I paused. She was obviously having trouble in the snow, but was safe. I had more important things to do than hold her hand, so I ran after the guys.

Or at least in the direction of the dragon fight. I could hear them colliding with each other overhead. Trees were getting trashed, and dragonfire was flashing orange over the leafless trees.

I wanted to see the action.

The road that had seemed obvious became less clear with every step. I slipped, finding myself up to my hips in snow. There were brambles beneath the snow, ones with nasty thorns.

I shoved my way through the snow, irritated that I couldn't just shift and fly above the trees. The forest seemed to break ahead of me, and I guessed I'd be able to see the fight from there. Vivid orange flames lit the sky as I hurried.

I was so anxious to see that I forgot to pay attention.

On the other hand, I got my wish to witness the action.

I tripped on a root buried under the snow and fell. Face-first. There was an instant when I was up to my eyes in snow, nothing but white; then I felt the snow give on one side.

It wasn't the end of the forest. It was a hill. A steep one.

I slid.

Down.

It was a toboggan ride without the toboggan. I snatched in every direction, finding nothing to grab, even as I tumbled down. I suddenly found myself on my back, staring up at a snowy sky. I was helpless to stop myself as I raced down the hill, spinning as I went.

Powerless to stop what was happening.

I SPIRALED TO A HALT a thousand years later, a blizzard's worth of snow piled under Alex's leather jacket.

"You okay?" Liam landed beside me with powerful grace. He

extended a claw to help me up. His green and silver scales gleamed so brightly in the sunlight that I had to squint to look at him.

"We couldn't grab you sooner." Garrett landed on my other side. It said something for my upbringing that having a dragon on either side of me wasn't at all remarkable. Their scales were really sparkly in the sunshine, so I had to narrow my eyes.

I shook the snow out of the jacket as Liam exhaled a gentle flicker of dragonfire in my direction.

I admired his control. "Very nice. Thanks."

"Easy," Garrett warned him. "You don't want to melt the ice."

That was when I knew we weren't in a clearing—we were standing on a frozen lake. Liam nodded, and turned the furnace off.

"Why didn't you just shift?" Garrett demanded.

"You might have gotten hurt this way," Liam chided.

"I didn't think of it." I was irritated and self-conscious.

They exchanged glances, their surprise clear.

I didn't want to get into it. Not yet. I gestured to the two dragons continuing to fight overhead, and changed the subject. Nick was taunting Adrian while Adrian tried to reason with him. "Who's winning?"

"No one," Garrett said. "The other *Pyr* is pulling his punches."

Adrian was larger, more graceful, and he *was* pulling his punches. Nick looked like an amateur, fighting out of passion, not strategy. Nick snarled and slashed at him again, but his claws didn't connect.

"Hothead," Adrian chided.

Nick breathed dragonfire and lifted his talons.

"Who is he, anyway?" Liam asked.

"Adrian." I shared his story, and Garrett frowned.

"I don't remember that story."

"Me, neither," Liam agreed. "I didn't think Sloane had any more cousins than Brandt."

"Maybe he's not who he says he is," Garrett suggested.

"He's *Pyr*," I argued, impatient that they were being difficult. "Obviously. And he knew where boot camp was."

Garrett spoke with care. "He could be *Slayer*."

"They're pretty much eradicated," Liam noted. They both tensed, as if they'd join the fight.

"But Donovan invited him to boot camp," I said.

Garrett frowned. "If Adrian told you that, you don't know that it's true."

"Wouldn't Donovan have mentioned that someone else would be here? Wouldn't Adrian have been at the house last night?" Liam asked. "Ouch," he added, when Nick took a hit and fell back.

Adrian might be losing patience, but he spoke to Nick with control. *"I told you that I was invited by your father. I have as much right to be here as you do."*

"And I say you're lying!"

"Donovan left Adrian an envelope, just like all of us," I shouted. Nick either ignored me or couldn't hear me—you can guess which seemed most likely to me. "That means Donovan *did* know he was coming."

"Left him an envelope? Where?" Garrett was surprised.

I pulled out my envelope. "Right where you'd think." They were so shocked that I knew they'd missed the mailbox. "It's a clue. You guys just failed the first test."

"Shit," Liam muttered.

Just then Nick launched himself at the pewter and purple dragon. He slashed, and Adrian flinched as one talon tore at the side of his face. Adrian pivoted with amazing speed, his eyes flashing even as red blood flowed over his scales.

I knew Nick was about to lose the fight, but Nick didn't see it coming. Adrian moved with lightning speed, hitting Nick hard.

When Nick lost the rhythm of his flight, Adrian went after him, striking him twice more, then giving him a wallop with his tail. He didn't cut him; he didn't burn him—he just thumped him.

Guess that was what you learned when the only person you could practice fighting with was your dad.

Nick, meanwhile, was falling like a rock.

Chapter 11

Nick landed hard on the frozen surface of the lake, cracks radiating from his point of impact. Adrian hovered overhead, the beat of his wings so slow that it seemed impossible for him to remain aloft.

"Fuck." Nick opened his eyes for a moment before he closed them again. He shifted shape, turning to his human form, winced, and exhaled in a long shudder. Garrett and Liam shifted shape to land by his side. The ice made ominous noises even with their lighter weight. I walked across the ice to join them.

"Nothing broken," Garrett said.

"But plenty of bruises." Liam grimaced.

"Looks like a lesson in manners to me," I said.

Nick glared at me. "I was defending you!"

"But I didn't need defending. You could have just asked."

Nick's lips set and I knew he wasn't convinced.

"Let's get him off the lake." Adrian swooped down and picked up Nick, who moaned.

"What about you?" I asked Adrian. "Are you okay?"

He gave me a look, appearing both touched by my concern and insulted that I could imagine the fight had hurt him. That was so *Pyr* that I almost laughed.

"I'll be fine, thanks." He lifted Nick high into the sky.

"He was looking for the cabin," I told the guys. "I'll bet he spotted it."

"Let's follow him, then," Garrett said. "Come on, Zoë; I'll give you a lift."

"Sweet talker," I teased. "You just want something in exchange." Garrett's grin widened; then he shifted shape. The glimmer of his garnet scales in the sun nearly blinded me again.

"Do you guys buff and wax your scales?" I joked. "They're so shiny."

"Protein," Garrett said. "Lots of protein is the secret to strong scales." I made a mental note to cross-check my own protein intake. I wanted to be serious eye candy in dragon form.

Whenever I managed to do it.

"I'll get those envelopes," Liam offered. "Where are they, Zoë? You can tell us, now that you've already won the round."

"In the mailbox by the road, of course." The guys groaned in unison that they'd missed something so obvious. I rubbed salt in that wound. "The little red flag was even up."

"Okay, now we feel stupid," Liam said.

That was nothing compared to how we all felt when a scream rang out. We turned as one to stare at the shore.

Isabelle.

We'd forgotten all about her.

And our mission as *Pyr* was to defend humans.

Oops.

ISABELLE WAS OKAY. MORE OR less. She'd wiped out trying to keep up, and had twisted her ankle. Those covet-worthy riding boots apparently had leather soles, which weren't so great in the snow.

I still loved them. I would have taken them from her in a heartbeat and saved them for city wear. The issue was that she had delicate, small princess feet.

Of course.

Garrett carried Isabelle to the cabin instead of me. I picked up the stuff she'd dropped—her purse and a small bag—feeling like staff following behind with milady's possessions. That wasn't entirely fair, but I reminded myself about popular girls as I walked.

You just couldn't trust them, not for a minute.

It wasn't smart.

I saw Liam fly overhead, all malachite and silver power, laden with duffel bags from the car. Presumably he also had the envelopes. Either way, he was carrying too much to scoop me up. I kept trudging through the snow.

I checked my messenger, thinking some commiseration with Meagan would be just the thing, and discovered that we were off the edge of the world.

Out of the range of any communications service.

Like the borders of old maps, where it said, "Here Be Dragons."

Ha, ha.

BY THE TIME I GOT to the cabin, there was smoke curling out of the chimney and I could smell food. I'd had time to think of Jared's almost-kiss—the one I hadn't received—which didn't exactly improve my spirits.

It would have been educational. An experience. A new sensation. That was the only reason I was curious.

Not because I had any expectations about something happening between us.

The cabin was rustic, just one room with a stone fireplace built into one wall. Exactly the way I'd seen it when I'd found Donovan. So that had worked, anyway. The fire was crackling on the hearth, a small stack of firewood beside it. There was an iron grille on a hinge that could be put over the fire.

It was simple, but that didn't usually bother me.

Nick was sitting on one of the four chairs that faced the fire, wincing as Isabelle wiped at his face. He was already developing a nice shiner. Adrian was beside the one counter that passed as a kitchen, taking inventory. Our gear was all piled in one corner, boots crowded near the door, and Garrett was surveying the firewood.

"So, how much food is there?" Garrett asked Adrian.

"A pot of vegetarian chili, some crisp bread, and oatmeal." Adrian dug in a cupboard that was under the counter. "About ten pounds of mixed onions, potatoes, and carrots. Raw."

"Great." Nick rolled his eyes. "How about some burgers?"

"No luck." Adrian shrugged. "We'll have to make do."

"Sounds like enough for a day," Liam said.

"Enough wood for one night," Garrett added. "If we're careful."

"Maybe we're supposed to be moving out by then." I really liked that possibility. "Maybe Donovan will come to get us."

"Nobody's going to come get us, Zoë. We're not little kids anymore." Nick slanted a smile at Isabelle that was anything but childish.

I refused to notice that she, too, looked unhappy with the cabin. We were not going to have anything in common.

"Maybe it's just not supposed to be an all-inclusive hotel," Adrian suggested.

"Maybe we're supposed to be self-sufficient," Liam agreed.

"We should look for Donovan's tracks," I said. "Maybe we can find him."

"If there were any tracks outside the cabin, they've been stomped over too many times now," Adrian said, and his reasoning made perfect sense. Donovan had been on the cusp of change—if he'd shifted and flown away, there would be no tracks. "I vote that we focus on getting through the night okay."

Garrett was leaning on the counter, watching Adrian, his arms folded across his chest. "And who was your dad again?" He was polite, but I heard his suspicion.

I bristled on Adrian's behalf, but he told the guys the same story he'd told me. It was a longer and more detailed version, but the gist was the same. I could almost feel the tension melting from the cabin as he spoke.

"So we're here and might as well make the best of it," Adrian said, so cheerful that I wanted to be part of the solution. "Who wants to cut firewood?"

Nick still watched Adrian with hostility. Maybe his wounded pride made him more antagonistic. "So you're taking charge now? Just like that?"

"No." Adrian spoke with care. "Just trying to figure out the plan. Got a problem with that?"

"Who asked you to?" Nick demanded, and Isabelle put a hand on his arm.

As if she were the one running his show.

"Take it easy, Nick," Garrett said.

"Take it easy? What's wrong with all of you?" Nick's voice rose. "We don't know this guy. We don't know anything about him, except what he says about himself. Why should we trust him?" Nick pushed to his feet. "Maybe he knows more than he's admitting."

"Like what?" Liam asked.

"Like where's my dad? He's always met us at boot camp."

A shadow filled the cabin, and it seemed much darker inside. More dangerous. I shivered, getting gooseflesh, as if someone were walking on my grave.

Adrian smiled. "I'm not answerable for your father. I don't know any more of his plan than you do."

"Still—" Nick started to argue.

"Still," I interrupted. "Adrian was expected, just like the rest of us."

"See?" Liam scooped the envelopes off the table and handed them around. Nick stared at his own envelope, some of his resistance dissolving when he saw that Adrian had one.

"There isn't one for me?" Isabelle asked.

Liam glanced at me, but I shook my head.

"Don't worry." Nick smiled at her. "We all know that *you* were invited." He sat down again and patted the arm of his chair. She sat down beside him.

No, she nestled against his shoulder.

I wanted to gag. Adrian rolled his eyes. I couldn't help but smile at him. Then I saw that there was still a bit of blood on his cheek.

"Are you okay? You should clean that up."

"It's nothing," he said. "It'll heal by morning. But thanks for asking, Zoë. It's good to know that someone's glad I'm here." There was something new in his eyes, something warm.

It wasn't reassuring at all to realize that I'd been right all along: that as soon as my period showed up, everything would change. First there had been that almost-kiss from Jared the Extremely Hot. And now Adrian was looking at me as if I were interesting.

That something I'd yearned for was finally happening didn't leave me any better prepared to deal with it.

I changed the subject. "So? What's in your envelopes? I've got one line, maybe from a riddle."

The guys went for the distraction like fruit flies after bruised bananas.

I did hear Adrian chuckle a little, though.

So maybe he wasn't so distracted.

And maybe I didn't mind that he came to sit right beside me.

I pretended not to notice that his leg bumped against mine. Instead, I pulled out my messenger and created a file for the clues, intending to compile them.

I made a few notes about riddles while I was there.

FIVE THINGS ABOUT RIDDLES

1. They're designed to fake you into making the wrong conclusion. It's like sleight of hand with words—that's what Lorenzo says. For his stage magic, he gestures to his right to make you look right, when the action is happening on the left.
2. They're one of the oldest forms of stories or jokes. Older maybe than the *Pyr*.
3. Dragons are supposed to be good at solving riddles. Maybe it's because we're both ancient ideas.
4. They can be funny or rude or both.
5. You can't solve a riddle by thinking straight. You have to think sideways. Outside the box. A little bit twisted. In an unexpected or unconventional way. Maybe that is why dragons are good at solving riddles. Maybe my being a dragon is why I'm good at solving them. Huh.

—————

I WAS THINKING ABOUT THAT as Liam handed out the envelopes. Was I looking in the wrong place for evidence of my Wyvern powers? Maybe.

"Okay, let's get to it." Garrett ripped his open.

"I'm starving." Nick got to his feet, grimacing as he limped toward the table. "Let's eat first."

"No way." Garrett tugged out his clue. "Boot camp is the first order of business. Zoë's already up a point for the day." He frowned at his note. Nick and Adrian tore their envelopes open as well. There was silence for a moment.

"'*I touch everyone, but no one catches me.*'" Nick shrugged.

"'*I am a city vast, thick with people but no streets,*'" Liam read, and I typed those two into my messenger.

"'*I am a boundless buffet from which everyone eats but no one fills,*'" added Garrett.

"'*Valued by all, sold by none, I have no price,*'" added Adrian.

"'*I slide before the sun, but make no shadow.*'" I contributed mine. I frowned at the five clues, thinking.

"Thought?" Garrett suggested.

"That doesn't touch anyone," Isabelle said.

"Smoke?" Liam offered.

"Who eats smoke?" Nick asked.

"Besides, it leaves a shadow," Adrian said.

Silence reigned. Then all of the guys looked at me.

"Well, Zoë?" Nick's manner was expectant.

I felt as if I should know the answer, but couldn't quite grasp the solution.

No pressure.

"I thought you were good with riddles," Nick teased. "Losing your touch?"

"You wish." That was more like our usual teasing. "I'll think of it. Maybe we just need some food."

The guys didn't argue with that. We heated the chili and dug in, and there was only the sound of happy consumption for a while. In no time, the pot was empty.

"What do you think the deal is with Donovan?" I asked. I was concerned, given how I'd seen him shimmer as he'd left.

Adrian nodded at the guys. "You've done boot camp before. What's your take?"

"Maybe we're in the wrong place," Isabelle said, and shuddered. "It's awful here."

"No, this is the right place," I said.

"How do you know?" Nick asked.

"I saw Donovan in this very cabin when I was sensing the other *Pyr* this morning." I let him make what he wanted of that. Isabelle's eyes widened.

"Where is he now?" Nick asked.

"I don't know. I can't find them anymore."

"They must be deliberately hiding," Adrian said, once again the voice of reason. "Donovan realized what Zoë could do and told the others to ensure she couldn't find them. Evens the playing field for all of us."

Garrett snorted and I felt their sudden displeasure. No, it was resentment. What could I say? I couldn't explain it any better than Adrian had.

The guys could cut me some slack.

"Maybe we're supposed to hunt my dad," Nick suggested after several moments. "Maybe we're supposed to stop for a meal, solve the riddle, and head out after him."

"Except Zoë isn't helping," Garrett noted.

"Anyone can solve the riddle!" I protested.

"But that's your thing." There was a new edge of hostility in Garrett's voice, one that surprised me. "We're each here for a reason, and using our skills makes us a better team. You could tell us where Donovan is, or you could solve the riddle."

He gave me a challenging look.

Trouble was, I couldn't do either.

And Garrett thought I was lying about it.

Why would he assume that I'd lie?

"Otherwise, why are you here?" he added softly. Our gazes locked and held, and it seemed that everyone else was watching. I was shocked that Garrett was turning against me. It surprised me so much that I wasn't ready to argue my own side.

How could he do that?

"Arguing won't solve anything," Adrian said finally, stepping between us. "It's not Zoë's fault. We have to work together."

"We should divide the area into quadrants, then fly out to find my dad, or whatever he's planned for us." Nick spoke with resolve.

Liam nodded. "At the very least, we'll familiarize ourselves with our surroundings."

"I think that's wrong," Adrian said, and Nick glared at him. He didn't flinch but just kept talking, and again, his words seemed to make everyone settle back into their chairs. "Who would defend Isabelle? Plus there's firewood for one night, used with care, so I think that means we're supposed to stay here tonight."

"Donovan does usually leave clear directions," Liam acknowledged. "Maybe there's another clue coming."

"Or maybe it's hidden here," Isabelle said.

"Maybe he's coming back," I suggested.

"We have the clue," Garrett insisted. "It's the riddle." His eyes snapped as he looked at me.

Adrian nodded, subtly taking charge. "Solving the riddle would give us more insight, but like Zoë said, some things can't be hurried. Let's work together to ensure that we're here and well in the morning."

"He could be right," Liam acknowledged.

"I think the first test is meant to be survival," Adrian said. "Can we survive on our own in the woods?"

"Of course we can," Nick scoffed. "That's a lame challenge."

"Maybe we *should* plan for the worst," Isabelle said. She wrapped her arms around herself. "Maybe we should get more supplies, show some initiative."

"Prove that we can do it," Garrett said. "Boot camp is a week long. Food for one night implies that we need to find the rest."

I didn't even think about the guys going hunting.

"There's got to be a town somewhere on this road." Adrian glanced out the window. "If we go now, we'll probably be back before dark."

"Hey, some of us could fly to a store," I suggested, but Adrian gave me a look.

"The Covenant," he said, and I blushed at the reminder. "How would you land outside a store in the middle of nowhere and shift to human form without anyone there noticing?"

I heard Nick catch his breath. "If you mean to drive, you're forgetting that my car's stuck." His tone was tight.

Adrian grinned. "How'd that happen?" he teased, as if they were old buddies. "Mine's not stuck."

Nick glowered.

Liam chuckled and ribbed Nick. "You'd think a Minnesota boy would know how to drive in the snow."

"Can't you push it out?" Isabelle asked Nick.

Garrett smiled. "Dragons don't need to work that hard."

"Even if Nick did wedge it into that snowbank pretty good," Liam teased. "Maybe he was just trying to impress you."

"Hey!" Nick's neck turned red.

But Isabelle turned to Adrian. "I have a bad feeling in this place. I don't think we should just sit here." She spoke with surprising urgency. "Let's take your car into town while the guys haul Nick's out of the snow."

Nick started to get to his feet. "I can drive to town."

"The light's already fading." Isabelle put on her coat again.

"It'll be too late. You look for another clue and I'll go with Adrian."

Nick looked like someone had just kicked him in the gut.

"You stay put," Garrett said to Nick. "Liam and I will get your car out."

"You'll just have to owe us," Liam joked.

"Big-time," Garrett agreed.

"But . . ." Nick protested.

"Find the clue that's hidden here," I told him. "Or solve the riddle."

He looked grim. "I don't like this."

"No one does, but we need to work together. Zoë?" Adrian asked, jingling his keys. "You coming with us?" He smiled. I had been tempted to stay with Nick, but Adrian's smile changed everything.

I was rewarded by Adrian's offering me the front seat.

Yup, Isabelle had to sit in the back.

Chapter 12

We drove for what seemed like forever before we found a town. In reality, it was maybe forty minutes, but every inch of the journey was exactly the same. The road just went on and on and on through the trees, with no sign of life anywhere. If anyone else had been driving, I might have thought he'd avoided towns on purpose.

But then, we *were* off the edge of the world.

And Adrian was part of the team.

The town we did find was small, small enough for us to have missed if we blinked. There was a post office, a gas station, and a pizza parlor. The pizza place also advertised burgers, wings, and fried chicken. The post office was also a drugstore and grocery— and it was where you paid for gas, too.

Adrian pulled in to fill the gas tank while Isabelle and I set out to explore the possibilities.

Such as they were.

"Does this even count as a town?" I asked.

"I don't care." Isabelle took a deep breath and shoved her hands deep into her pockets. "I just had to get out of that cabin. It's horrible there."

I knew exactly what she meant, but pretended otherwise. The place had given me the creeps, too. "What do you mean? Too rustic?"

"No." She was emphatic. "Something really bad happened there. It has terrible energy. I wish we didn't have to go back." She shuddered as she opened the door to the post office and store. Bells rang on the door, and a woman looked up from behind the counter.

"Well, we have to go back," I said, putting a half dozen cans of soup into a basket. "It's not like there's a choice. It's boot camp."

But Isabelle wasn't behind me anymore.

I found her in the aisle that offered a small selection of alcohol. She grimaced, then grabbed a bottle of sparkling wine. "Beggars can't be choosers," she muttered.

"What are you doing?"

"Making sure I get some sleep in that place."

Before I could argue, the bells rang again. Adrian had come in to pay. He grinned when he saw what Isabelle had chosen. "You legal?"

"I thought you might buy it for me." She smiled. "For us." Her elbow dug into my side, warning me to agree with her. The notion of being on the same side as Isabelle was so surprising that I didn't manage to say anything. "Zoë likes bubbles, too."

She was just making a guess, but it did sound good.

After all, there were no adults around. Why shouldn't we get a bit wild? Plus, recent experience had shown me that bad behavior could be rewarded.

I was ready for another bonus.

I nodded, trying to look as if I drank sparkling wine all the time. "Sounds good to me."

"Well, you two can't drink alone." Adrian took a second bottle from the shelf. He also grabbed a case of beer and a bottle of bourbon. He winked at me, conspiratorial. "One sip will do you."

It would do me. I couldn't drink the hard stuff, but I didn't admit any more weaknesses. I was aware that I was the little high-school girl hanging with the two über-cool college students. I tried to act like I belonged.

Adrian was looking better by the minute. I wished there was something I could do to be part of the cool club. Otherwise, I would just be the kid tagging along.

I couldn't instantly become five years older. I couldn't spontaneously develop great breasts. My best shot was looking like conquering my dragon powers.

ASAP.

I was sure we'd be carded at the register and Adrian wouldn't be able to buy stuff. I could beguile the clerk, I decided, and be part of Team Cool.

We took the soup and the booze, as well as some other groceries—cereal and milk and bread and hot dogs and buns. A massive jar of mustard because they didn't have small ones. Isabelle and I agreed to pass on the tofu hot dogs, which had an expiration date of the previous month. She took processed cheese slices instead and a couple bags of nuts.

The woman at the register didn't even check Adrian's ID. She was too busy watching some game show with the volume turned off.

So much for my contributing to the cause.

ADRIAN SNIFFED APPRECIATIVELY AS HE balanced the beer on the back bumper of his car and unlocked the gate. "There is something about pizza and beer."

"It does smell good," Isabelle agreed.

I turned toward the pizza shop. "As opposed to raw carrots and onions."

"Cheese slices and soup." Isabelle grimaced.

There was one car parked out front of the pizza shop and I could see the fender of one parked around the back. As I watched, a delivery guy came out with one of those padded carriers and took off in the car that had been parked out front.

Adrian shook his head. "Bet they won't deliver to the cabin. It's off the edge of the known world."

I was startled that his words echoed my own thoughts. "Here be dragons," I muttered, and he chuckled.

Isabelle sighed. "I guess we'll have to have soup. At least it will be hot. A pizza would be stone-cold by the time we got back anyway."

"Too bad they don't lend out those padded carriers," Adrian joked, turning to get into the car.

I froze. I knew right then and there what I could do to impress Adrian. "Maybe they could be persuaded to give us one."

"You're not going to beguile them!" Adrian's eyes twinkled.

I bit my lip. "It would be wicked."

He laughed at my token argument. I did love the idea of our surprising the guys with hot pizza and beer.

"Wicked?" Adrian shook his head. "*Wicked* is bigger stakes than that, Zoë. It wouldn't even be *naughty*." He nodded, eyes gleaming. "Mischievous, maybe."

"It would be wrong." Isabelle folded her arms across her chest. "I forbid you to do it."

Adrian widened his eyes and looked at her. He let his pupils change, and I was awed by how smoothly—and how quickly—they became vertical slits. "You forbid her?" he repeated quietly, the dragon in his tone.

Isabelle took a step back. "It would be wrong and you know it. That's not what beguiling is for."

I smiled. "But isn't boot camp about mastering new abilities? Maybe I need the practice."

Adrian said nothing—he just handed me a couple of twenties. I could see the approval in his eyes, though.

Before Isabelle could give me a lecture, I headed for the pizza shop. I could practically taste the melted mozzarella.

On the way, I reviewed everything Lorenzo had taught me.

And crossed my fingers.

WHAT CAN I TELL YOU about beguiling?

Beguiling is a special dragon power. Essentially it's a kind of hypnosis that works on humans. It's very handy—for example, in persuading humans that they haven't just seen a human transform into a dragon before their very eyes.

Tone of voice is critical to a successful beguiling. The dragon speaks low and slow, in a melodic tone, for best results. The human is fascinated and begins to repeat whatever the dragon says.

The other key to beguiling is the dragon lighting flames in his (or her) eyes. Humans are fascinated by fire and stare at those flames, which then makes them susceptible to believing whatever the dragon tells them.

Everything I know about beguiling I learned from Lorenzo, the dragon magician whose show in Las Vegas has run since the Ice Age. (Or maybe since the 1990s. Either way.) Lorenzo beguiles roughly five thousand people five nights a week, and twice on Sunday. Make that five thousand twenty-two—the ushers fall for it, too. Lorenzo is the best at beguiling—and a couple of summers ago, he took me as an apprentice.

The best thing about beguiling is that it's one dragon thing I can (usually) do pretty well.

IT WAS ALMOST TOO EASY.

I ordered three jumbo pizzas—one meat-lover's special, one with double pepperoni, and one with my fave combo: black olives, green peppers, and feta cheese.

After I'd paid (I wasn't *that* mischievous) I leaned over the counter. I caught the guy's sleeve with my fingertips. He was maybe thirty, skinny, not unattractive. He could have used a shave. He looked at my hand, then into my eyes.

I smiled.

He blinked. Maybe girls didn't smile at him that often.

Or maybe I was coming into my Wyvern-ness.

I conjured the flame in my eyes, just the way I'd been taught. He frowned and looked more closely, fascinated by the flames, yet doubting what he saw. I widened my eyes and he stared.

I dropped my voice low, to that precise melodic pitch.

"I'd like them to take out," I said, starting with something easy.

"To take out," he echoed. "Sure."

"Even though I have to go far."

"Go far," he repeated, scowling slightly.

I was losing him. I tried for something he'd find easier to agree with. "I hate cold pizza."

He almost shuddered as he repeated my words. "I hate cold pizza."

Okay, we had a connection there. I turned up the flame, widening my eyes and letting him see more of the fire. He leaned across the counter, intrigued—or snared—and clutched my hand. I could feel his pulse, heard it skip, then accelerate.

I had him.

I needed to make it count.

"Cold pizza is gross."

"Gross," he agreed.

"Plus a waste of a masterpiece."

He almost smiled. "Waste of a masterpiece."

"I'll need an insulated carrier."

He nodded. "You'll need an insulated carrier."

"Just like the delivery guy uses."

"Just like the delivery guy uses."

"You could give me one."

"I could give you one." He said it just as easily as that.

I smiled.

He smiled.

"You'll forget you ever saw me," I added.

"I'll forget I ever saw you."

"And you won't remember anything about the carrier. It'll just be gone."

"Just be gone." He was twitching a bit, knowing on some level that he had to check the pizzas.

I let his sleeve go and hoped for the best. His sense of timing was right—the pizzas were done. I held my breath as he slid them out of the oven and put them into boxes.

They smelled like heaven, and my stomach growled in anticipation. That made him smile.

I halfway thought the beguiling wouldn't work or that I'd have to start over, but he pulled out a big padded green carrier from under the counter. As if he did it all the time. He loaded those three boxes into it, added a bunch of napkins and a menu, and sealed it shut.

"Hope it's hot when you get home," he said, pushing it across the counter with a smile. "I hate cold pizza."

I snatched it up and practically flew back to the car. I was so excited at what I'd done. Isabelle took one look, then got into the backseat of the car and slammed the door. Adrian grinned at me as if I were the most incredible chick in the world.

This was the good stuff.

We loaded up and headed back to the cabin, the car full of the smell of hot pizza, just as the first stars were coming out.

I couldn't wait to see what the guys said.

Maybe they'd even be glad I'd come to boot camp.

THE GUYS FELL ON THE pizzas like a pack of starving wolves. I guess hauling cars out of snowbanks is hungry work. The mood in the cabin was even worse than it had been, as if the solitude of the place was feeding dissent between us. I hated it. Isabelle retreated to one corner with a big glass of wine and a carrot. She refused to take even one slice of pizza.

"But it's good," Nick said.

"It's stolen goods," she retorted, taking a gulp of wine. Nick looked at me.

"Not true," I argued. "I paid for the pizza."

"If not the carrier," Adrian teased. The guys demanded to hear the story. Nick and Liam laughed that I'd done it.

"The Wyvern can beguile," Liam teased. He licked his finger, touched it to my shoulder, and made a hissing sound. "She's hot stuff."

"Isabelle's right." Garrett was stern. "That's not what beguiling is for."

"Then let's throw your pizza in the snow." I surprised myself with the challenge. "You can have yours cold."

Big surprise—Garrett didn't go for it.

He backed off, wariness in his eyes. Nick gave a low whistle, then winked at me. "Have another drink, Zoë. Things are getting interesting."

I knew he was daring me, so I did just that.

The thing is that I wasn't feeling so proud of my beguiling. It felt like a really juvenile trick I'd pulled and a waste of my powers. I wondered what Jared would think. I was pretty sure he'd agree with Isabelle.

The wine made me feel edgier than usual. Spoiling for a fight, which wasn't like me. When I closed my right eye, I could see little orange sparks inside the cabin, like static electricity. It seemed to be drawn to each of us, clustering around Garrett and Nick with particular strength.

So I was back to losing my mind again. It should have felt like familiar territory.

I poured myself another glass of wine.

I'd never been drunk before. I'd had a sip of wine once in a while, even a glass a couple of times. Meagan and I were too squeaky clean to get invited to parties where other kids got wasted.

All of a sudden I missed Meagan, and wished I were sharing the sparkling wine with her instead of Isabelle.

Isabelle came back for more wine, still disapproving. The guys were getting loud and boastful, the beer eliminating what few inhibitions they had in one another's company.

This time, Isabelle grabbed her coat and headed for the enclosed porch. It had to be freezing out there, which said something about her opinion of our company.

It wasn't ten minutes before Nick seized the bottle of sparkling wine and headed in pursuit.

"Hey!" I shouted. "Some of that's supposed to be for me."

But Nick didn't even look back.

"Private party," Liam said, with a roll of his eyes.

My disquietude grew as quickly as I got drunk. I was feeling woozy, but I didn't care. It dulled the edges of disappointment, if nothing else.

Adrian handed Liam another beer. Adrian poured himself a shot of bourbon, baring his teeth after he threw it back. "Hair of the dragon," he said with a grin.

"What's that stuff taste like, anyway?" Garrett asked around a slice of pizza.

"Liquid fire," Adrian said, and Garrett reached for a glass instantly. Seemed he'd do anything for any kind of fire. "You can try it, but take it easy."

In no time, Liam and Garrett were daring each other to drink shots faster and faster.

Meanwhile, the pizza was gone and the beer stock visibly diminished. Adrian was drinking more slowly, kind of savoring his bourbon. He seemed to be enjoying how much they liked his treat. I finished my glass of wine and went to get more, a little tipsy on my feet.

I opened the door to the porch, surprised by the silence. Had Nick and Isabelle gone for a walk in the snow? They couldn't be *that* drunk.

The bottle shone on the table in the moonlight, still a third full. I headed for it, stumbling as I went.

That was when I saw them. Two shadows entangled on the Adirondack chair, making little purrs of pleasure.

I stared.

It was Nick and Isabelle, making out like they'd invented it.

But Nick was supposed to have a destined future with the Wyvern. With *me*.

My only excuse is the alcohol. Otherwise, I would never have done what I did.

I grabbed the bottle of wine, put my thumb over the top, and shook it. Then I sprayed them down. "Time for a cold shower!" The wine was gone in a matter of seconds.

"Hey!" Nick roared.

Isabelle yelped. "My coat!"

"Zoë!" Nick leapt up, intent on defending his female of choice.

Against his female of not-choice.

I saw him shimmer, on the cusp of change.

I saw his eyes shine amber.

I dropped the bottle and ran back into the cabin, slamming the door behind me. I knew I'd just pushed him too far.

Oops.

"ZOË WANTS TO PLAY GAMES," Nick said. He'd lunged into the cabin and the guys had turned to stare at him. I'd made it to the far side of the cabin, putting a good bit of furniture between the porch door and myself. Isabelle came inside behind him, looking both wet and flushed.

Nick had a dangerous glint in his eye. "Maybe it's time to see what our Wyvern can do."

"Maybe not when you're drunk," I retorted.

Just FYI, I was feeling pretty sober right then and there. Terror will do that to you.

"In Donovan's absence, I'm setting the rules," Nick continued as if I hadn't spoken. He peeled off his watch, a piece of precision equipment that he'd scored the Christmas before, and handed it to Isabelle. "Whoever can shift the fastest wins the point for today."

"I'm in." Garrett pushed to his feet. Liam just blinked at the guys, the bourbon having hit him hard.

"We'd better take this outside," Adrian advised. "Not enough room in here for four dragons."

"Five," Nick corrected, glaring at me. "Assuming Zoë's not completely full of shit."

I eyed each of them in turn, seeing their doubt. I supposed it was time to come clean.

"I've never done a full shift yet," I admitted, even though it nearly killed me to do so. "Only partway."

"Like we're going to believe anything you tell us now," Garrett said with a snort. His attitude stung.

"I said I'd try," I said to Garrett.

He spread his hands. "I see no progress. Go ahead—change

my mind." Then he marched out of the cabin, letting the door slam behind him.

"Maybe it's time you tried harder." Nick followed Garrett. En route, he pulled off his sweater and chucked it on the couch.

Isabelle trotted behind him like an obedient dog, his watch in her hand. "Can you show me how this works?"

He paused and smiled for her, all his antagonism gone. "Like this." He slid one arm around her to show her how to use the timer, so kind and thoughtful that I knew I'd been crazy to think there could ever be anything between us.

Destiny or not.

Only Liam and Adrian waited for me, concern in their gazes. "What's up with them?" Adrian asked, and I had no answer.

"You okay with this?" Liam was holding on to the table, quite unsteady on his feet.

"Doesn't matter much, does it?" I pretended to be indifferent, even though my heart was pounding.

What if I couldn't shift?

I really didn't want to try for the first time in front of everyone. Not when I was sloshed and they were wasted. Not when I'd been spooked by my dragon's anger the last time. That smelled like an accident about to happen.

I wanted to be completely on my game when I let myself shift. That wasn't now.

So I knew what I'd do.

I *wouldn't* shift.

I'd steal Nick's clothes when he shifted, and hide them until he calmed down.

That could take a while, but I'd wait.

Dragons can do patience, you know?

SO HERE'S THE INSIDE STORY on shifting shape. It's not instant. Anyone who has sharp powers of observation, like the *Pyr* do, can see this incremental change. You'll have to just trust me. The body changes shape, shifting from human to dragon form, in the blink of an eye.

But within that blink, two other things happen: The dragon pulls his scales over himself like a coat of mail. It's like reaching back for the hood on your sweatshirt, then hauling it over your head.

At the same time, he stashes the clothes he was wearing in human form. I've told you before about the hazards of not hiding clothes fast or having them stolen.

No surprise that this combo makes for some wild eye candy. Probably good that it happens so fast. This might be why witnessing the shift is rumored to make some humans lose their marbles.

It also takes practice to be smooth at this transition. No one nails it the first time, or even the hundredth time. Shifting itself, even as little as I've done, is overwhelming.

So this exercise is like folding your laundry and putting it away in the same moment that your house is being hit by a tornado.

The guys are *guys*. Folding clothes was not going to be in their skill sets. I knew they'd stink at this.

And I knew I could use that information to my advantage.

Maybe even to distract them from the deficiencies in my own skill set.

As plans went, I thought this one had definite promise.

By perfect coincidence, it also was the only plan I had.

Chapter 13

I walked outside to the clearing beside the cabin. There could have been a million stars glinting overhead. The only sounds were the whisper of the wind in the trees and the crackling of the ice on the lake. The forest was dark on either side. It was cold enough to slap a person sober.

Almost.

I wrapped my arms around myself as I took my place in the impromptu circle the guys had made.

"Ladies first," Nick said, bowing toward me. His tone was mocking and so was his gesture. He never used to be such a jerk.

But then, I'd never interrupted one of his seductions before. I checked him out with my left eye, and those orange sparks were radiating around his head.

I wouldn't be the one to tell him he looked like a saint.

"Show me what I'm up against first."

His eyes flashed; then he gestured to Adrian.

"So now *you're* in charge," Adrian said. He sounded amused.

"Believe it." Nick was adversarial, his gaze darting between Adrian and me. If I hadn't known better, I'd have thought he was jealous. "You first."

Isabelle held her finger above one button on the watch, probably the one that made it work like a stopwatch. Actually, I thought Nick was just being inclusive because he was sweet on her. In reality, only we dragons could assess our relative speed with any accuracy.

"Go," she said.

Adrian shimmered vivid blue and shifted shape.

He was fast. I didn't catch one glimpse of his clothes.

He wavered again, just for a heartbeat, just long enough for me to remember that it had happened before. And that I had forgotten it. Then I forgot it all over again.

I remembered how gorgeous he was, all pewter and purple and silver colors, sleek, muscled power right to the tip of his tail. The starlight gleamed on his scales, making him look like a precious treasure. It was enough to make a girl sigh with longing.

I couldn't stop myself.

Nick inhaled sharply.

Adrian settled back on his haunches, bared his teeth, and smiled at Nick with dragon confidence. I could feel the guys' agitation, even as I applauded and Adrian bowed to me.

He'd set a tough benchmark.

Nick pointed to Liam. Isabelle reset the watch, held up her hand, then said, "Go!"

Liam straightened and threw his hands toward the sky. He shimmered, but then faltered. The blue shimmer around his body sparked, faded, then burned brighter once more. When he shifted, he fumbled with his clothes.

He staggered even in dragon form.

Isabelle shook her head, saying what we all knew already. "Too slow."

Liam looked as if he had more pressing troubles, like his need to ditch the bourbon. He headed for the forest, not making anything near a straight line.

If you've never seen a dragon puke, trust me—you can do without the view.

Nick gestured to Garrett. They eyed each other, and I knew that neither of them wanted Adrian to win.

I kind of did.

Especially since they were both being such jerks.

Strange how Garrett had even more of those orange sparks clustered around his head than Nick. Maybe they were affecting his brain.

Isabelle gave Garrett a mark and he roared with fury, shifting so quickly that the blue of his shimmer nearly blinded me. It was as if he had been struck by lightning.

Or he had generated it.

Either way, the blue flash was so bright that I had no idea where he hid his clothes. He was suddenly in front of us, resplendent and gleaming in his dragon form. His garnet scales were gorgeous and rich in hue, the gold edges making him look like a real prize.

There was a challenge in his eyes, as well as a whole lot of pride when he looked at Isabelle.

"You're in first place," she told him. It was an unnecessary confirmation of an obvious truth, but maybe saying it made her feel a part of it all.

Adrian offered one claw in congratulations. Gracious. I liked that. Garrett smiled as they shook.

Funny, but dragons always look hungry when they smile.

Nick eyed me, but I shook my head. "Lady's choice," I said when he might have argued. "After you."

Isabelle gave him a kiss on his cheek, then reset the timer. As soon as she gave him a mark, I was ready.

Nick spun as he began to shimmer, probably trying to do some flashy dance move. As if there were going to be extra points for style.

I didn't care. His choice meant that he lost track of me.

He spun. He shimmered.

Isabelle stared, transfixed.

I dashed behind her and was right beside Nick when he shifted. I saw his clothes blur as he tried to fold them away. I grabbed, tugging them out of his grip. I had his jeans and his T-shirt, and that was good enough.

I definitely had surprise on my side.

He roared as he finished his shift, then snatched at his clothing. His talons sliced through the air.

I was already out of range.

"Three wishes!" I shouted, and ran as if my life depended on it.

Chances were good that it did.

IF YOU HAVE EVER RUN drunk through a snowy forest in the middle of the night, you might have an idea how dumb my choice was. I didn't have my coat, but there was no chance of my getting cold—I was sweating as I ran as fast as I could. I also had no real plan as to what to do with Nick's clothes, something I realized when he was breathing fire and flying right behind me.

A distinct lack of planning there.

My chances of outrunning him, at least so long as I was in human form, were minimal at best.

My chances of negotiating or even talking reason to him were about nil. He was furious.

I blamed the wine for messing me up.

He shouted, then breathed a plume of fire, scorching my butt and my best jeans.

"Hey!" I shouted.

"Thief!" he roared. "Come on, Zoë. Shift already! Let's square it up the old-fashioned way."

I realized then that he would hound me until I changed to dragon form.

Because he wanted to wrestle in front of Isabelle and impress her with his abilities. Which showed exactly zero concern for my fears.

I wasn't going to play.

I ducked under a branch and into a thickly grown section of the woods, turned hard, and headed back toward the clearing. I was practically crawling, brambles grabbing me from every side, the jeans and T-shirt tucked under my elbow. There was a gap in the trees ahead, and I ran more quickly, hoping to cross it unobserved.

Fat chance.

I was right in the middle when my boots sank into soft muck. It was swampy, which was why the trees didn't grow there. How could the muck not be frozen? It wasn't, though, probably because it was deep. I'd broken through the veneer of ice and was sinking fast.

Nick came peeling over the trees, all hot orange fury. He saw me, laughed, and dove like an arrow toward me. Garrett hung back, watching. He wasn't going to help me.

Oops.

I tried to run but the muck grabbed at my boots, pulling me in past my knees. I struggled but only sank deeper. I panicked.

I heard a whistle just then and looked up to see Adrian cutting through the air, sleek and strong.

He collided with Nick overhead. "You can't attack the Wyvern," he cried as he and Nick locked talons. They spun end over end through the sky, propelled by the force of their collision.

"Get lost. This is between Zoë and me." Nick took a swing at

Adrian with his tail. Adrian grunted as the blow hit home. Neither of them was fighting as cleanly as they had earlier.

It looked like a grudge match. Garrett was watching, staying out of it.

For the moment.

I grabbed a tree branch and hauled myself closer to the other side of the muck. It was heavy work. Gym class cubed, not squared. Meagan would have laughed at that feeble math joke.

I was just thinking how much I would have appreciated some help when Liam's old-speak slipped into my thoughts.

"Take my claw," he whispered, clearly trying to keep the others from overhearing. I knew it wouldn't work. They'd hear him.

Whether they'd do anything about it was debatable. Nick looked pretty busy.

Liam's silver talon shone in the starlight. I reached for his claw, taking a chance. He looked pale and tired, courtesy of the bourbon.

But he was powerful. He hauled me out of the muck with ease.

It was possible that it would have been easy for me in dragon form, too.

"Wait!" Just before I was clear of the swamp, I dropped Nick's clothes and kicked them down into the mud with my boot. I wasn't able to push them in all the way, but they were still a mess.

Then Liam took flight, soaring high above the trees. He dragged me into the sky, holding my hand, then caught me up against his side. It was awesome to fly, and I wanted to stretch out my arms to feel more of the wind.

This was what I wanted most of all.

I thought of Jared then, and wished I'd played our last moments together differently.

Would I get another chance? I hoped so.

"No!" Nick bellowed. I looked back to see him fling Adrian

aside. He pursued us, hot on Liam's trail. He fired off a plume of dragonfire and I saw orange flames brilliant against the night. The fire was coming straight at me, which had to be an accident.

Liam spun to defend me, taking the fire's onslaught across his back.

I felt him stiffen in pain.

I smelled his scales burning.

And I heard the rhythm of his wings falter.

Just before we fell out of the sky.

Shit.

LIAM AND I CRASHED INTO the top of a tree. Its branches were bare for the winter, but its wood was plenty hard enough. The collision knocked all the snow from its branches and the breath out of me.

Liam was out cold.

"You should have shifted to save him," Nick scolded when he arrived.

"You shouldn't have breathed dragonfire on him," I snapped.

"That was for you."

"Nice."

"You shouldn't have stolen my clothes."

"Arguing isn't going to solve anything." I ignored Nick and looked at Liam's wound. About a dozen of the scales on his back were burned and misshapen, some skin left bare by the damage. It looked pink.

Like a sunburn.

It made him vulnerable. My chest tightened and I felt awful at my role in this.

Now I really wanted to puke.

"He'll be all right," Adrian said, hovering beside us. "He'll sleep off the booze, then just need a scale repair."

"And who's going to do that?" Garrett asked quietly, his tone full of recrimination.

"This is *not* my fault," I said.

Neither Nick nor Garrett appeared to be convinced. So they were going to turn against me, one at a time, were they? First Garrett was angry with me and now Nick. Maybe it was a good thing that Liam was out cold.

At least Adrian wasn't giving me a hard time.

Maybe boot camp showed you who your real friends were.

"Is everyone all right?" Isabelle called. "Nick? Are you hurt?"

I turned my back on Nick and Garrett and talked to Adrian. "Can you carry Liam back to the cabin?"

I figured I'd walk by myself.

I wasn't much for the company of my so-called friends.

IF I'D DISLIKED THE CABIN before, I hated it then. You could have cut the air with a knife. We got Liam into his sleeping bag—he'd shifted to human form while Adrian had been carrying him and passed out again—then Garrett banked the fire.

I made one last trip to the outhouse, glanced down to the dock, then couldn't look away.

I stood there, snared by the sight.

Isabelle was on the dock, washing Nick's clothes. There was a hole in the ice, one that opened to a jagged bit of dark lake. A midnight star. Starlight was all around her, the sky a gazillion hues of indigo all around.

Then there was Nick. He hovered just above her, so beautifully golden that it made my heart ache. At her gesture, he breathed fire to dry his laundry with the heat of a flickering yellow flame.

Perfect. He was so light against the darkness. She could have been that princess, her hair lifting behind her, her face lit by the flames he breathed. My throat was tight and I knew I should look away.

But I couldn't. There was something magical about them together, something *right*.

I would have loved for it to not be so, but it was.

Isabelle laughed at him as he made the flames dance, then reached out to caress his scales. They both froze. I knew his eyes would be gleaming amber. I knew she would have given him anything, right then and right there.

My heart stopped when he took his clothes and landed on the dock, shifting back to human form so smoothly that I never saw the transition.

He was just Nick then, Nick in his T-shirt and jeans, Nick with his fabulous shoulders and amber eyes. I knew he was smiling at her, that one corner of his mouth would be higher than the other in a crooked smile that had always destroyed me.

But that smile was for Isabelle. Not for me.

They locked into one hummer of a kiss, one that seemed to go on and on forever. No chance of their getting cold.

I watched. And if I cried a little for what would never be mine, then that's between you and me. If I did, I did it silently.

Because sometimes even hot guys you've known all your life are out of your league.

When they finally parted, Isabelle framed Nick's face in her hands.

"Nicholas," she whispered. I could hear the one word even at a distance.

But no one ever called Nick by his full name.

Maybe it was a British thing.

Maybe I wasn't doing my mental health any favors by watching this.

I walked away, knowing that one day—maybe soon—I'd paint that scene. In full color. I usually drew my dragons individually, although they tended to look like the dragons I knew. Maybe it was time to push the limits and do a full scene. I smiled at the idea that maybe I wasn't trying hard enough.

Maybe I'd give the finished work to Nick and Isabelle.

Either way, I knew I'd never forget what I'd just witnessed.

THE WINE CHURNED IN MY gut, doing a tango with the pizza. I felt awful when I got back inside the cabin, awful in too many ways to count. The cabin seemed even smaller and darker than it had before, and I was getting a headache.

Adrian pushed the furniture toward the walls, and we laid out the sleeping bags in a row. I crawled into mine, then peeled off my jeans to sleep. I had my hoodie and underwear and heavy socks. It was a fashion statement, let me tell you, but it was warm.

I slipped my rune stone into the kangaroo pocket of my hoodie. I put in my earbuds, but stopped myself in time.

No. I was never again going to listen to the tune Nick had sent me. That dream was over.

I WASN'T SURPRISED WHEN I dreamed of snow.

In fact, I was relieved. I dreamed of snow blowing inside the cabin and melting before the fire. The others were all asleep. The doors and windows were still closed.

But the snow drifted in as if the wall closest to the lake were missing. I played the eye game, and there was no cabin when I looked with my left eye.

In fact, I was all alone when I peered through that eye.

I was back on the endless snow-covered plain, with one big honking tree close to me.

There was no sign of Granny.

Or her knitting.

That was a bit disconcerting.

The wind whistled through my hair and around my bare

legs—yes, even in my dream, I was wearing the same thing I'd worn to bed. Let me tell you, it wasn't the most primo choice for a night in a blizzard.

So if Granny wasn't here, what was the point?

There was something red on the ground, something intermittently obscured by the blowing snow. I knelt down and cleared a space with my hands. I was actually standing on a ridge of red rock.

And it was carved all over with symbols. I pushed away snow as quickly as I could, but the wind made that a challenge. I'd seen symbols like that before. I pulled out my rune stone.

It was the same red rock.

And there was blood running in the carvings, staining the marks dark red.

Just the way my rune stone had been the night before.

I could see the spine of rock extending a good distance in either direction before the shape of the land changed. Had my rune stone been chipped off this ridge?

If so, could I find the place where it belonged?

Was I supposed to put it back?

I looked up, startled to see that the huge tree was in full foliage, despite the season. Its leaves were vivid green and they rustled in the wind. I looked more closely and noticed something swinging from one of its boughs. I couldn't figure out what it was and couldn't get a better look without climbing the tree.

That seemed like a bad idea.

There was a hole by one of the tree's roots. That root wound down into the hole, so there must have been water at the bottom. When I leaned over it, I could see the stars reflected waaaaaaaaaaay down there.

A well, then. Huh. I wondered whether it was frozen. Maybe the tree root kept the surface open.

There was something odd about the well, though. I had a sense of it as being dangerous.

Not water you'd want to drink.

Water that might give you more than you expected when you did drink from it. Yes. That was it.

I shivered and straightened, looking up into the tree. From here, the swinging weight was obviously a person.

Who had been hanged.

Ick. Although I knew I needed to try to help. It was a guy, but he was so still that I knew he was dead. I was too late. He swung, a noose around his neck, his body limp. He was naked and I saw he had a feather tattoo on his left biceps.

But instead of his right arm, there was a black-feathered wing.

At that moment, the wind blew through the branches and his body turned around in the flying snow. He spun and I could see his face. His skin was tanned darker than mine, his hair black. He was staring right at me, his eyes as dark as obsidian.

It was the guy from my room.

From school.

The guy whose face I'd seen in the stone.

I stared in shock.

And he blinked, as if surprised to see me there.

"*Unktehila*," he said, just like last time.

Then he reached for me.

Okay, I screamed.

I ran.

I fled into the snow, wanting only to get away from that tree and the corpse that wasn't one. It made no sense that someone could hang like that and still be alive, but I knew he was.

And I was scared shitless of him.

In the distance, there was a pinprick of light. It was orange and flickering, like a bonfire. Exactly what I needed. It couldn't be that far away if I could see it.

I headed straight for the fire.

The snow started to fall then, swirling around me in fat flakes, much as it had earlier that day near the cabin. The sky was filling with clouds, fast-moving clouds with pewter bellies that obscured the sky.

A sense of dread blossomed within me and grew like wildfire.

I kept my gaze fixed on the fire, starting to panic that I wasn't getting closer faster. I glanced back and the tree was gone, as if I'd left it a thousand miles behind.

I freaked.

I ran across the snow, racing toward the bonfire. It seemed to take forever to get to it, but I finally did. It was huge, the flames probably twenty feet high. An inferno. I stretched out my hands toward its heat, slipping in my rush to get closer.

And then it disappeared.

As surely as if someone had flicked a switch.

Worse, there was no sign of where it had been.

I was all alone, surrounded by white and cold.

Chapter 14

I woke up with a gasp, my heart pounding and sweat running down my back. The guys were sleeping all around me, the fire down to glowing embers on the hearth. It was snowing again outside, but inside everything was normal.

Except that Isabelle was sitting up beside me, her eyes wide and her hands on her mouth. "His name is Kohana," she whispered.

No! We could *not* have shared a dream.

"I don't know what you're talking about," I said, flopping back down into my warm sleeping bag. I turned my back on her, facing Adrian, eyes open.

Isabelle exhaled shakily. She settled back into her sleeping bag. I could tell by the rate of her breathing that she was wide-awake.

One thing was for sure: this Wyvern gig could have used a

manual. I wasn't going to think about the fact that Jared had the closest thing to one in his possession.

In fact, I wasn't going to think about him at all.

And I wasn't going to think about Garrett turning against me.

Or Nick being angry with me.

Or Liam getting hurt because of me.

I had a crick in my neck. My head was pounding and my tongue felt thick and icky. My stomach was still unhappy. I decided right then and there that I didn't like sparkling wine after all.

I knew I had to get out of that cabin. I'd suffocate if I stayed. The sky was turning pearly gray, but the cabin seemed filled with an oppressive darkness.

I couldn't stand it one moment longer.

I tugged my jeans into my sleeping bag to warm them up a bit, then pulled them on. I sorted my boots out of the pile by the door, grabbed Alex's leather jacket—which I was starting to hope I could keep for the duration—and headed to the outhouse.

IT WAS SNOWING LIGHTLY. The sky looked as if the storm clouds were settling into place, intending to bury us alive in fresh snow.

Not that I was getting negative or anything.

I felt better, though, just getting out of there.

I pulled my rune stone from my pocket as I walked. It had changed again. The *F* tree looked more insubstantial than it had before. Like it was fading. I couldn't begin to imagine what that meant.

I was in the outhouse when I heard footsteps; then someone coughed. I was bundling back up when voices started to whisper.

Practically begging me to eavesdrop.

"She can't be holding out on us." Liam sounded cranky. "I don't know why you'd think that."

"I can't *not* think it. Nothing else makes sense." Garrett spoke in an undertone.

"Do you think anyone has any aspirin?"

"Never mind that. The Wyvern traditionally stayed away from the *Pyr*, didn't she?"

"So? You mean she'd deliberately hold out on us?"

"What else could she be doing?"

"But why?"

"To teach us that we can't rely upon her, maybe. I don't know! Wyverns are supposed to be mysterious, too."

"I don't know. Doesn't seem like Zoë."

"Then what's she doing here?" Garrett challenged. "She doesn't shift; she won't solve the riddle; if she has any foresight, she's not telling."

"Hey, maybe she's learning. . . ."

"Maybe she's not playing for the team." Garrett's voice turned hard. "That's what I dreamed."

"What?"

"That she betrayed us all." Garrett was grim. "I had the same dream over and over again, like a warning. I mean, look at you. You took a hit for her and she did *nothing* to help you. She didn't even break your fall."

Liam sighed. "Okay. I thought it was weird that she didn't solve the riddle right away."

"Yeah," Garrett said. "I thought we were getting that riddle in the first place to make her part of the team."

"But she didn't figure it out."

"Either that or she didn't tell us the solution. Maybe she's keeping it secret to give herself an advantage."

"I don't know if that's fair. Zoë wouldn't do that."

"Isn't it? My dad said the last Wyvern helped him make the connection to fire, so I should ask Zoë for help."

"And?"

"She said she wasn't sure she could do it." Garrett snorted. "It was a lie. I could tell. Maybe she wasn't sure she *wanted* to do it."

"That's harsh, Garrett."

"No. Harsh is you getting injured and me not being able to repair your scales because I don't have the full power of the Smith."

"Maybe she doesn't know how to do what you want," Liam suggested.

"Come on! She's the Wyvern."

Liam's tone turned thoughtful. "Maybe she's here because she's *not* the Wyvern. Maybe Donovan is calling her bluff. Maybe that's her test."

"Well, that sucks. I don't think we should have to do without a Wyvern, not if her powers are meant to help us come into our own. I think we should *make* her help."

I'd heard plenty.

I kicked open the door of the latrine hard enough that it swung all the way back and banged on the outside wall.

Liam and Garrett nearly jumped out of their skins.

"Gee, why wouldn't I want to help you guys?" I demanded. "Seeing as you all have so much faith in me. Seeing as we're all such good *friends*? One day in the woods and you're turning against me, just like that." I snapped my fingers.

I didn't wait for an answer, just marched past them.

"Well, what are we supposed to think?" Garrett said, his tone hostile. "It's not like you've done anything to participate."

"I found the riddles!"

"But you didn't solve them."

Liam eyed me and spoke more quietly. "Are you holding out on us, Zoë?"

That was it. You can probably guess what happened next.

Yup. *That*.

THE CRIMSON TIDE RAGED THROUGH me, claiming me body and soul. It filled every vein, every crevice, every nerve in my body, heating it all to red-hot. It shorted my circuits and overwhelmed me completely

The dragon was loose, and I was completely lost in the maelstrom.

There was no blue shimmer. There was nothing I could control. There was nothing I could stop or start.

The change happened fast, ripping through me and changing my shape so quickly that it left me dizzy. One second I was indulging that flicker of anger; the next I was an enormous dragon. I didn't manage to hide my leather jacket in the heat of the moment and it fell to the snow.

My senses were even sharper than before, and when I turned to tell Garrett off, flames erupted from my mouth.

On the one hand, I felt awesome power and pride in what I could do. (I was finally *doing* it!) On the other hand, I was terrified.

And furious.

Uh-oh.

The guys didn't have a chance. I roared and leapt at them. I swiped at Garrett with one claw and caught him across the side of the face. Four long scratches marked his cheek and started to bleed. He fell back in the snow, his eyes wide with fear.

Of *me*.

He scrambled backward like a crab. He never even blinked, not wanting to risk losing sight of me. He shimmered on the cusp of change, but I breathed fire again.

"Easy, Zoë. I was just joking. Really." He was stammering, freaking out.

I'd never seen Garrett afraid before.

"Take it easy, Zoë," Liam added, hands held high in surrender. "Deep breath."

That was when I realized that I *was* a freak, just like Suzanne was telling everyone at school.

Because the dragon was running me.

No more. I'd rather hurt myself before I injured my friends more than I already had. I turned away, threw myself at the forest. I had to get control of myself and figure out how to shift back.

Nobody tried to stop me.

Nobody begged me to stay.

You know, I couldn't blame them. I tried to feel for my dad, being in desperate need of some dragon advice, but he was still out of range.

Boot camp just kept getting better and better.

Not.

"ZOË!"

I ignored the shout. It was, after all, a woman's voice. One with a British accent. Three guesses who was hunting me, and the first two don't count.

I was perfectly happy sulking quietly on a rock far from everyone I knew. I was back in human form, having been able to shift once guilt replaced my anger. I didn't care if it was starting to snow. I didn't care if I was cold.

I was a bona fide freak.

As well as a failure, a disappointment, and a delusional chick.

Worse, I didn't know what to do about any of it.

Even though I didn't answer, Isabelle found me anyway. Maybe she *was* psychic.

She wore her white down-filled winter coat with fake fur around the hood, and her boots were slipping in the snow. She was carrying the leather jacket that Alex had lent to me. She came to a sliding halt before me, held out the jacket, and smiled.

Tentatively.

"We have to talk," she said, her breath making a white puff in the cold air.

"I don't think so." I started to turn away, but her next words stopped me.

"I don't believe you meant to hurt the guys."

I was both curious and skeptical. "Why not?"

She gestured vaguely with one hand and frowned. "Look, I don't know exactly why, but I feel that it's the truth." She smiled again. "I know it."

That didn't make me a whole lot less skeptical of her.

But curiosity was winning the day. Even if she was trying to trick me, I couldn't figure out why.

I told you that I like a puzzle.

I took the jacket and tugged it on. "What did you want to talk about?"

Isabelle glanced back toward the cabin, as if fearing she might be overheard. It wasn't exactly a long shot, given the superhearing of the *Pyr*. She lowered her voice and stepped closer. "Something weird is going on. Maybe you'll be able to figure it out with me."

"I'm listening. But you know, a whisper draws attention. Makes people want to eavesdrop."

She nodded, then looked around, uncertain.

I rummaged in my pocket, pulled out the notebook and pencil that I always have—in case I have a desperate need to draw— then handed both to her.

She smiled, her eyes lighting with a pleasure that made me feel like less of a loser. She grabbed the pencil, flipped open the book, and hesitated. I know she'd just found one of my dragon drawings, but I didn't want to talk about it.

I looked away.

If I'd had a newer messenger, I could have drawn on it and secured the file with bunches of passwords. It would have been private forever, or for as long as I'd wanted it to be. Paper has its limitations.

But I had bigger issues right now than a lack of gadgetry.

She considered me, then turned the page. She scribbled for a moment, then handed the notebook back to me.

I want to talk about dreams, she had written, which startled me. *Particularly the ones I have about you. And about Nick.*

Bingo. With three short sentences, Isabelle had my undivided attention.

WE WALKED IN THE SNOW, away from the cabin. We found a bunch of rocks on the side of a frozen river. Isabelle looked in every direction, brushed the snow from a big rock, then pulled a deck of cards from her pocket. She shuffled them and drew one, putting it faceup on the rock.

Then she stared at it, unblinking, as the snow fell steadily all around us. I stepped closer to have a look.

Curiosity doesn't kill the dragon.

Just so you know.

The card was bigger than the playing cards I knew, and I didn't recognize the illustration on it. The guy on the card looked like he was about to step off a cliff—and he seemed to be whistling. It said, *The Fool,* at the bottom and had a zero at the top.

Null and void. That pretty much summed up the current tone of my life.

"Fresh starts," Isabelle said with satisfaction. "I drew it right side up, which means an auspicious beginning. Taking a chance, maybe on faith, and making it work." She smiled at me. "Which means that telling you about this is exactly the right thing to do." Then she took the pad of paper, sat down on the rock, and started to write.

It might as well have been an essay. I sat down beside her, listening to the wind in the woods. I wondered about my ability to shift, how I could do it only when I was deeply pissed off, and fretted that I'd never get control of it. I worried about the discord between me and the guys, and wondered what I could do to fix it—especially since everything I did just made it worse.

I pulled out my rune stone and ran my thumb over the symbol etched into its surface.

That was about beginnings, too.

As I waited for her, I turned those clues around in my thoughts. When in doubt, solve a riddle, right? I pulled out my messenger and mulled over the clues.

> Valued by all, sold by none, I have no price.
> I slide before the sun, but make no shadow.
> I touch everyone, but no one catches me.

The answer was something invisible, yet pervasive: something we all took for granted even though we needed it. Not smoke. Maybe thought.

Lust, maybe.

But I wasn't going there.

> I am a boundless buffet from which everyone eats but
> no one fills.

Something apparently limitless. Self-propagating.

Lust could be like that, from what I'd heard.

I had a hard time believing that this boot camp's theme was lust. I rubbed my stone harder.

> I am a city vast, thick with people but no streets.

I'd heard that one or something like it before.

Air. Of course! One of the four elements, perfect as a focus for boot camp. I straightened and looked around, amazed that I'd missed something so obvious.

I thought about going back to share my revelation with the guys, but wasn't so hot to do that. They might not want to talk to me at all.

I heard Jared's voice in my thoughts then.

A dragon girl, afraid?

Yeah, pretty much.

But maybe it was time to ditch that perspective.

"MAY I HOLD YOUR STONE?" Isabelle asked, startling me with the reminder of her presence.

"It's just a rock," I said gruffly, and shoved it back into my pocket. I felt rude, but she didn't seem offended. Instead she held out the notebook for me. I took it back and read what she'd written.

> I dreamed of you Friday night in Minneapolis. We were together, you and I, and we were both large white birds. Swans, maybe. And we were flying together, not saying anything. It was easy to be together, as if we were old friends, as if we had no need to chatter about this and that. I felt a connection with you.
>
> And I thought that was pretty strange, given that you and Nick obviously have had something going on in the past, yet it seems that he and I have some potential for the future. You probably don't want to hear this, but I've been dreaming of Nick all my life—and my dreams always come true.
>
> Last night, I dreamed of being drawn to a bonfire. I was in some cold place and it was snowing. And as I walked to the bonfire to get warm, it suddenly disap-

peared. I was left in a blizzard to freeze. And I woke up, terrified, to see the same look on your face. Did you have the same dream? I think you did. Maybe you know what it means.

Do you know anything about the guy who was hanging from the rope?

Maybe you know why I want to call Nick Nikolas.

Maybe we need to work together to make our dreams—and our destinies—come true.

What do you think?

I read it twice and looked away before responding. I had not been in a hurry to become pals with Isabelle or help her make a permanent connection with Nick. And I still wasn't in a hurry to tell her any of my secrets, either.

She was waiting, though.

On impulse, I asked what I really didn't want to know. No point in having doubts. On the notepad, I wrote, *What do you dream about Nick?*

She smiled.

She blushed.

She looked away and knotted her hands together. It was interesting to see her so discomfited. With clumsy fingers, she rummaged through her deck of tarot cards and deliberately chose one, turning it so I could see it.

The Lovers.

Well, that pretty much said it all, didn't it?

Chapter 15

"It's getting dark," I said, pushing to my feet. "And my butt's cold. We'd better head back."

"Wait," she said. Isabelle had chosen another card, but I hadn't noticed it in her hand.

The second card was Death.

I had a bad feeling of my own, then, as if I were going to be the cause of someone dying. I was doing a fairly crap job of playing for the team, and didn't see how to bring my dragon powers around quickly.

Isabelle watched me for a long moment. "There's a storm coming," she said finally, then put her cards away.

That wasn't half of it.

I strode back in the direction we'd come, not really waiting for her. It was funny, but the closer we got to the cabin, the more I resented Isabelle. Maybe she was turning the guys against me.

Maybe she was stealing my dreams—or maybe she was psychic enough to get glimpses of them.

Lots of nasty thoughts seemed to breed in my mind without any help from me. They felt toxic and poisonous, but I couldn't get rid of them.

I didn't like having them in my head, but couldn't ditch them. It was like an ear worm, the chorus of a catchy song that you can't quite get out of your memory.

I spun to face Isabelle. I scribbled in the notebook while she got closer. She really was no good at walking in snow, and it wasn't just because of her boots. I handed her the notebook instead.

What do you know about the last Wyvern?

Isabelle shrugged, then took the pencil. *That there was one, and she died.* She met my gaze, apparently finished.

I was sure she was lying.

I would have snatched the notebook back, certain our time of girly bonding was over. Doomed, maybe.

"There's something else," Isabelle said. *It's Adrian,* she wrote. *I don't trust him. . . .*

I didn't let her write any more. I guessed where this was going. She had to be jealous of his interest in me.

You can't have all the guys to yourself, I wrote, and she blinked in surprise. Then I shut the notebook and shoved it into my pocket again.

Isabelle watched me for a moment, then swore.

That made me blink.

"I hate this place," she said, surprisingly fierce. "It's wicked here; you have to feel it, too. It's making us fight with one another, and ruining everything."

"You weren't fighting with Nick last night." I had to say it but managed to stop myself there.

She frowned. "But we can connect emotionally only when we

leave that cabin behind. It's like there's something in that place, something that disguises the truth. Or turns it bitter. Something evil."

I wanted to argue, but she was right. I didn't dislike her nearly as much away from the cabin as within it. In the forest, that simmering resentment was diminished, and I could even see that we had some things in common.

I'd hated the cabin from the first as well.

And I'd never felt unappreciated by the guys before arriving at the cabin.

What was the deal with those orange sparks? I needed to look for them while I was sober, see if they were real.

"But how could it do that?" I asked her. "Why?"

"I don't know, but there's something powerful at work." She met my gaze again. "Nasty. I think someone's trying to turn us against one another."

A test of Donovan's? I had a hard time believing that.

I thought about the older *Pyr* disappearing from my Wyvern radar. Was it really their choice? Or my inability to track them?

Or was something wrong?

I shivered. Before I could formulate good questions, Isabelle tugged her zipper up higher and headed back to the cabin at a crisp pace. Maybe she thought I didn't believe her.

I followed her slowly, thinking things over.

And there was that song Nick had sent me. Why had he done that?

It was time to find out.

I HEARD THE STEADY TAP of a hammer before we could see the cabin. I knew exactly what the guys were doing and I hurried. I loved seeing a Smith at work.

There were two dragons outside the cabin. They looked especially magical in the falling snow, one malachite green and silver, the other garnet and gold.

Nick stood close by in human form. He wore heavy gloves and had a pair of tongs, and was heating Liam's damaged scales for Garrett to work upon. They must have been loose, and Garrett worked them free. Adrian, also in human form, watched. I wondered whether he'd ever seen a Smith before.

Garrett had obviously brought a small jeweler's forge with him, and he had a fire roaring within it. The flame burned a rich gold, lighting up the dragon scales and the faces of the other guys.

It looked like the repository of an ancient hoard. I smiled, my chest tight with a fierce love of what we are.

The snow swirled around the guys, piling on the roof of the log cabin. It landed on Liam and Garrett, adorning their wings and tails, and dusted the hair and shoulders of Adrian and Nick.

Another scene to paint. It was too perfect. I studied them all once more, greedy for every last detail that would make the painting more real.

Was this my destiny? To document my own kind? To create an illustrated record of what we are?

Maybe to create a manual for the next Wyvern.

Garrett was focused on his work, intent upon repairing a scale that must have come from Liam's back. The scale itself was all green whorls, outlined in a thin edge of silver. Nick heated it on the forge; then Garrett hammered it, working it gradually back into shape.

Liam lay in the snow, watching us approach with gleaming eyes. Isabelle continued to the cabin, hunched down in her fluffy coat, but I hesitated on the perimeter of the forest.

As much as I wanted to be part of this, I doubted my presence would be welcome.

Nick started at Isabelle's arrival and smiled in her direction. Soon she stood beside him, keeping her hands shoved in her pockets, watching. Warming herself by the forge, maybe. Adrian smiled at me and waved.

Garrett glanced up, perhaps sensing Liam's interest, and his gaze locked with mine. I saw the four long wounds on his cheek, so much larger in his dragon form, and the wariness in his eyes.

I had done that. I had scarred his cheek and put the doubt in his eyes.

I saw the scorched scales on Liam's back: the three that had already been repaired and the four still waiting.

I was responsible for that, too.

I'd never failed any course in my life, but I was failing Wyvern 101.

Or maybe just Dragon 101.

"*Can you fix it?*" I asked Garrett in old-speak.

He shrugged and returned to his work.

I couldn't blame him.

The others remained silent. Watchful. I felt the mood of the cabin pressing against me, provoking my anger and resentment. I could have insisted that I'd been unfairly treated, that the guys should pay. I could have started a fight.

But I knew I had to move past whatever ominous power this place had. That was the test. I had to do something different to break its influence.

"*I solved the riddle,*" I continued in old-speak. Nick glanced up. Garrett's lips tightened. "*It's air.*"

No one said anything.

I dared to walk closer to the group and spoke aloud. "Air governs unions, ideas, negotiations. Thoughts and dreams. Reasoned discussion. Logic."

I saw Garrett flick a glance at me; then he breathed a slow and steady stream of fire upon the scale he held. The forge had heated it to the point that his dragonfire could just provide the last burst of heat. Quinn worked with a forge most of the time, too, relying solely on dragonfire only when there wasn't a choice. The scale glittered in Garrett's grasp, and I marveled at how adept he was. He had already learned so much from Quinn. I sensed his passion for his craft and understood his desire to be the best.

I had to figure out how to help him. That dark force whispered at me, picking at my doubts, but I forced myself to not listen to it.

These were my friends.

I knew that in my heart and had to hold fast to it.

Garrett turned the scale in his talons, heating it evenly, coaxing the hole to mend. I watched him fix three scales, working with steady patience even as the light got poor.

The clouds were getting darker and the snow was falling more thickly. Nick shifted shape and focused on keeping the embers glowing hot for Garrett. But the last increment of heat, the part that made the scale repair possible, had to come from the Smith.

The last scale was the worst one, and I knew that Garrett had been working up to it. It had a big hole right in the middle.

A hole that was too large to patch.

No matter how Garrett heated it and coaxed it, that hole kept opening again. If it wasn't fixed, Liam would have a spot that was vulnerable.

Unarmed.

I couldn't let that happen.

I knew that dragon scales could be healed with jewelry. Often a mate contributed a piece of her own treasure to help heal an injury sustained by her dragon of choice.

I pulled off my malachite and silver earrings and walked closer, offering them to Garrett on the flat of my hand. "You'll need these, I think."

Garrett faltered. He was that surprised by my gesture. He

looked between the earrings and me, uncertain. "But only a mate can give a gift to mend the scales of a *Pyr*. . . ."

"Liam can't wait that long. It could be years before he meets his destined mate and has his firestorm." I stretched my hand out.

"Centuries, even," Isabelle added.

"Doesn't a friend count, too?" I asked.

Garrett studied me in silence.

"Take them," Nick murmured.

"Thanks, Zoë," Liam said quietly.

Garrett accepted the earrings with care. I felt his talon brush my palm, and our gazes met for a second. He checked the earrings and I saw his relief. I smiled, knowing that he'd confirmed that the jewelry was pure silver. He was a craftsman, and picky about his materials.

I watched him heat one so the silver was fluid, and he worked it with dexterity. Each earring had one large oval stone and one small round one. He arranged them into a diamond shape, spreading the silver in between to make a badge. As it took shape, I saw his confidence grow that he could make the repair.

I wanted to help him.

When an adult *Pyr* has his scale repaired, with the help of his mate, they achieve a balance. We all have a link to two elements— fire is usually a gimme—and the circle of the four elements is completed with our partner's complementary affinities.

I wondered whether that was what made scale repair work.

Could we replicate that?

Even without Liam's having a mate?

I thought about our respective natures. Garrett's main connection had to be with fire, and he was already honing his affinity with it. He was passionate, seldom angry, but when he was angry he made it worth the trouble.

What about Nick? I thought of Nick as practical, powerful, stubborn, and strong. Confident in a different way. Rooted. One of his affinities must be with the earth.

And Liam was everybody's best friend. He was the one who understood before you even said anything, the one who could forgive and forget. Water had to be Liam's affinity.

What if mine was air? The Wyvern was associated with dreams and foresight, both governed by air. I drew and I solved riddles—more air, in the realms of imagination and intellect.

We had all four elements covered among us! Could we secure Liam's scale repair if we managed to pull together?

The idea excited me. I wanted to make it happen.

Meanwhile, Nick heated the scale. Garrett heated the other earring. He fused the earrings together into a kind of a medallion, one that looked like it had a silver rope around it.

A medallion that perfectly fit the hole. Liam bared his teeth as Garrett fused the pieces together. He worked both the back side and the front of the scale to secure it, making Liam's coat of armor complete again.

When he stepped back, nodding with satisfaction, it looked to me as if my earrings and the scale had become one. There was no clear line to show where one ended and the other began.

I liked that.

I liked it a lot.

"Fire," I said, gesturing to Garrett. He smiled in sudden understanding. The repair of an adult dragon's scale ended with this ritual acknowledgment of the elements, and I knew he got it. He proved that by breathing a short stream of flame upon Liam's mended scales.

"Earth," I said to Nick, and he braced his hands on Liam's shoulders.

"Water," I said to Liam, and he nodded in understanding.

"Here," Isabelle said, bending to lift a drop of moisture from Liam's cheek. She placed it carefully on the mended scales and it hissed.

"Air," I added, then bent to blow across the repaired scales.

"All for one and one for all," Nick concluded with satisfaction. There was a moment when we smiled at one another, when the darkness of the cabin's mood seemed to have disappeared.

Then Adrian cleared his throat. "What about me?" he asked lightly, and I was ashamed that I had forgotten him.

How could I have done that?

"Old joke," Liam said, lying to cover for me.

Adrian shrugged and smiled as if it didn't matter. But something had changed. We were edgy with one another again.

And I couldn't explain why.

MAYBE IT WAS THE STORM.

Isabelle had been right: there was a storm coming, and it was moving fast. I hadn't been paying attention while Garrett worked, but the truth was inescapable.

The snow was falling faster by the time Liam's scales were repaired, and the sky was the color of smoke, even though it was only midafternoon. The wind stirred, making the snow dance in spirals.

The air in the cabin was so charged that it felt as if the whole thing would blow if someone dropped a match. Isabelle had nailed it in one. I was haunted by Jared's words, even as I watched whatever was at work in the cabin affect the guys.

You're coasting, Zoë, and that's not going to cut it if you really want to be the Wyvern. In fact, it doesn't cut it for pretty much anything.

Don't you hate when an extremely hot guy also proves to be right?

I had to solve the puzzle of the cabin's power over us. Whether I ever saw Jared again or not. I really wished I had his book to refer to. But I was determined to work through the clues I had, looking for loose ends. There were a lot of them.

"Why did you send me that song?" I asked Nick. "Where'd you get it in the first place?"

"What song?"

"The one you sent me when our dads decided I was coming to boot camp."

I know Nick well enough to know when he isn't putting me on. "I never sent you a song."

I pulled out my messenger and showed him the message. He was completely confused. "You're right. It looks like it's from me. But I never sent it."

"What kind of song?" Isabelle asked. I put it on audio and let it play. Agitation rippled through the cabin and Isabelle backed away. "Turn it off. It's awful!"

"It's kind of catchy," Adrian said.

"It's *wrong*!" Isabelle said, almost shouting. Nick went to her side, as if preparing to defend her, and the air crackled in the cabin.

Against what?

I had an idea then. I played the eye game as I turned on the music again. With my left eye, I could see glimmers in the air. They seemed to emanate from my messenger, circle around the ceiling, then target the guys.

The brightest ones clustered around Garrett. There was a dimmer cloud around Nick, but Liam seemed to be able to repel them somehow. Adrian had none around him.

By playing this song, I'd brought this dissent into the cabin? This was my fault, too?

"Turn it off!" Isabelle cried, making a snatch for my messenger.

I did, even as I tried to work out what could be happening.

It was a puzzle, after all. I needed more information. I sat down at the table, shoved my messenger away, and pulled out my notebook. "What do you guys know about the last Wyvern? What have your parents told you?"

"Why?" Liam asked. I should have expected my first ally would be Liam. That affinity with water again.

"Because I don't know everything I'm supposed to be able to do. It would be nice to have a clue."

"Dead Wyverns don't give clues?" Adrian asked. It sounded like he was trying to lighten the mood by making a joke, but it fell flat.

"Erik didn't give you a hint?" Garrett asked.

"I think my dad is waiting to see what I figure out for myself. Or what the *Pyr* tell me. My mom said her name was Sophie."

"Sophie died," Liam said.

"She showed my dad how to connect with his legacy," Garrett said. "She was okay." The implication there was as clear as crystal, but again, I didn't bite. I thought that maybe if I didn't play along with the negativity in the cabin, it might be undermined.

It was worth a shot.

In fact, this might be a boot camp test, set up by Donovan. Maybe he had sent me the song, using Nick's account. He would have had easy access to it, after all.

If the theme was air, as the riddle indicated, spells and magic were governed by the element of air. Maybe—since he was the one worried about Mages—he was trying to teach us how to fight them.

If that was the case, there had to be a way to break this spell. I was growing excited, determined to pull the guys together on this challenge.

"But she wasn't *supposed* to engage with the world," I said, keeping my tone upbeat. Liam pulled up a chair beside me and I smiled at him in encouragement. "That's the thing. The Wyvern is supposed to remain aloof, kind of beyond it all. I wonder whether that's why she can see farther."

"Because she's above it all?" Isabelle suggested. She sat at the table, too. I felt the tension among all of us start to ease.

We were winning!

I shrugged. "Maybe. But Sophie, she got involved. And she died, I think young."

"It would be helpful for you to know what went wrong," Isabelle agreed.

"I'd like to avoid making the same mistake. If there was one."

"How did she get involved?" Nick took a couple of steps closer. With my left eye I could still see those orange sparks circling overhead, as if seeking a target.

Liam snapped his fingers. "I remember this! She and this *Pyr* were the ones who destroyed the academy where the Elixir was forced into near-dead *Pyr*. Like my dad. The Wyvern and this *Pyr* sacrificed themselves to ensure that no more *Pyr* could be made into shadow dragons."

"But who was that *Pyr*?" I asked, seeking both information and cooperation. "Someone's uncle or brother?"

Nick frowned. "No. He was some kind of outsider." He sat down beside Isabelle.

"An outsider?" Adrian echoed.

"He was the first of the Dragon's Teeth Warriors," Garrett said, his tone more normal than it had been. "I remember that story now. He was different, hard to understand, my dad said. He'd been enchanted for a couple of thousand years, after all, and the world had changed. A lot."

"Like Drake?" Liam named the current commander of the Dragon's Teeth Warriors.

"Yes, but not like Drake." Garrett shrugged. "Maybe like Drake before he got used to the way the world had changed."

Now we were working together, and it felt good.

"But why did he sacrifice himself?" I asked. "I mean, I can see the Wyvern working for the universal good, but why him?"

"Because he knew she was right?" Liam suggested.

"Because she asked for his help?" Nick offered. "The Wyvern isn't supposed to be a fighter, after all. Maybe she wanted to go in with some muscle."

"That's still a big move," I said. "To commit to a mission that you won't survive."

"It must have been because he loved her," Isabelle said. We all turned to look at her. She smiled with confidence. "It's the only thing that makes sense."

In a way, it did.

And in a way, it didn't.

Which meant there was still a piece missing.

"I wonder whether she loved him." I stared into the fire, drumming my fingers on the arm of the chair. It wouldn't have been a very nice thing to trick a *Pyr* into going to his death. I couldn't imagine a Wyvern doing that.

Because I wouldn't do it.

If she loved the *Pyr*, why wouldn't she have wanted to be with him? Live with him, and get involved in the world in a more basic way?

If she didn't love him, it would have been an even more improbable thing for her to do, like killing an inappropriate suitor instead of just ditching him.

An inappropriate suitor.

I had it!

Chapter 16

"You're right!" I said to Isabelle, unable to hide my excitement. "She loved him and he loved her."

"Sooooo?" Liam said, dragging out the question.

"But they couldn't be together." I was certain I'd solved the riddle. "That was why they chose to sacrifice themselves. They could make a difference to the world—and they couldn't have had a life together anyway."

"Is that supposed to make sense?" Nick asked.

"They were both *Pyr.*"

"Okay," Liam said.

I could see that the guys weren't following my line of thinking. "Okay. Each of you will have a firestorm with a human woman."

"Right," Nick said.

"And the firestorm will result in the conception of another *Pyr*."

"We know all the basics, Zoë."

I ignored Garrett's tone. Adrian was hanging back, and I smiled at him. I was sure that if we all worked together, we could beat the spell. He folded his arms across his chest and stayed in the kitchen area, though.

I felt that sense of working together start to fracture, but I kept talking. "But what about me? We don't mate with our own kind, which means that I must be going to have a firestorm with a *human* guy."

(I instantly thought of Jared, but let's just keep that between you and me, okay?)

"Maybe Wyverns don't even get to have firestorms," Nick said.

I ignored that troubling possibility.

"Even if they do, I still don't get it," Liam said.

There were suddenly more orange bits of lightning zipping around the ceiling, and the cabin started to darken. I talked faster. "Sophie was the Wyvern. The guy she died with was a *Pyr*. If they were in love, their love defied that one-human-one-dragon convention."

Oh. They all sat back in sudden understanding. And I got thwacked in the brain with a realization of my own—I could never be with Nick. Not in that way.

For exactly the same reason: we're both *Pyr*.

Duh.

"They couldn't be together," Isabelle said with excitement. "Ever. Unless they were dead—like Romeo and Juliet. I think you're right, Zoë."

"So they made a choice to do something together that would leave a legacy for the *Pyr* and the world." I held up my hands, happy with my solution and expecting applause.

I didn't get any.

In fact, only Isabelle and I were still on the same page. The guys were looking around, bored maybe with the notion of romantic love, seeming irritable again. I closed my right eye and the vivid orange light overhead nearly blinded me.

Okay, we hadn't beaten it yet, but we'd made some progress.

I needed a new plan. There were still lots of errant puzzle bits to fit into the big picture.

The not-dead guy in my dream, for example.

I hunkered down in front of the fire to doodle and think sideways about puzzles.

IT WAS ADRIAN WHO EVENTUALLY sat on the floor beside me. It was quite a bit later, and Isabelle was making soup for dinner. No one was talking much, the impatience rising with every passing hour. The cabin was cold, despite the blaze of the fire, and Garrett was rationing the wood.

Adrian's shoulder leaned against my knee and I could have reached out to bury my fingers in his dark curls. "I'm sorry the guys are so tough on you," he said quietly. "You can't do everything, and you can't learn everything overnight. They forget that it took them years to hone their skills, such as they are. How long have you been at it?"

My heart glowed. "Two days."

"See? It's different for you. I wish they'd back off."

Okay, I liked the sound of that. It made me feel all warm and fuzzy. "Thanks."

"No problem." He smiled at me, and I smiled back for a long moment. My heart started to pound a little faster.

"You could be wrong about Sophie, you know," he murmured.

"How so?"

"Well, everyone likes a love story, but what if it was something else?"

"Like what?"

Adrian hesitated, so I slid out of the chair to sit beside him on the rug.

"Go on, tell me."

He gestured that he wanted to write something. I turned to a fresh page of my notebook.

What if she did something for herself, and this Pyr *guy just got caught in the cross fire?* He wrote more quickly. *Or what if she had a plan the* Pyr *didn't like and he was trying to stop her?*

My eyes were wide.

What could the Wyvern want to do that the *Pyr* wouldn't like? I'd never thought of the Wyvern acting against the *Pyr*. It was an astonishing idea. She might be evasive or inaccessible, but she didn't plot against the others.

Adrian's eyes were really dark as he watched me work through this; then he bent to scribble again. *What if she felt unappreciated, and acted for herself, not the team?*

That was a pretty compelling possibility.

I looked and saw that Adrian had more to say about this—and I wanted to know what he was thinking.

I took the notebook and pen. *We should talk.*

Adrian nodded. *Tomorrow.*

Then he tore the page off the notebook, crumpled it up, and tossed it into the fire. Was it my imagination that the flames devoured that piece of paper more greedily than I would have expected?

LATER THAT NIGHT, I DREAMED of my dad.

I had to be dreaming, because I was back in the snowy other-world, in the middle of a frozen lake that looked a lot like the one down below the cabin. My dad was sleeping on the ice. That was strange, but it seemed consistent with Granny's world.

I'd never seen him look so peaceful.

I moved closer and looked at him. I knelt down in front of him, and his eyelids didn't even flicker.

That was when I knew something was wrong.

My dad, remember, is a dragon. He never really sleeps. In fact, I'm not sure I've ever seen him out cold. His eyes are always open a little slit, and, if you look carefully, you can see the glitter of his eyes. He's always monitoring the situation, ready to respond.

Ready to fight.

Or defend the hoard.

Maybe *hibernating* is a better choice of word than *sleeping*. Or *dozing*.

But in my dream, he was dead to the world. He didn't notice me standing before him. No flicker. No response. I walked right up to him and he didn't respond. I waved my hand in front of his face, even snapped my fingers close to his nose.

"*Dad?*" I asked in old-speak. "*Dad?*"

He didn't move. Not one muscle.

I panicked. I reached out to grab his shoulder and shake him awake.

"*Dad!*"

As soon as I touched his shoulder, he rolled to his back. Limply. His head landed on the ice with a thump and his mouth fell open.

He still didn't wake up.

That was when I saw the blood that stained the ice. There was a dark red cloud of it, slowly spreading wider. In places it was darker, as if it had run down into the carvings.

Snakes and circles and lightning bolts.

Just like the carvings on the red rock.

I WOKE UP, HEART POUNDING with terror. I sat straight up. I might have yelled.

It was cold in the cabin, and I could see brilliant sunshine outside the windows. The sky was scrubbed-clean blue—the storm had passed.

I closed my eyes and tried to feel my dad's presence, tried to find a current or a glimmer or some sense of his being out there in the world. And I couldn't find him.

At all.

After that dream, I was freaked.

I was terrified that something had happened to my dad.

Maybe to all of the *Pyr*.

Seeing blood in my dream hadn't exactly been reassuring.

What was I going to do?

What *could* I do?

I got up, tugged on my clothes, and left the others sleeping. My thoughts felt more clear outside, as if the wind had blown away my doubts and worries.

Where would I start to hunt Donovan? He had been in the cabin just before we arrived. He had prepared to shift into dragon form at the sight of something.

And he had vanished into thin air.

By choice? Or not? I was starting to think option B, but that didn't give me any clues.

Then I recalled that this lake looked a lot like the lake in my dream, the one where my dad had been, well, down. It beckoned to me.

I chose to trust my impulse.

IT WAS INCREDIBLY COLD, COLD enough to freeze your lungs with one breath. The little hairs inside my nose felt like icicles, and even my gloves weren't enough to keep my fingertips from going numb. I had my shawl wrapped around my head, and my ears were cold before I even got to the shore.

The snow was deep, too. We must have gotten six feet of it the night before. Again, I considered how strange it was to have such a wintry April. Had Donovan overlooked that variable in his planning? Was that what was wrong here?

No. It was more than that.

At least I'd been right about one thing: my dad had been on this very lake in my dream. At night instead of in the morning, but I recognized it as the same place. I slid out onto the surface—with the snow on top of the ice, my boots didn't get enough traction.

My dad had been far from shore, in the middle of the lake. So that was where I headed.

Away from the shore, the wind had blown the snow away from the ice. The ice was buffed smooth, like a mirror, very slippery underfoot. I made slow progress, and my fingers got colder, but I carried on. I heard the guys wake up. I heard them arguing and knew whatever spell was on the cabin was working its worst.

I ignored them, focusing on my own quest.

I walked for ages. I was so far away that I couldn't hear the guys anymore, even with my keen *Pyr* hearing. The sun rose over the line of trees, burning a path high into the bright blue sky. I thought about the ice melting beneath my feet, but knew it was too thick for that.

It creaked, though. That was spooky. It murmured on all sides, groaning and shifting beneath the sun's touch. I was far from the shore and all alone—if I went through the ice, I'd die before anyone even guessed I was in trouble.

Still, I kept going. The shape of the trees around the shore of the lake was almost right. I was nearly at the spot, although I didn't know what I expected to find there. Where was my dad? Why did I have this sense that I'd failed him?

And that it mattered big-time.

"Zoë!" someone yelled.

I heard the beat of dragon wings and spun to scan the sky.

A dark gray dragon was flying straight toward me. I had a moment to hope—my dad is onyx and silver in dragon form—before I saw that the proportions were wrong. My dad was bigger, leaner, more powerful than this dragon. Older.

This dragon was shadowy and insubstantial, and my dad was not. I squinted, looked again, and realized I'd been wrong.

But he was pewter and purple.

Adrian!

He'd wanted to talk. The middle of the lake was a good choice. I waved.

He came closer and I felt a flicker of dread. I attributed it to the long shadow of whatever haunted that cabin. He shifted shape just as his feet touched down, an elegant transition that I longed to master.

"Are you okay? I was worried about you."

"Thanks. You wanted to talk about your idea."

Adrian nodded. "You know how I said that my dad has kept himself apart from the *Pyr*?" I nodded. "Well, that's not exactly true. He's been hanging out with different *Pyr*. Actually, it's a group of different shifters. They're committed to learning more about their powers and becoming more than what they already are." He held my gaze. "That's where I met Sophie."

I was shocked. "You *met* her? When?"

"She didn't die, Zoë."

I gaped at him.

"That's just what the *Pyr* say. The truth is that they didn't appreciate her any more than they appreciate you." Adrian winced. "And when she figured it out, she left them. She made a choice to follow her own path."

My father had lied to me? But Adrian kept talking, and the more he said, the more plausible it sounded.

"She's worried about you. She said she'd been trying to send you dreams, but wasn't sure it was working. So she asked my dad to send me here."

"Why?"

"To invite you to join her. She thinks that two Wyverns will be able to change the world."

"But that's what the Wyvern is supposed to do, along with the *Pyr*."

"Those days are past. That's what she said. The Wyvern can work with the *Pyr* only if she stays apart from them. If she gets involved, well, it doesn't work out."

"What does that mean?"

"She says they betrayed her, Zoë. Because she was different, they used her to get some academy destroyed. She didn't know. The *Pyr* she loved didn't know. The other *Pyr* lied to her. They set her up and he got killed. She only barely escaped, but she decided she'd never go back."

It sounded all too plausible.

But still, my dad couldn't have lied to me.

He wouldn't have. "So maybe they're not lying now. Maybe they really don't know she's alive."

"Come on, Zoë. Can't your father feel the presence of every single *Pyr* on the planet? He knows; he's just not telling you." Adrian cleared his throat. "Just the way he hasn't told you about the other *Pyr*, the ones who chose the other path. The ones who don't report to him."

I still couldn't wrap my mind around the idea of my dad being deceptive. He tells it like it is, whether you want to hear it or not. "But . . ."

"Your father has his own agenda, Zoë," Adrian insisted. "It's time for you to choose yours. Come with me and talk to Sophie, at least."

"Talk to her?" It seemed like a decent offer.

A very reasonable suggestion.

Then why did I not want to go?

"You can learn the truth from her." He smiled and put out his hand. "I'll take you to her. We'll be back before the guys even notice that we were gone." He shrugged. "Unless you decide that Wyverns should stick together."

I was torn in a way that shook me. I wanted to do as he suggested, wanted to put my hand in his with all my might. Yet a little voice deep inside me was screaming, *No, no, no!*

It reminded me of what humans said about beguiling, if and when it was explained to them.

It reminded me of what Lorenzo said once about beguiling—that you can only really beguile a human into believing something he or she already wants to believe.

Or doing something that he or she really wants to do.

And I didn't want to do this.

There were no flames in Adrian's eyes.

Still, his words were making me consider a choice that I normally wouldn't make. What was going on?

I felt a shadow pass over me and shivered.

I glanced around and everything looked normal.

Until I closed my right eye.

IN GRANNY'S WORLD, PART OF the sun was obscured. It looked as if someone had taken a bite out of one side of it.

No, it was the shadow of the moon falling over the sun.

The solar eclipse Rafferty had mentioned. There are times when it's good to be an attentive student, and this was one of them. (Don't tell my mom I admitted that.) I also have a thing for eclipses, given that important firestorms of the adult *Pyr* are triggered by lunar eclipses.

Call me a romantic.

There was supposed to be a solar eclipse on Monday at about

noon. It wouldn't be visible in Chicago or even in Minnesota—I'd done an assignment on it a couple of months before and remembered that—but with my freaky eye, I could have been standing right beneath it.

The strange thing was that the eclipse was creeping me out, making all the little hairs on the back of my neck stand up and quiver simultaneously. And I *like* eclipses. I knew it was just the shadow of the moon blocking the sun, just a trick of location and light, but it felt like a warning. Danger was approaching.

Something snapped into focus.

Something broke.

Something lost its hold over me. I suddenly knew that what Adrian was telling me was bullshit.

Sophie was dead.

My father hadn't lied to me.

There could be only one Wyvern, and if Sophie was alive, then I wasn't the Wyvern.

But I *was* the Wyvern, which meant she was dead.

Sophie was not with some other group of *Pyr*. There was no other group of *Pyr*, because my dad would have told me.

Someone must have lied to Adrian.

Fortunately, I could set him straight.

I turned back to Adrian and what I saw silenced anything I was going to say. In fact, my mouth fell open.

Holy frick.

What was he?

Chapter 17

Right in front of me, Adrian flickered and shifted, rotating through a bewildering number of forms.

First he was a dragon, but a ghostly one. The edges of his dragon shape were blurry and he seemed insubstantial, even with my right eye. The eclipse's light was merciless. I saw that my fleeting impression each time he'd taken dragon form—that there was something wrong with his dragon form—had been right on the money. How had he made me ignore that? I had a second to wonder, and then he shifted again.

With my left eye, he was a griffin.

Then he was a unicorn.

He was a basilisk.

He was all of those things and more, changing rapidly between forms. I knew that if I blinked I'd miss at least three. Those forms, though, were substantial. How were they different from his being a dragon?

And how could he take so many shapes?

The eclipse swept away even more. Not only did I recall those moments of doubt over Adrian looking wrong, but I suddenly remembered Adrian's scent when he'd first arrived. I recalled how I had been surprised by that initial whiff of it, back when he'd pulled up beside the driveway.

And I knew with complete conviction that he wasn't *Pyr*.

I wasn't sure what the hell he was.

How had he fooled us? The flickering of his forms continued, adding a whole suite more.

He was a snake.

He was a Medusa.

He was a manticore.

He was a Harpy.

I felt like I needed to sit down and put my head between my knees. There was something deeply wrong with this.

Wicked.

Unnatural. That might sound strange coming from someone who hangs with dragon shape shifters, but trust me—his rapid shape shifting was wrong.

"You can see me," Adrian said, his surprise clear. I knew then that it would have been smarter to have hidden my reaction from him, but it was too late.

I nodded. "Whatever you are."

A minotaur.

A boar.

A Sphinx.

A different man. An older one. Which was he really?

Was he *human*?

"Maybe that makes it easier." He spoke with a smooth confidence, but this time his words didn't reassure me. They sounded oily. Manipulative. Powerful and dark.

Like the mood in the cabin.

I suddenly had the solution to the riddle. I knew then what Adrian had done. He'd cast a spell over all of us; he could enchant with the power of his voice. That was how he'd made me believe that he was *Pyr*. I could see the same glimmers of light as I'd seen in the cabin.

But they were emanating from Adrian.

He was some kind of sorcerer.

And this was an offer he didn't intend for me to refuse. He'd used deception only because the truth wasn't so pretty. I continued to watch him as he changed shape.

A deer.

A serpent.

A phoenix.

A dragon again. Again the dragon form was less real than the others, more shadowy.

Why was it different?

"Can you stop it? Or just slow it down?" I asked. I couldn't look away, but watching him shift so quickly made me want to puke. My brain couldn't deal with it. (And yes, I thought of those humans losing their minds when they witnessed our shift.)

Adrian stopped.

He was in human form, looking just like the guy I'd met at the side of the highway. I remained suspicious. His edges wavered as he surveyed me, proof that I'd nailed it in one when I'd wondered whether he was actually any of these forms.

"Thanks." I took a deep breath and concentrated on looking at him with my right eye. He was less fluid that way. "What *are* you?"

Adrian smiled, and again I was not reassured. "The future."

"I guess I don't understand."

His words flowed gently, as soothing as the current of a lazy river. That was how he cast his spell: with his voice. I recognized it now. He'd persuaded us to stay put when we would have gone after Donovan with his suggestions. He'd convinced us about his credentials—which had to be a lie—with his story. He'd tempted us to get drunk and distracted us from what we'd known we should do.

With his words.

But now the river of his spell was one that rolled right past me, leaving me on the shore. Now I could see how dirty the water was. Thanks to the light of the eclipse, the illusion was completely shattered.

I looked at Adrian with my left eye. His form was dark and a bit twisted. It wasn't real. He wasn't real. Granny was showing me the truth. I felt like I'd gotten hit in the head with a rune stone.

Adrian had deceived me.

He'd lied to my friends.

He'd probably hurt Donovan.

I had a horrible feeling he knew what had happened to Rafferty and my dad—or that he'd been a part of something nasty. He was no friend, although he'd pretended to be one.

Remember, Zoë. Just as you're more than you seem to be, so is everyone else. I heard Jared's parting words. Forewarned in this case hadn't meant forearmed.

I had no time to feel dumb. I had to fix this.

I reached inside myself and I tried to summon the shimmer. I intended to ensure that Adrian paid the price. I meant to embrace my legacy and use it for good.

The problem was that I couldn't find the shimmer.

Had he done that to me, too?

ADRIAN CONTINUED, TRYING TO PERSUADE me. "I'm where Sophie went, Zoë. This is what we can become, shifters like you and me. We can rise beyond the limitations of our innate forms and become so much more."

He was excited enough that this might be the truth. I hid my disgust and pretended to be interested. What I was really doing was trying to figure out how to get out of this situation.

Preferably alive.

Here, shimmer, shimmer . . .

"Tell me more."

"All the *Pyr* are doomed, except those who choose this other path. Like Sophie did. That's why they cling to you and lie to you—they're afraid."

"That makes sense. The guys have been pretty tough." I wanted him to keep talking while I kept trying to coax the shimmer to show itself.

It was better than panicking.

"Why does the world need the *Pyr*?" he asked. "The traditional role of defeating *Slayers* is fulfilled."

"But there is the Earth to defend, and the elements to guard."

Adrian snorted. "A task we can do better when we have more skills. But don't just believe me—come with me. Let Sophie tell you about it." As he spoke, I felt his words slide into my thoughts, trying to enchant me into doing what he wanted.

The very fact that he felt the need to cast a spell meant that going with him wasn't such a great option. Problem was, I really didn't know what Adrian could do. I fingered the rune stone in my pocket, figuring it was the only weapon I had if plan A didn't work.

Here, shimmer, shimmer . . .

"All you have to do is take my hand," Adrian said smoothly. He reached out toward me and smiled.

In that same moment, in Granny's world, the eclipse became complete. The shadow of the moon had slipped fully over the sun. Everything was dark, except the corona of fire of the obscured sun. It was like night, but reddish in a creepy way.

Something danced over my skin like quicksilver, and I shivered as I looked down. There a glinting light moved over me—a red glow changing to a blue shimmer.

Yes! The sight thrilled me.

I followed it and felt where it had been hiding in my mind.

As if the eclipse's light showed me the way.

I felt more confident. I felt the shimmer stir and dared to believe in myself. It was mine. I was running it. I was going to shift and stay in control.

And then I'd kick Adrian's butt.

Adrian stepped closer, taking my silence for submission. "Come and talk to Sophie about the better side."

"Oh, I don't think so," I said, shoving my hands into my pockets and offering Adrian a smile. "I think I'll just stay put. But thanks for the offer."

"Oh, no," Adrian said. He became darker then, and more ominous. His form swelled larger, large enough to make me nervous. "This isn't an invitation you can refuse."

"I just did."

Adrian roared and switched to his dark dragon form with lightning speed. He lunged toward me, snatching with those silver talons, his teeth bared. Even shadowy, they were scary. My heart skipped in terror.

I would be toast.

Unless I could pull this off.

I hauled hard on that shimmer.

And I felt it come on demand.

Woo-hoo!

THE BLUE SHIMMER THAT HERALDED the shift crashed through me like a tidal wave. It was different from the red current of anger, but every bit as powerful. It was cold and cleansing, similar to a wall of water that would flood everything in its path. It ripped through me, pushing down barriers, shoving everything aside except the essence of dragon.

It felt right.

It was a part of me, not some alien beast taking control of me.

I welcomed it. It didn't need much encouragement to claim every molecule of my body, seize me heart and soul, change everything it touched.

This was my destiny.

This was my power.

And it arrived with explosive force.

Right on time.

The shift happened in a heartbeat. One second, Adrian was closing in on me fast, and I was a scrawny teenage girl, looking like lunch. He could destroy me and there'd be no witnesses.

The next second I was soaring above the lake, massive wings unfurled behind me. I was beating the air with them, soaring higher, stunned by the weight and mass of myself.

I'd done it!

I'd shifted and I was still in charge.

For one instant, Adrian simply stared. I seized the moment and I had a look myself.

I was a dragon, all right, a long, slender white one. My scales had a glitter to them, as if I had been born of the ice itself, and there were long white feathers trailing from my shoulders and tail. My talons could have been made of glass.

Not just a dragon. I knew now about the color, now that I'd seen Sophie.

I am the Wyvern.

With my left eye, under the light of the eclipse, I looked fluorescent. I glowed like those stars my mom had stuck on my bedroom ceiling roughly a zillion years ago.

But I had no time to feel triumphant. Adrian snarled; he turned and dove toward me.

And I remembered that I had no idea how to fight.

Oops.

My time as the Wyvern might be very, very short.

I shouted in old-speak, calling to the guys to help, but having zero confidence that they would do so.

Who knew what spell Adrian had laid on them before he left the cabin? I was on my own.

Maybe this was my test. I raised my talons in the traditional fighting pose. I turned to face Adrian straight on, and resolved to do my best.

Even if it wasn't going to be nearly good enough.

Any doubts I might have had about Adrian's intent didn't last long. He fell on me with force, knocking me sideways through the air with a heavy body check. My wings faltered as I lost my flying rhythm. He took advantage of that to slash at my side, cutting across my gut with four of his sharp talons.

This wasn't just fun and games. He meant to kill me.

I yelled in pain as my blood dripped onto the ice far below us.

Adrian circled around for another hit. "It doesn't have to be this way, Zoë. You could just come along quietly."

"Then what?"

"Sophie's waiting."

"Sophie's dead!"

He shook his head sadly, shifting to a flying horse. "They lied to you, Zoë."

His shift came at exactly the right time to remind me of his deceptiveness. He'd say anything to get me to go with him.

Which meant I shouldn't.

"No. You're the one lying to me."

"Stubborn." Adrian lowered his head, shifting to dragon form again, and dove toward me, breathing dragonfire. His eyes glittered, visible through the flames, and he moved like nothing I'd ever seen before.

I needed a plan.

Fast.

I yelped and lost my rhythm as I tried to fly faster. It was track day all over again, hurdles crashing on every side. For lack of a better strategy, I decided to go with incompetence.

I pretended to faint in terror and let myself fall.

It was strange, dropping through the cold air. I kept my eyes open a slit and watched the ice get ever closer. I steeled my nerve, telling myself to keep my pulse slow, to not give myself away. It was nearly impossible.

I could only hope that he didn't have *Pyr* perceptiveness.

Adrian took the bait. He came after me, altering his trajectory. He was diving fast, really fast, and that improved my chances of success.

Could it work?

Five seconds to impact. Max. I watched the ice as I felt the heat of him drawing closer.

Three. I kept my body limp.

Two. I poised to flee.

One.

In the last instant, I came to life. I flapped my wings with all my might. I turned my course, heading straight up.

It wasn't pretty but I got the job done. I faltered—no gymnast here—then shot into the sky.

Adrian missed me, his talons slicing through the air just below my tail. I flew harder when I felt the current of air as he passed me.

Adrian was so surprised that he didn't have time to turn. He slammed into the ice, smashing his shoulder into it and making it crack.

That made him shift through a couple of forms again. He skidded across the surface of the lake, rolling to his back as he tried to stop his slide, swearing all the way. I didn't dare watch. I flew straight up, my heart thundering.

Could I get far enough away from him for it to matter? I doubted it.

Talk about a primer in dragon fighting.

With the ultimate stakes.

I glanced down to see a bull stamping on the ice, breathing red smoke. He had eyes that could have been made of fire. Then he bounded into the air, shifting to a dragon again.

He shot skyward like an arrow launched from a bow.

Shit.

Adrian accelerated with an agility I could only admire, and once again targeted me. Holy frick, but he was fast. I realized he'd been *really* holding back when he'd fought with Nick.

It wasn't encouraging that even Nick hadn't managed to best him.

And Adrian hadn't been trying to kill Nick.

I raced toward the sky with no hope of outrunning him and no backup plan. Flying farther and faster for as long as possible was the best I could do.

I didn't get far enough. Adrian grabbed me from behind and bit at the tendon of my wing in one shoulder. I looked down, saw how far I could fall, and panicked.

"Bad choice, Zoë," he said softly.

I had pretty much nothing to lose at this point. I spun in his grip, then locked my tail around his. He bucked against me and nearly pulled free.

But not quite. I slashed at him with my talons, caught him across the snout, and ripped the skin from the corner of his eye to the edge of his nostril. He bellowed in pain, then belted me.

I tumbled through the sky, rolling end over end and unable to stop myself. I hit the ice and skidded across the surface. My left eye gave me a vision of bodies floating beneath the ice.

Pyr corpses.

All the *Pyr* I knew.

I'd dreamed of my dad being hurt and hadn't been able to feel the presence of the older *Pyr*—because they were in danger, too.

And I'd been too stupid to trust the instincts I'd been born with.

That was going to change.

If I survived this fight.

Adrian soared after me, pursuing me without urgency. He knew he'd won and was gloating. He settled beside me on the ice, then poked me with a talon.

"Stubborn, aren't you?" he muttered. "Such a waste. You could have ensured that at least one of the *Pyr* survived. Oh, well, you'll live on in stories, just as you always have." He shifted to a lion and bent to rip open my guts.

He planned to eat me alive.

As if.

That he didn't care whether he deceived me or turned us against one another told me everything I needed to know about his moral code and so-called vision for the future. How dared he attack us? How dared he attack me? Anger tore through me.

And I let it.

No, I channeled it and put it to work.

Fury flooded my body, giving me incredible strength. I opened my mouth and the dragonfire spewed in a torrent. It was white-hot. Way beyond orange and yellow, this stuff was fierce. The hungry flames sizzled against his chest, setting his lion fur alight. Adrian hollered in pain.

Even better, he let go of me.

He ran and I pursued him. He shifted on the fly, slipping into alternate forms in rapid succession. I had the sense he was search-ing for a specific one, maybe one that came in a fireproof suit, but he didn't find it.

I singed feathers. I fried fur. I burned scales and I roasted skin. I blew fire high and I blew it low. I followed him across the ice, hearing it crack, leaving pools of water behind us, taking flight when he did. No matter what he did, I kept the furnace on.

Or his toes to the fire.

Either way.

He was the one who was toast.

Chapter 18

*I*n the same moment that the guys shouted and cleared the shore, flying high in their dragon forms, the sun slipped free of the moon's shadow in the alternate dreamworld. The red tinge disappeared from the light, no matter which eye I used, and everything returned to normal.

And after one ripple of his dragon form—it rippled the way the surface of a lake ripples in the wind—Adrian looked substantial and *Pyr* once more.

It was obviously an illusion, but how did he do it?

Could the guys even see that his form was unstable at first?

Adrian smiled at me. I took that as a bad sign.

"Help me!" he screamed to the guys. "She's gone crazy. She's trying to kill me!"

"He attacked me!" I shouted. The three guys hovered in flight, keeping their distance from me. They looked good in their dragon forms, sparkling like jewels in the sunshine. Adrian appealed to them, looking more pathetic than I could believe.

That stupid orange light was hanging around the guys, as if its sparks had followed them from the cabin. This was also a bad sign.

And it became more radiant with every word Adrian said.

"Right," Adrian said with disdain. "And why would I attack the Wyvern?" He shook his head, his voice turning to that persuasive, easy tone again. The orange light brightened with every word. "I tried to help. She was stranded out here on the ice. I thought something was wrong. I came to help her back to the cabin and she went crazy on me. She could have just said no!"

"Wait a minute," Liam began to argue, but I felt their hesitation. The orange light wound around them like snakes.

"He's lying. He tried to kill me out here—"

"Look!" Adrian interrupted and whimpered. "She *burned* me."

The guys halted to consider this—and their doubt was almost tangible. But I knew who had made Garrett dream of me betraying the *Pyr* and given him the idea that I was holding out on them. I knew who had turned the guys against me, and why the cabin felt so oppressively hostile.

And I knew his voice was the strongest weapon he had against us.

"He's not *Pyr*," I argued. "He's here to destroy us. . . ."

"You were the one who let Liam get hurt," Nick said.

"And you were the one who stole Nick's clothes in the first place," Liam added.

"Don't you care about anything but yourself?" Garrett asked me.

I could see those invisible spell lines dancing all around them, weaving into a net that would trap them.

And it was all coming from Adrian.

"I don't think she does," Adrian said. "I just tried to help."

"No! It's a spell. . . ."

"Right. Like the story that you don't know how to take dragon form." Nick shook his head. "Looks like you've nailed it pretty well."

"She can't even tell us the truth," Adrian said. "It's like we're her enemies, not her friends."

I saw their expressions harden and knew his charm was working.

"Yesterday was the first time. . . ."

"Enough lies, Zoë," Garrett said.

"Yet you were thumping Adrian the first time you ever fought?" Nick challenged.

"When Nick couldn't touch him?" Garrett shook his head in disbelief. "We're not stupid, Zoë."

"Maybe we're better off without a Wyvern, if she isn't going to play on our team," Adrian said, his tone sly. "Maybe we shouldn't have anyone on the team we can't trust."

"But . . ." Liam said.

"Adrian is casting a spell," I argued. "He's turning us against one another."

"No. You're the one trying to turn us all against one another." Adrian said, so soft and persuasive. "Why?"

"I'm not the bad guy here!"

"All I did was try to bring her back to the cabin," Adrian said to the guys. "All I did was try to help her."

"You were trying to kill me!" I shouted. I saw the orange sparks get brighter, gathering more tightly around Garrett and Nick, and knew I was in deep trouble.

"Maybe we should just talk about it," Liam suggested.

"I think we've heard enough," Nick said, preparing to face off against me.

"*Now,*" Garrett commanded in old-speak.

"No! You liar!" I would have screamed a lot more at Adrian, but Garrett came after me in a frenzy. His talons were extended and he was closing in fast.

Garrett launched a torrent of dragonfire as he dove. His eyes gleamed with malice and I saw that the spell light was completely surrounding him.

Holding him in its thrall.

Making him want to hurt me.

And neither Nick nor Liam was going to stop him.

Holy shit.

I flew straight at Garrett, though. I snatched at his claws, wanting to get this part over with. (I told you about the perils of arm wrestling with Garrett.)

We locked talons in the traditional fighting pose, wrestling and thrashing furiously. I ripped free of Garrett's grip as quickly as possible, although I knew I'd be sore for a while. I went for his back, wrapping myself around his wings and upper arms. I wouldn't be able to hold him, but maybe he'd lose altitude.

He did.

I saw the light of the spell winding around us, binding us both. It made me dizzy, polluting my mind with Adrian's hatred.

It made Garrett seethe.

And gave him new strength. He spun suddenly and belted me. I managed to duck the worst of the blow. I snapped at him, livid at what the spell was making him do. Something in my eyes made him back away. I chased him, breathing fire and lashing my tail.

"We should help her," I heard Liam say.

"Let them work it out," Adrian said to him in that oily and persuasive tone. I sensed the guys struggling against this argument.

Before they accepted it.

The next thing I knew Garrett pivoted abruptly, launching a

volley of blows that I was hard-pressed to block. He was all over me, and all I could do was duck and flinch. I definitely had made a mistake in not being more enthused about gym class.

Then Garrett hit me right on the temple. I spun in pain, trying even so to keep myself aloft. Before I hit the ice, he caught me from behind in a tight bear hug, one that I feared I'd never escape.

He started to squeeze the life out of me.

Then I felt him take a deep breath. He was going to turn his dragonfire on me.

Shit.

I squeezed my eyes shut and wished with all my heart that I were anywhere in the world other than where I was right then.

The incredible thing was that my wish came true.

I FELT DIFFERENT.

Different from when I was filled with the blue shimmer of shape shifting or even with red rage. I felt neutral—cool as a cucumber, my mom would say—and that was a relief. I still had four long, bleeding wounds on my abdomen and they hurt more than ever. As a bonus, I was nauseated and dizzy.

And freezing.

But I wasn't over the lake anymore. And I wasn't getting cooked by Garrett's dragonfire. I was in the snow. It was cold. And judging by the size of the trees surrounding me, I wasn't a dragon anymore, either.

Either that, or I'd ended up in some magical forest.

(Which wasn't out of the question.)

I also felt like I was really going to puke.

I kept my eyes closed until that wave of nausea passed, then had a look at myself. I was as white as milk. My skin was smooth, not scaled. I had webbed feet and an undeniable compulsion to flick my tongue.

I was a salamander.

Okay, I knew this was another form that the Wyvern could take, and while it was fab that I could do this, too, it would have been much more helpful if I had any clue as to *how* I had done it.

Never mind how to change back to my own self.

Where in the world I had ended up would have been a useful detail, too.

I glanced around and realized that I wasn't in the forest exactly, but in the middle of a clearing. A long, narrow clearing. With two trenches worked into the snow, one of which I was sitting in. Yes, the snow was packed down into distinctive patterns. I wasn't used to seeing tire treads as wide as I was tall. . . .

I did the math, just as a car appeared. It wasn't going that fast in the snow, but those tires looked as if they would squish me before I could get away.

I squeaked.

I leapt out of the trench o' death.

And I sank way down into the snow. It didn't matter how much I scrambled and struggled. My efforts just made me sink down, down, down. I'd never get out of here.

Well, maybe when the snow melted.

If I survived that long.

The car stopped right beside me. I could see the gleaming blue paint.

Nick's car was that color.

This was not good. Nick wanted to kill me because of Adrian's spell. I panicked. I fought to dig a tunnel through the snow. Maybe I could disappear—white on white—if I could just put some distance between us.

I didn't get far before someone snatched me up.

I squeaked and squirmed.

"Hi, Zoë."

Isabelle. It would be an understatement to say I was shocked. She knew it was me.

How?

Why?

How had she known where I was?

"I *knew* I'd find you up here," she said quietly. "I had a premonition, and I had to follow it. And here you are, but hurt!" She wrinkled her nose. "I bet you feel awful, too."

She didn't seem to be talking about my wounds. I tried to speak and was a bit surprised when it worked. "Why?"

"Rafferty says moving through space makes him feel terrible. Nauseated and dizzy. You need something to eat and to drink; plus you need that bleeding stopped."

"But the guys are trying to kill me!"

A fierce light dawned in her eyes. "They'll have to get past me first. Come on."

I decided I was going to have to like Isabelle, after all.

She got back into the car and held me in her lap. She unwrapped the end of a granola bar and I had a bite; then she dabbed at my wounds with a tissue. "They look like surface cuts."

"They hurt."

"I'll bet. There's a first-aid kit in the glove box." She put me on the passenger seat and eyed me. "You'll have to shift back to human form. I can't bandage a salamander."

That made sense.

If I could just do it.

"I won't look," she said. She put on her seat belt, then put the car into gear again. We started to roll slowly along the road, and I realized the cant was uphill.

She was leaving the cabin.

"I don't suppose you know how to drive," she said. "I mean, I do, but everything is backward. In this snow, it would be good to have a driver who wasn't distracted by the gearshift being on the wrong side."

I closed my eyes, looked for that sweet spot in my thoughts, and hoped like heck I could shift.

I did. It took a bit to take hold, long enough for me to despair; then it happened really fast.

In fact, I changed so fast that I didn't have time to think about position. As a salamander, I'd been lying on the seat—in human form I was in exactly the same pose, but my forehead banged on the door to the glove compartment and my legs were all folded up in a strange yoga posture.

"That was graceful," I muttered as I swung myself around.

"Well, you did it. That's good." Isabelle flashed me a smile. She pointed to the glove compartment and I got out the first-aid kit. I pulled up my shirt and wrapped some gauze over my cuts. They'd mostly stopped bleeding. Isabelle handed me the rest of the granola bar.

"You should drink some water, too." She gestured to her purse in the back and I found a new bottle of water there.

I did as she instructed and felt roughly 10,645 times better.

Give or take.

"I drew a card this morning," she said, frowning at the road. "The Hanged Man."

"Sounds optimistic."

She half laughed. "It's not good. I knew it was a sign that I should leave, somehow; then I could see the two of us leaving together. I had the strongest sense before I left the cabin that I'd find you on this road. Maybe that made me watch extra carefully, but when I saw a white salamander, I knew it had to be you."

"Not a lot of newts out in the snow."

She laughed for real then. "No. Especially not any that shimmer blue as they appear. I'd have missed you without that light. Feel better?"

"Yes, thanks. I'm glad you were here." I meant it, too. I smiled at her. "I'd have been a newtsicle otherwise."

She laughed at my joke, even though it was lame, and I found myself smiling even more. I liked her.

In fact, maybe I needed her help.

Because the sad fact was that I'd not listened to Isabelle, or paid attention to my dreams in which she featured, simply out of jealousy. (I tell you, Granny is one tough cookie—when she pulls aside the veil, she really goes for it. That solar eclipse had left me with buckets of revelations.) I had been petty and unfriendly. With my impatience to be Wyvern, I'd set something in motion that had worked against all of us.

And by my own logic—*Pyr* plus human equals mating—Nick was out-of-bounds to me anyhow. We could never be more than friends. Or at least, we could never be in a romantic relationship and have anything come of it.

That had been the last Wyvern's mistake, and it would have been really stupid for me to make the same one all over again.

I suddenly remembered one bit of my dream.

The present is where the past shakes hands with the future.

And I'd shaken hands with not just Sophie, but Isabelle, too. So we should be allies. I was good with that. I surrendered to Granny's wisdom and insight.

Like Jared said, I'd been the one doubting my powers.

I believed now. I'd shifted. I'd moved through space. I'd even taken shape as a salamander. I was stepping into my destiny. All I had to do was survive Adrian and break the spell he had over the guys.

Then figure out how to save our dads, whatever had happened to them.

No pressure, right?

BEFORE I COULD ASK FOR Isabelle's help with all of the above, I heard the low thrum of a motorcycle engine.

It was coming closer.

I don't know beans about motorcycles, but I would have bet you my Wyvern powers that it was a vintage Ducati.

Being ridden by an urban pirate.

Oh, yes.

My luck was turning. Big-time.

"Can we go any faster?" I was even leaning forward.

"Not without visiting the ditch."

I flung open the door of the car and jumped out into the snow.

"Where are you going? What's wrong?" I knew the moment that Isabelle heard the bike, too. "Oh!" she said, and coaxed the car to accelerate.

On foot, I was still faster than she was. And impatient, too. I wanted to see Jared, and I wanted to see him now.

If not sooner.

Isabelle kept driving behind me, but there could have been wings on my feet.

Suddenly, the bike engine stopped.

No! He couldn't leave!

I ran faster, determined to change his mind.

Then I heard the steady crunch of footsteps in the snow, along with the sound of a bike being rolled.

Closer.

Right. Jared had said there was too much snow for the bike. He wouldn't leave it behind on the road, but the obstacle wasn't going to stop him, either.

What was not to love about that?

I raced around the curve in the road and skidded to a halt. It was Jared. And he was here. Against the odds.

He didn't just look dangerous and sexy.

He looked uncomfortable.

If his face hadn't lit at the sight of me, I would have been a lot more worried than I was. As it was, he glanced away and frowned, then pointed a finger at me. "Look. I couldn't just leave you here. Not with that guy."

Meanwhile, Isabelle stopped the car behind me and got out. Eavesdropping shamelessly. I was really starting to like her.

Jared continued, his tone defensive. (As if I would have issues with his presence. Right.) "He might look okay, but he's trouble, and he has bad intentions toward you—"

"She knows," Isabelle interrupted in that chirpy British way of hers.

Jared blinked. "Excuse me?"

I strode toward him as I explained. "He just tried to kill me, and now he's set the guys on me. Actually, that's what he's been doing all along. He's made a spell. He's not *Pyr*, even though he seems like it."

"Then what is he?" Isabelle asked.

"A Mage," Jared said with conviction. "They're spellcasters, intent on taking control of everything."

That made sense.

"He's been casting a spell since we got here," I said. "Turning the guys against me, keeping us here. He showed himself when I refused to go with him." I shuddered, feeling Jared watching me.

His lips tightened. "Never believe those guys." His tone was bitter. "They change the deal after they have you powerless." Then he studied me, as if trying to confirm that I was okay.

I liked that a lot.

So, of course, I blushed. And I had to change the subject. "How do you know about Mages?"

"They've been trying to recruit me for years." He frowned. "They recruit humans who have a natural ability to cast spells, take them as apprentices, and train them. I knew what he was right away, but I'd promised Donovan that I'd leave you here."

I understood. "And you can't break a promise to Donovan."

"I tried to think it was part of Donovan's plan." Jared shook his head. "I tried to do what I'd promised. I went to Sioux City. But it drove me nuts. I called Donovan, but he didn't answer his phone. I finally drove back to Minneapolis, but Alex said there'd been no sign of him. That's when I got worried."

"My dad?"

"Alex called him, but your mom said he'd disappeared, too." He swallowed, as Isabelle and I exchanged worried glances. "They can't find any of the *Pyr*, which meant I had to get back here and find out what was going on."

I couldn't help thinking of all the blood in my dreams.

"You wanted to check on Zoë anyhow," Isabelle said, and Jared shot her a look. My heart skipped a beat at his expression. He had been worried about me.

"Got a problem with that?" Jared said, and Isabelle held up her hands in mock surrender. Then she winked at me. I blushed more and Jared pretended not to notice. He made a sound of frustration. "You can't call anybody in this place."

"We're off the map," I said. "Here be dragons and all that."

"Not funny, Zoë." Jared was stern. "The *Pyr* are in trouble."

"I know, but I can't find them, either. At the library was the only time I was able to sense the other *Pyr*." I had a sudden realization. "No, I felt for them on this road, when I was with Adrian. And the connection was broken right then."

"By him." Jared grimaced. "I should never have left."

"His spell was meant to keep us all here," Isabelle said.

"And distracted." I was thinking about pizza and beer, about the way Adrian had turned the decision to staying put instead of seeking Donovan. We'd been duped.

I was afraid of what the price of that might be.

"Which means whatever has happened to the other *Pyr* required all of you to be out of the picture for a while." Jared was grim.

I felt more grim.

I heard dragon wings.

Shit.

"Here they come," I said, scanning the sky. I knew the two humans with me wouldn't hear the sound just yet. "They must have heard me."

"How are we going to break Adrian's spell before Zoë gets hurt?" Isabelle asked. She clutched my hand and I felt her fear.

"Hold the bike," Jared said with determination. "This is what I do."

Excuse me?

Chapter 19

You know, I'd never considered myself to be a damsel in distress, much less one in need of a rescue—having a mom who calls herself a rabid feminist will do that for you. On the other hand, Jared's protectiveness was working for me in a big way.

It was sexy.

Plus, there had to be some reason why the Mages wanted to recruit him. I didn't know much about spells or spellcasting or whatever magic Adrian could do. But I'd seen its effects, and I knew enough to be worried.

Even though I knew that Adrian's spell wasn't a whole lot different from beguiling, what spooked me was that he had made two of my three best friends believe not just that they should hate my guts, but that they should try to kill me.

Whatever he was tossing out there, it was powerful stuff.

So, while I was scared crapless of dragons shredding me alive,

I was afraid for Jared, too. He hadn't signed up for the Mages' advanced spellcasting program, which meant he might not know all the tricks he needed to win.

All of this ensured that the withdraw-with-smelling-salts-and-await-the-outcome option was out of the question.

Since I wanted to live with myself after this day.

"Hide," Isabelle suggested to me in an undertone. Jared was staring at the sky, preparing to do . . . something.

But hiding was the damsel choice, and I was a dragon.

I reached into my mind for the blue shimmer and gave it a poke. It was easier to find now that I knew where it lived. The shimmer danced over my flesh, much as I would imagine it felt to shower in minty mouthwash. I felt alive and tingly, as if I were stepping into my destiny.

And I was.

I summoned that cool blue tide and coaxed it to greater power. I held on to it better this time, keeping control a little bit longer, before it swept through me with a vengeance. The wave crashed through me and over me, inundating me with its power. I barely had time to fold my clothes away and hide them beneath my scales.

Isabelle and Jared, fortunately, weren't watching me. They were staring at the sky.

I stretched my wings and roared, excited to be getting the hang of this. I was a white dragon again and right on time.

Isabelle jumped as I launched into the sky, savoring the power in my wings. I caught a glimpse of Jared's proud smile, had an instant to enjoy it; then the guys came screaming over the tops of the trees, their scales gleaming in the sun. They moved at incredible speed, driven by fury and bloodlust.

Snared in a nasty spell.

One that had gotten meaner. With my left eye, I could see the radiance of it, and the places where it burned hotter.

Like before, it was brightest around Garrett, then around Nick. Like shooting sparks. Liam was fending it off somehow. We'd have to figure out how and why later. Adrian was sending out more magic threads, feeding the spell.

I flew higher, moving out in front of the two humans I'd go down defending. I saw Jared moving his hands, as if he were making a snowball. But there was nothing in his hands.

No, wait. With my left eye I could see a jumble of light in his hand. Purple and green lightning, dancing together, being bent into a sphere. And I could hear him humming, just barely.

And as he hummed, the light grew brighter. He was conjuring something, and he needed time.

Time I was going to give him.

The guys flew lower.

They extended their talons.

Four against one.

No pressure.

I took a deep breath and lifted my claws in the traditional fighting pose, as ready as I'd ever be. My heart was thundering in terror.

I hovered over Jared and Isabelle, shielding them. I couldn't rely on the guys to remember our mission to defend humans, not when they were under the influence of Adrian's spell.

Not when he'd made them forget so much else.

"Traitor!" Nick cried, and spiraled toward me. I noticed the gleam of his scales, the power of his flight, the angry glow in his eyes.

But that anger wasn't really Nick's. It was the result of Adrian's spell.

I breathed a stream of fire, challenging him. The plume of flame flicked brilliantly in the cold air and I saw Nick's surprise. He'd expected me to back off.

He could get ready for another surprise or two.

It's traditional to trade taunts, and he took the initiative.

"*You can't win,*" he taunted in old-speak. "*Surrender the fight now.*"

"*In your dreams,*" I retorted. "*You're just afraid you'll lose to a girl.*"

His eyes flashed like molten gold and he lunged at me.

Yikes.

"Wait!" Liam cried. "Isabelle's here!"

"I'm not going to hurt Isabelle," Nick snarled, just as he locked talons with me, some twenty feet over Jared's head.

Nick wasn't just joking around either—he hit me like a brick wall. The force of the collision sent us end over end. We locked all four claws, our tails lashing as we tumbled through the air. It was all teeth and talon and fire. I was fighting for my life.

"Don't hurt Zoë," Liam cried, launching himself at Nick. Garrett snarled and attacked Liam, the pair of them wrestling.

Jared kept humming that strange tune.

Just before we hit a tree, I ducked and pushed back against Nick's grip. He stumbled in surprise and I seized the moment. I struck him with my tail and raged fire at him for his stupidity.

"*I'm on your side, you moron!*"

"*As if!*" He came after me again. We wrestled through the sky, biting and scratching and striking. It wasn't a pretty fight, and we were both getting a lot of minor injuries. I could hear grunts as Liam and Garrett fought, too.

This wasn't right!

"*Adrian's cast a spell!*" I shouted at them in old-speak. "*Don't listen to it!*"

Nick snarled. "*Adrian's the one on our side.*"

"Idiot!" I thwacked Nick across the face with my tail and snapped at him. I didn't really want to hurt him. Nick backed away, but clearly didn't have the same urge to play nice—he was aiming to take me down.

He was also ready to play dirty. He drove his shoulder into those cuts on my stomach and I faltered in pain.

"Nick!" Isabelle shouted in dismay. "Don't hurt Zoë."

"It's her or us." Nick breathed fire, then shot after me again. I spun at the last minute to backhand him, anger giving me strength. I slammed him in the cojones with my tail at the same time that I punched him under the chin.

Then he was the one reeling in pain.

His eyes gleamed and I knew he'd make me pay for that. I blew a long torrent of dragonfire after him, proud of myself for its sheer quantity. I was hoping to keep him at a distance, knowing it was a long shot.

All the while, I heard Jared's humming, rising beneath my wings like a tangible force. When I glanced down at him, Adrian gasped.

"What are *you* doing here?" Adrian sounded surprised, maybe a bit worried. Nick fell on me heavily, wrapping himself around me in a wrestler's clinch. I couldn't look at Adrian. I was busy trying to breathe.

"You must have missed me," Jared said, his voice all melodic and soothing. I looked down to see him smiling with a strange serenity.

I caught a bit of his mood, though, as I listened to that humming. I felt calmer. I breathed more slowly. It was as if a cool breeze had blown in from the ocean, pushing away dark clouds and stale air. I felt invigorated. Clean.

And Nick's grip loosened enough for me to wriggle free. I quickly put some distance between us.

Liam and Garrett stopped fighting.

What was going on? All three guys were staring at Jared.

Hovering in the air, their leathery wings beating.

"I wanted to catch up, hear your news," Jared continued in that same singsong voice. "How is the Mage plan for world domination coming along? Still looking for recruits stupid enough to sign on?"

"What are you talking about?" Garrett looked between Adrian and Jared in confusion.

Whatever Jared was doing was working.

How could I help him?

"You know each other?" Nick sounded sleepy, as if he were awakening from a dream.

Or a nightmare.

"He's lying." The darkness grew with every word Adrian uttered. "We only met on the road the other day. He's trying to trick you. Don't be fooled!"

I guessed and closed my right eye. I could see the shadow of that dark spell roiling like thunderheads, pushing back against the clean wind, snapping with orange light. A battle was beginning—one for the hearts and minds of these three *Pyr*.

I could see the effect of Adrian's words upon the guys. I found his argument a little bit persuasive myself, even though I knew it wasn't true.

"What's a Mage?" Liam asked.

"A liar!" Isabelle shouted. "Someone who pretends to be a friend but isn't. Adrian's not *Pyr*, and it's his fault that everyone has been fighting. He enchanted us in that cabin."

"He was supposed to keep us busy while our dads were in danger." I noticed that all three guys started at that news.

"Don't be ridiculous. I'm trying to save you," Adrian said in that soothing tone. Shadows multiplied all around us, at least in my left-eye view. "You've been deceived. I was the one trying to fix things. I was trying to continue in the spirit of boot camp. . . ."

The dark cloud grew with every word he uttered.

"I was following Donovan's rules for boot camp, learning new skills and helping others," Adrian continued. "I played for the team—unlike one of us."

With my left eye, I saw his words foster the doubts within the guys, turn their minds against what they knew to be the truth, and gather like a storm.

Not just any storm.

A storm with a precise target.

Yours truly.

"But which team?" Jared shouted. "You were keeping them busy while the Mages destroyed the *Pyr*!"

"No!" Adrian cried, insulted.

"Yes!" Jared roared. He gestured then, as if he were throwing a baseball. That ball of brilliant light flew into the air and exploded amid the guys.

I'm not sure they could see it, but even through the bright flames of dragonfire I could—with my left eye. In fact, I think it burned my retina. The released sparks of blue and green shot out in all directions, making Adrian cower.

Jared sang with vigor. It was the same tune he'd hummed, but now it had words. Words in another language, words that I didn't understand. It sounded old. Powerful.

And the words seemed to guide those waves of light. They moved in straight lines, changing direction at the command of Jared's song.

The Mages had wanted him because he was a spellcaster, too. It must come naturally, like being *Pyr*.

I was in awe of his abilities.

The battle had moved to new ground.

JARED'S SONG WAS LIKE THE sun breaking through the clouds. I understood that it was shattering the hold of Adrian's spell, burning it away, maybe. The guys stared at the light he directed, the anger fading from their eyes.

"Get her! Get him!" Adrian cried, to no avail.

Maybe spellcasting *was* like beguiling. Maybe what a person wanted to believe took precedence, or let them choose which spell to heed.

When they had a choice.

I felt a wind again, a steady, cool wind that pushed back the clouds. With my left eye, I saw Jared's song in the air. I saw the sound morph into new beams of light, sine waves of light, sound waves that changed their frequency based on the rhythm of his song.

It was Jared's battle cry, a song launched into the air to attack, becoming more demanding with every bar. The geek in me adored the eye candy. Purple and green and electric blue.

Adrian retreated, proof that he could see or sense them, too.

Liam was closest to Jared, and a beam struck him right in the heart. He lost his flying rhythm for a second, like he had stuck his finger in an electrical socket. His shocked expression said it all.

Then Liam turned on Adrian, scowling at him. "Liar!" he cried, and breathed fire. "You tried to make us destroy our Wyvern!"

"Jared's trying to bewitch you! He's dividing you!" I heard desperation in Adrian's tone. He continued to create shadows and dark clouds. "Close your ears. Don't listen. You'll all be forced to act against your will."

His words weren't as compelling to Liam as they once had been. Even Adrian seemed smaller and more insubstantial than he had been. And his dragon form was rippling like a flag in the wind.

"He made you guys target Zoë," Isabelle said. "He tried to recruit her; then he wanted to kill her."

"It's part of a plan to eliminate the *Pyr*," I added.

"So he wanted us to do the dirty work for him." Liam breathed a stream of fire at Adrian, who yelped. "He wants to destroy our Wyvern."

"No," Garrett said. "It was Zoë who didn't support us."

"She's the one betraying us," Nick agreed.

"And she's still doing it!" Adrian shouted. "Can't you see that Zoë is fighting back in her own way? She can't even do it herself. She has to use a human sorcerer to persuade you. Doesn't that say it all?"

I worried that Adrian might convince them, but Jared's next beam of light struck Nick in the chest. Nick fell back, shocked, but I knew from the look on his face when he eyed Adrian that the spell over him had been shattered, too.

"Adrian is the one who got us drunk," Nick said, hostility in his tone.

"So you wouldn't leave the cabin," Isabelle agreed. "Adrian's the one who stopped you all every time you talked about trying to help the *Pyr.*"

"No," Garrett insisted. "What's wrong with you guys?" He turned on me and I knew he was going to attack.

Again.

"You're still enchanted," Nick said, putting himself between Garrett and me. They began to wrestle, Nick trying to stop Garrett from coming after me. "Give it up!"

"We're going to lose this chance!" Garrett cried.

"That story about Adrian's father was all a lie." Liam was disgusted. "And we believed it."

"This is the lie!" Adrian insisted, mustering his spell and focusing on Garrett. Nick and Garrett fought hard, Garrett decking Nick. Nick fell back and I had a moment to be afraid.

When I looked into the burning anger in the eyes of the next Smith.

"Remove the traitor," Adrian hissed, and Garrett lunged for me. *Uh-oh.*

Liam and Nick snatched at Garrett, but he was too fast and

evaded them. There was no one between us. I lifted my talons, knowing I'd lose this battle but determined to go down fighting.

Jared kept singing, and a third beam hit Garrett when he was just a couple of yards away from me.

The tension rolled out of him as if his body were relieved to be freed from the spell. He fell toward the ground, limp like a rag doll.

"Wait! Don't be tricked!" Adrian cried. "Move now, while you can."

Garrett flapped his wings. He straightened, lifting his head proudly. He exhaled a puff of smoke and his scales glittered as he turned his gaze slowly. . . .

On Adrian.

I saw Adrian swallow. I heard the leap of his pulse. And I saw the terror in his eyes.

"We already were tricked." Garrett's words were low and hot. "And now you will pay for what you have done." He pointed at Adrian and the three *Pyr* targeted the impostor. They lunged toward him even as he tried to flee.

Jared's spell was faster. The light beams raced ahead of the guys and struck Adrian like barbs. Or arrows. One after another after another fell on him and he couldn't flee. He was in that much pain, which worked for me.

I watched, enthralled, as Jared's song changed.

WITH THE CHANGE IN BEAT, Jared's light beams were transformed, too.

They became long, like ropes, or maybe serpents. I was sure I saw a forked tongue or two. They rippled through the air with a definite purpose. He raised his voice, and they convened on Adrian.

Adrian tried to sing and fend off the spell, but he clearly couldn't do both. The spell waves wound around Adrian, binding him from head to toe in a brilliant net of blue and green and purple. He shifted shapes in rapid succession, just as he had before me, and I felt the astonishment of Isabelle and the *Pyr*.

He was a bull, a mermaid, a unicorn, a monkey. . . .

Jared sang louder and louder. I could see the sweat on his forehead, but he didn't give it up. His hands were clenched into fists, his voice strong and deep. Rich. The bonds of light kept getting tighter around Adrian, despite how he struggled. In moments, they were so close together that he had become a wriggling bundle of light.

Adrian roared in agony, or maybe in pain.

Jared stopped his song.

And Adrian fell to the ground.

The spell was complete. I couldn't see the light anymore, not with either eye. Adrian was rolling around on the ground, helpless. Well, he was swearing as he writhed.

I shifted shape, unfolding my clothes with greater dexterity than before. I was getting in the groove of this shape-shifting stuff.

And it felt good to be just a skinny chick again.

Jared strode toward Adrian, every line of his body filled with purpose. He looked as if he were going to throttle his opponent.

Adrian glared at Jared. "I won't tell you anything."

Jared smiled, looking as hungry and unpredictable as a dragon. "We'll see."

Just as Jared reached for Adrian, a brilliant bolt of orange light fell out of the sky. It was like lightning, but the wrong color.

And it struck Adrian, flashing brilliantly as it slapped him across the face. He screamed.

When the light faded, Adrian was gone.

Jared stared at the sky, shook his head, then came to my side. He looked exhausted, as if he'd just performed a concert, his hair all wet at his temples. But those green eyes were locked on me, filled with a concern that made my belly do flip-flops.

"You okay?" he asked, his voice low.

"I'll be fine." I swallowed, his intensity making me nervous. "Did you send him away?"

Jared looked displeased. "No. Someone collected him."

"Probably to make sure he didn't talk."

He nodded and I knew he was irritated. Then he flicked a quick smile at me, his eyes warm. "Thanks for giving me cover, dragon girl."

I felt that blush again, but it was okay. "Thanks for breaking the spell." We stared at each other for a long moment, one that left me all tingly and warm.

I wanted to kiss him. Or I wanted him to kiss me.

But had he come back for me or the *Pyr*?

He was a major dragon fan, but I wanted him to be a Wyvern fan.

There was no good way to ask, not without sounding needy, and I wasn't going there. I gestured to the place Adrian had been. "What did you do there?"

"A binding spell, after the counterspell." He shoved a hand through his hair. "I've never done two back-to-back before." His quick conspiratorial smile made my heart leap one more time. "Guess I just needed the right motivation."

"Thanks."

"Least I could do, after screwing up."

"Did you recognize him the other day?"

Jared shook his head. "I don't know Adrian. But I did recognize what he was." He grimaced. "I should never have left, no matter what Donovan had said. I didn't want to mess with his plans for boot camp, but I should have trusted my instincts."

"Someone gave me that advice a while ago. It's good."

"Yeah. I guess it is." Jared grinned. Then he reached out and took my hand, giving my fingers a tight squeeze.

It felt really good.

Like coming home.

You know what I was thinking? *Pyr* plus human equals a good pairing. Could Jared, the hottest guy I'd ever known, really be the one for me?

I had to hope.

Chapter 20

I squeezed Jared's hand, my throat all tight, and once again had nothing clever to say.

"We should take care of your wounds." Isabelle joined us, her hand clasped in Nick's. He'd already shifted shape and looked a lot less cocky than usual. I glanced at him and he averted his gaze, the back of his neck turning red.

"I'll heal," I said to Isabelle, as if I were a bold, confident chick who survived dragon fights all the time. No biggie. *Uh-huh.* "And we've got more important things to do."

"You okay?" Liam asked as he landed on my other side. He shifted quickly, concern in his eyes.

"All good, Carrots. Thanks for holding fast."

He grinned and squeezed my shoulder. "I didn't do anything on purpose."

"Maybe it's an affinity thing," I suggested.

"Hey, Zoë," Nick said. I was sure I'd never seen him shuffle his feet like that. "I'm really sorry."

"Too bad we didn't get to see you lose to a girl," I teased, and he shoved a hand through his hair, not smiling.

"I'm not sure it would have shaken out that way." He sighed. "You did come on hard, Zoë. Good job."

I returned his smile. "I'm just glad Jared got here before you served me up medium-rare."

"I made a big mistake. . . ."

Isabelle squeezed Nick's hand. "You couldn't help it."

"But I was wrong. Zoë could have been really hurt."

There wasn't much anyone could say to that.

Garrett landed then and shifted shape with that grace I so envied. (Practice makes perfect, right?) Without missing a beat, he dropped to one knee in front of me, his head bowed. "Forgive me, Wyvern," he said, his voice thick.

And the others seemed to hold their breath. I felt like a queen, her court waiting as she judged a wrongdoer. I knew they'd support whatever I decided.

It was kind of weird to feel so influential.

But I was the Wyvern. I knew that.

I had to do this right.

The fact was that Garrett had doubted me. He had challenged me. He had burned me. He had broken the most basic rule in the *Pyr* book by trying to do me injury.

But he had been enchanted, as well, and it had been one powerful spell. I certainly couldn't have guaranteed that I would have acted any differently.

I had to forgive him.

Jared's lips tightened and I saw his nostrils flare as he glanced at me. He wasn't in agreement with me.

Again, I was startled that he knew what I was thinking before I said anything. How did he do that?

"You were under the influence of an evil spell," I said to Garrett, my confidence growing as I spoke. "I can't hold that against you, because you didn't choose it. I made mistakes, too." I held tightly to Jared's hand, liking that his grip was sure even though he disagreed with me. I felt like we could be a team. "I owe all of you an apology for not trying harder to master my powers."

The guys protested, Nick and Liam closing in for a group hug even as I tugged Garrett to his feet.

"You couldn't have known, Zoë," Nick said.

"I still think that I made the bigger mistake," Garrett said.

"It's not your fault, Zoë," Liam said.

"Friends?" Isabelle offered with a smile. I nodded and smiled back. It might have been a big, shiny, happy moment, but Jared cleared his throat.

"Actually, it *is* Zoë's fault, in a way."

"How so?" Nick bristled.

"A spellcaster has to find something to work with, a bit of resentment or anger or jealousy, in order to work a dark spell like this one." Jared shrugged, but he didn't let go of my hand. "You need a hook for your bait."

"So I let him in," I said, realizing the full import of my jealousy of Isabelle.

Jared nodded. "In more ways than one."

I had an idea then who had really sent me that song.

JARED DIDN'T EVEN LISTEN TO all of the song before he pulled my ear buds out of his ears with disgust. "It's a jealousy spell," he said. "A nasty one."

"I didn't send it to you," Nick insisted, but I knew that already.

"We have to trust one another from this point onward," Garrett said, and we all nodded. "Airing doubts is the only way they get resolved."

"Air!" Nick said. "Wasn't that supposed to be our lesson this year? That's communication."

"And spells," I said.

"Dreams," Jared noted, which made me think.

"But Donovan didn't set this up," Isabelle argued.

"I think all of the older *Pyr* are in trouble," I told them. "Adrian was supposed to keep us busy while they were captured. Then he was trying to draw me in, too."

"But what happened to Adrian?" Nick demanded.

"He's not working alone," Jared said. "Someone summoned him with a spell, someone a lot stronger than Adrian is."

That didn't bode well for us.

"Someone who didn't want us to learn anything from him." Garrett nodded. "How can we help our dads if we don't know where they are?"

Everyone turned to look at me.

I looked at Jared. "What do the Mages want?"

"To use the world as their plaything. To be rich and powerful, to do what they want without answering to anybody." Jared grimaced. "They don't care who they destroy, not on the way to getting more for themselves."

"That's why you didn't join them?" I had to ask.

He smiled. "Right. Not my style."

"What changed?" Nick asked. "We've been hearing all our lives that they're no real threat."

"Maybe they've added to their powers," Jared said.

"But how?" Liam asked.

I remembered all the forms Adrian had taken and guessed. "Shape shifters. It's got something to do with shape shifters."

"The guy we both saw in that dream had a wing where his arm should have been," Isabelle said. "I think you're right, Zoë. He was a shape shifter in trouble. He was looking for help from you."

Jared smiled at me. "And what do we know about the Wyvern and dreams?"

"I can't control them, not yet."

He gave me a look and didn't have to say anything.

It was time to try.

I reached into my pocket and pulled out the rune stone. That guy on the tree—Kohana—had something to do with the red ridge of rock. I ran through all the clues again, trying to find which piece of the puzzle I'd missed.

I found an unexpected one.

"Wait a minute," I said. "If Adrian basically crashed the party, why was there an envelope addressed to him?"

"Do you still have the envelopes?" Jared asked. "Because I'll bet that it *wasn't* addressed to him."

"His name was written in my dad's handwriting."

"No. It was probably a glamour." Jared headed toward his bike, giving my hand a tug so that I followed him.

I did.

Like we were together.

"A glamour?" Garrett echoed.

"It's a spell," Isabelle said. "One that makes a thing look like something it's not. Like fairies leaving coins at night, coins that turn out to just be leaves the next day."

I had a thought. "Is that how he managed to look like a dragon?"

Jared nodded. "It was another glamour. An illusion. Didn't you see how it wavered when he was under duress?"

I nodded. "He just couldn't do everything."

"Right," Jared agreed.

Isabelle pointed to the cabin. "Let's see if Jared is right about the envelopes, too." The others went with her, talking to one another with excitement. I liked that we had our familiar rhythm back.

I really liked that Jared was holding my hand. That he'd come back to help me. That he was a spellcaster and one who wanted to use his abilities for good. Our shoulders bumped as we walked. My heart was doing the skippity-bip and I could have danced on starlight. Which meant, of course, that I had nothing clever to say.

"I've got the book," Jared said, as if it were no big deal. "You might want to have a look at it before you try the dream thing."

That was it. I couldn't resist any longer. I leaned across the teeny space between us and I kissed his cheek.

Just like that.

And the world stopped.

We stared at each other, oblivious to anything or anyone else. How could he have such green eyes? I could have stared into them forever.

"Well," Jared murmured finally, his voice sexy-low and his smile crooked. "This Wyvern *is* bold, after all."

I was blushing down to my toenails. Rooted to the spot. Snared in his gaze.

Maybe he'd enchanted me.

If so, it was a spell I wasn't going to fight.

"Zoë!" Nick called from ahead, and I realized I was being a dolt. Jared probably thought I was some lovesick kid, making an idiot of myself over the first guy who was impressed by my so-called abilities. Pathetic. I turned away and would have bolted to the cabin.

But Jared didn't let me.

He gripped my fingers even more tightly, tugging me back toward him. He caught my neck in his hand and smiled down at me. "It looks good on you, Zoë," he murmured.

I loved how he said my name. His fingers were wrapped in my hair, the strength of his hand turning my knees to butter. I stared into his eyes and couldn't imagine anywhere I'd rather be.

"Me, neither," he whispered, startling me that he *could* read my thoughts.

Then he kissed me.

Oh.

MY FIRST KISS WAS DEFINITELY worth the wait.

"*Earth to Zoë,*" Nick said in old-speak, his words tinged with both impatience and amusement. I straightened and ended the kiss with my usual clumsy style. We bumped noses and I almost tripped myself stepping back.

Some things, apparently, would never change.

Jared didn't seem to mind. His gaze searched mine. "Thunder or old-speak?"

I liked that he knew some of the drill. "Old-speak. They're waiting on me."

"Maybe they should get used to it," he said with impatience. "There's only one Wyvern, and you can't be everywhere."

He was right. I could *choose* where I wanted to be. And I was a rare commodity.

It didn't feel so bad to be special, now that I could actually do some Wyvern feats.

Although there were other skills I wanted to work on, ones that had nothing to do with the *Pyr.* I longed to kiss Jared again, to just linger there and perfect my technique.

But there had been all that blood. . . .

"We have to help the *Pyr* before it's too late," I said.

"Probably the responsible choice," Jared said, that twinkle in his eyes telling me that he might have decided otherwise.

"Come on; you're not so irresponsible as that." I had to tease him, just to check.

That dangerous grin flashed. "Gotta keep people guessing."

"You don't fool me. You came back to help me."

"Like I said, that's not all I came back for."

Jared reached into the saddlebag on the bike and pulled out a clothbound book. The red cover was faded, and the edges rubbed down. I couldn't even read the type embossed on the front cover, but my heart leapt all the same.

He opened it to the title page and handed it to me.

"'*The Habits and Habitats of Dragons: A Compleat Guide for Slayers*, by Sigmund Guthrie,'" I read aloud. I took the book with reverence. I held it in my hands. It had to hold all the secrets I yearned to know; I couldn't wait to start reading. "I wonder how he knew so much about us."

"Ask your dad," Jared said. I was confused but he didn't elaborate. He flipped through the pages, leaning close enough to make my heart flutter.

"Where did you get this again?"

"You don't want to know."

"Actually, I do. Because if you're not going to let it go, I'd like a copy of my own, and if you know a shop that stocks this title, I want to go there."

He smiled at me. "I lied about the shop."

"Then . . ."

"You don't want to know, Zoë."

"Wrong."

"I'll trade you—the story for that flight."

"You should just tell me anyhow."

He smiled, proof that he wasn't going to tell me. Not now, anyway. So I made an effort to concentrate on what was important.

Jared was *helping* me.

I looked through the book, taking advantage of the opportunity. The pages were yellowed on the outer edges, and worn soft. The margins were huge to my eyes, and the type was tiny. I saw that it was organized like an encyclopedia, with many short entries sorted in alphabetical order.

"Here. Read this." He turned to the entry entitled, "Dreams."

"I've got to push the bike. I don't want to leave it out here. Go ahead of me; I'll catch up." Jared smiled quickly, then turned his attention to the motorcycle. I watched him check it over—he didn't fool me about being irresponsible—then ease it off the stand and begin to push it.

He'd protect anything he cared about.

Could that include me?

I had to believe that mastering my Wyvern-ness could only help increase my appeal to a guy who was a fan of dragons.

This called for intensive study.

You could say I was motivated.

I walked beside Jared, reading as I went, a skill I'd mastered a long time before. (It worked brilliantly at home, in the loft, but I had been known to collide with a wall or two in other places. The forest had no walls, so I figured I was good to go.)

> Dreams—Similar to visions, dreams are generally viewed as involuntary or "given." Visions, in contrast, occur while the individual in question is conscious, albeit in a more meditative state than is usually described as wakefulness. Visions can occur involuntarily, as well, but may be deliberately conjured.
>
> The Wyvern is traditionally considered a source of dreams for the *Pyr* themselves, and associated with the ability to dispatch dreams to individuals. There are stories of the Wyvern sending a message to a *Pyr* or group of *Pyr*, warning of a future event that would be the result of current actions or advising of an unanticipated threat. Less commonly, there are tales of the Wyvern sending a *Pyr* a memory, generally not one of his own, in order to provide insight to his current circumstance.
>
> As for the Wyvern herself, it is implied that she can direct her own dreams in order to see past, present, and future. It must be noted that the link between the Wyvern and the *Pyr* has traditionally been a loose one, so that such dreams were accepted by the *Pyr* as rare

gifts of counsel, not to be ignored. On the majority of occasions, the Wyvern does not involve herself in earthly affairs, perhaps choosing to abide in dreams herself.

I closed the book and continued to walk, not really seeing what was in front of me any more clearly than when I'd been reading. I pulled out the red stone and thought about the guy I had seen hanging from the tree. I shivered. He'd turned up first, my first clue. I knew he had some connection with the stone. He'd said something to me, something I couldn't remember, probably because I hadn't known what it meant.

But that gesture of reaching out one hand had said it all. He'd been appealing for my help. Had he been responding to Meagan's visioning session? Had we awakened him? If so, I had an obligation to him.

Plus, he'd had that feathered wing instead of an arm. He was a shifter, like us, even if he changed to a different creature from a dragon.

Isabelle was right.

I had to go find him again. I had to help him.

And I'd bet my rune stone he'd tell me what I needed to know in order to save the other *Pyr*. He was our best shot at saving our dads.

Whatever the Mages had done to them.

I paused to wait for Jared, turning the stone over in my hand as he parked the bike beside Nick's car. I could see that he was dissatisfied with this spot, probably because the bike would be exposed to the elements. I'd bet that bike was usually tucked into a nice warm and dry garage.

"Tough being reckless and irresponsible," I teased.

His eyes danced. "Best choice possible, I guess. It'll have to do." He considered me then. "You look like you have a plan."

"I do. Thanks for the book." I offered it to him, not sure

whether it had been a gift or a loan. (You know which option I was hoping for.)

Jared smiled, took it, and tucked it under his arm. I had a moment to think that that must be that—that the kiss was no big deal to him, that he'd act as if we were just friends—then he took my hand in his again.

As if there were no doubt that was where my hand belonged. He'd taken off his gloves, and his grip was warm around my fingers. Strong. Protective, even.

I could live with his carrying the book.

THE GUYS WERE OUTRAGED WHEN we got to the cabin. Before I could ask what was going on, Liam shoved a pile of envelopes at me.

"Look at that!" he said. "Jared was right."

They were the envelopes from the clues that had been left in the mailbox. There was one addressed to me, one to Nick, one to Garrett, and one to Liam.

The last one, though, was addressed to Isabelle. I frowned and flipped through them again. "Where's the one to Adrian?"

"There isn't one," Garrett said, his disgust clear. "The clues are all the same, though."

"But you all thought this one said 'Adrian'?" Jared took the envelope carefully and I saw him flinch when he first touched it. He examined it with care. "It *has* had a glamour on it."

He put it aside, his manner thoughtful. I thought he maybe didn't want to touch it any longer.

"What's bothering you?" I asked.

He was surprised that I'd guessed his reaction. "I didn't think he was that strong a Mage. After all, I beat him, and I haven't had any training."

"So?" Nick asked.

"So a glamour, especially one that holds for very long on an innate object, takes experience and power."

"Not like the illusion of him being a dragon?" I asked.

"It's easier to manage a glamour wrapped around your body," Jared said. "Like keeping your coat closed. He wasn't holding this most of the time. That's tough to do."

"Maybe he just let you win," Nick suggested.

"Maybe." Jared frowned and drummed his fingers on the table. "But I'm thinking about that lightning bolt that snatched him away."

"He has powerful backup," Liam said.

Jared nodded. "Who was also maybe the one who supplied the glamour on this envelope."

"Okay, how do you fight a Mage?" Nick turned to Jared.

Jared smiled. "You meet fire with fire. Counter each spell with another stronger one, ideally one that can turn the first one to your own favor. It's like a riddling contest, where each tries to anticipate and best the other."

I could tell that he liked that part of it, which meant a liking for puzzles was something we had in common.

"First of all, we need to know where to find the Mages, however many there are," Garrett said. "And to figure out what they want."

"Then we can fight them," Nick said.

"No," I argued quietly. "I need to find the answer in a dream."

Jared watched me, a slight smile playing over his lips. I could see that the guys were uncertain, although Isabelle was as sure as Jared.

"The guy in the dream," she said.

I nodded. "He asked for my help. I want to see if I can get back there. Maybe we can make a deal."

Chapter 21

*I*t was surprisingly easy to fall asleep, even with all of them hanging around and watching me. Sometimes just knowing that something can be done makes it easier to do it.

(I knew it wasn't a universal rule. Knowing that teenage girls grew breasts had so far done nothing to increase my cup size.)

Or maybe I was just exhausted.

I closed my eyes and relaxed. I breathed more slowly and made my heartbeat slower. It occurred to me that this must be like going into a trance to breathe dragonsmoke—something I'd yet to do because you have to breathe dragonsmoke while in dragon form. I let calm radiate through my body. I called to the dream and was surprised by how quickly it came to me.

I ran on instinct then, there being no Wyvern manual. I had the idea that maybe some of the deal was wired right in and didn't require instructions. It might just work.

Jared would say I chose to believe.

I directed the dream. I wanted to go back to the red rock and the tree. I wanted to return to the part-bird guy.

The dream took me, all expenses paid.

Careful what you wish for.

As soon as I saw the red rock under the snow, I freaked a bit. I was terrified of going to this place, since I'd been scared shitless there. Why did I keep seeing blood on that stone? My heart took off at a gallop, and the dream lost focus. Adrenaline worked against me for a few minutes, and I had to try again, calming myself and starting from the beginning once more.

I felt Jared take my hand in his.

He'd sensed my unease.

His touch immediately made me feel better.

And you know, the contact also made it easier for me to stay calm. Maybe it was more than that. He was humming something softly, something that seemed to wind into my ears and push me toward that dreamy place.

Whatever he did, it worked. I saw the red rock through the snow beneath my feet. It was like a replay of the dream I'd had before. I was on the same spot, living the same dream one more time. I suspected that I had to do the same things to get to the same ending.

I bent and brushed the snow away, noting the carvings on the rock.

I compared my rune stone with what I was seeing. I felt as if I were reenacting a ritual, and that if I got any part wrong, the dream might veer off to destinations unknown.

One that didn't include Kohana.

I looked left and right, just as I had before, peering along the length of the red stone ridge as if I'd never been there before.

I noticed the well at the root of the tree, approached it, looked down. It was just as dark as before. Just as spooky.

I looked up, afraid he wouldn't be there.

He *was* there, swinging bonelessly.

Terror struck my heart cold, just as it had the first time.

I saw the feather tattoo on his shoulder, along with the black feathered wing where his right arm should be. I felt the wind gather and braced myself for his swinging body to turn toward me.

It did.

He looked into my eyes.

He lifted his hand.

He said it again: "*Unktehila.*" It was more obviously an appeal this time. Maybe I was listening better.

Instead of running, this time I nodded.

He watched me in silence. I climbed the tree until I was over him. It wasn't any easier than it would have been in real life—the tree's bark was smooth—but I had to cut him down.

I realized a bit late that I had no tools. Although . . . the rune stone was sharp on one side. I sawed through the rope with my stone, but progress was slow. I despaired that I would get the job done.

He looked up at me, which was a shock.

It was even more shocking that he was laughing at me.

"*Unktehila,*" he said again, then exhaled with his teeth bared.

I got it. *Unktehila* meant *Pyr.* I was a *dragon* and he knew it. He was reminding me that there were easier ways to get this job done.

Duh.

No wonder he was laughing at me.

I tried not to blush and failed completely. I heard him chuckle but ignored him.

I was busy. After all, I wasn't sure whether I was working with a time limit. I summoned the blue shimmer and let it push through my body, shifting my shape. It was so easy now, since I'd witnessed that eclipse.

Was that what I'd been waiting for?

I had no time to think about it. I caught up Kohana's weight and hovered beside the tree. I felt him check out my scales with his one hand, tentatively, which was odd.

Not feeling me up. Just curious.

Distracting me just when I didn't need to be distracted.

I focused the stream of dragonfire on the sturdy rope, ensuring that I didn't scorch the tree. Damaging this tree had to be a very bad move. I could sense it. It took a bit of concentration to keep the stream of fire thin. My personal blowtorch burned through the rope, which gave with a crackle and a flurry of sparks.

As if I were sharpening a knife.

It took more dragonfire to break the rope than I'd expected. The sparks that flew from the rope were that odd bright orange, too, brighter than fire usually was.

When the rope was frayed, Kohana pulled it loose with an impatient gesture. He flung it away, as if it were a poisonous viper.

And I understood. It had been bewitched. I'd broken the spell that had held him captive.

Wow!

I saw him smile; then he flung up his arms.

He shifted in a glorious halo of yellow light. It was like staring into the sun: radiant and warm.

He became a large bird, one covered in gleaming black feathers. He was far bigger than any bird I'd ever seen, but still much smaller than me in my dragon form.

But talk about fast. He shot into the sky, and I sensed he couldn't get away from this place soon enough. The night sky was thick with stars, more stars than I'd ever seen in my life. I marveled as I raced after him.

He left me completely in his dust.

Way above the ground, up where the air was thin, he waited for me. I was a bit out of breath when I reached his side.

He bowed his head, hovering in the air with slow, steady beats. His eyes were such a brilliant yellow that they could have been burning orbs. I saw something that looked like crooked spears in his talons.

"There is an old idea that once one being saves the life of another, their lives are forever entwined," he said. I didn't exactly hear his words like normal language. I kind of felt them, and understood instantly. It was like telepathy, but not invasive.

A variant of old-speak? Or something special for dreams?

His eyes blazed. "That rope was wound with a spell."

"By the Mages?"

He nodded, then flung one of the bolts in his talons toward the earth. It hit the ground with a flash, and was accompanied by a boom of thunder. "But even they could do it only in such a sacred place."

"In dreams?"

"We're in the dreaming, but the site is real." He indicated the red rock far below us. "It's where Mother Earth herself speaks of past, present, and future."

"So it's a good place." I wondered where exactly it was. I wondered whether I could get there in real life.

"It was. The Mages are using its natural power against those who would revere it."

I made a guess. "Is my dad trapped there, too?"

He nodded. "And the others. You can save them all. I wasn't sure before, but now I know that you can."

"Why?"

"Because you came back into the dreaming. You found the same spot in the same dream, and you changed the end of it. Your dream power is strong." Although his words were flattering, his tone wasn't very positive. I wondered why. "Of course, you won't be able to do the rest, not unless I help you."

I had a feeling that wasn't the number one item on his to-do list, despite the new bond between us.

Or maybe this was a test.

"I saw you at school. In my room and in the stone. Like you were stalking me."

He smiled a little. It was a disquieting expression, as if he were laughing at me. "You summoned me. Didn't you know?"

Of course I didn't. And I had just about nothing to lose in seeking more information. "Maybe you can help me out with the details a bit. What exactly are you?"

"I am a *Wakiya*." He spoke with pride. "You might call me a Thunderbird."

"You called me *Unktehila* before."

"It is what you are."

"I'm *Pyr*." I said this with new confidence.

He made a dismissive gesture.

"But how can you know my kind and I don't know yours?"

"Don't you know the story?" He spoke with disdain.

I shook my head. He didn't explain and I knew somehow that he wouldn't. Okay, on to plan B. "Well, can you tell me more about the Mages?"

He looked away, impassive. "They learned a feat in the jungles of the Amazon from other magicians. They learned that to eat the flesh of the last of a species is to gain the powers of that race."

I suddenly understood Adrian's shifting. "Those are the forms of all the shifters they've eliminated?"

He nodded. "They believe that when they finish the task, when they have eliminated and devoured the last of every kind of shifter, their powers will multiply by a thousand."

I guessed. "Thunderbirds and dragons are left."

"Also wolves and cats."

"But he became an eagle. There still are eagles."

He shrugged. "Some shifters are closely related to other species that do not shift. Eagles with no power to change are those that survive. The eagle shifters are gone." Before I could even formulate more questions, he continued. "We are but four species left of dozens."

That there had been so many kinds of shifters was news, but I hid my surprise. I knew the *Pyr* kept to themselves, but I'd always assumed it was just from humans. Now I knew better.

"Help me save the *Pyr* and I'll help defend the *Wakiya*."

He smiled at me, so enigmatic that I had no idea what he was thinking. I had a moment to feel doubt; then he pivoted.

And he was gone.

KOHANA FLEW TOWARD THE EARTH, a gleaming spear of obsidian. I raced after him, lacking his powerful grace. He dipped low over the big tree, zooming over it like a fighter pilot at an air show. As he did so, he threw two more of the spears from his talons.

Like the first, they fell as lightning bolts, striking the earth with force.

An orange lightning bolt of a Mage spell erupted from the rock face, targeting us, but Kohana spun away. I had no time to warn him before lightning flew from his eyes. It made a great illuminating flash, like heat lightning, as he glared at the orange bolt.

That orange spell was cooked to cinders before it got fifty feet off the ground. The cinders fell to the earth, like soot on the snow.

"That won't hold them for long," he muttered, spinning to rocket away. He flew low and fast over a snowy forest.

I wondered where the heck we were going, but it was taking all I had just to keep up with him.

Yet another indication that I really did need to try harder in gym class. Otherwise, this dragon stuff was going to kill me. It was all high-octane action.

When I saw a highway snaking through the forest, with tractor-trailers on it, I realized that this dream place *did* exist in real life. It was part of our world. And Kohana was showing me how to find the red rock once I left the dream.

He was helping me!

I had a good look to orient myself. I could see towns scattered around, and a city far off to one side. Without a map, that wasn't a ton of help—except that the red rock was in the opposite direction.

Meanwhile Kohana dove toward a frozen lake, targeting a cabin. I raced after him, heart pounding as I tried to catch up. There was a blue electric car parked at the top of the hill outside that cabin, a motorcycle close beside it.

Hey! I knew where we were! I was going to shout to him, but everything went black.

I opened my eyes in the cabin, among my friends.

Just like that.

And there was a dark-haired guy leaning against the fireplace, his arms folded across his chest. He stood perfectly still in the shadows. He was barefoot and bare chested, wearing only jeans, and there was a feather tattoo on his left biceps. His eyes were dark and glinted with humor. He evidently enjoyed that the others didn't realize he was there.

"WELL?" JARED DEMANDED, GIVING MY fingers a squeeze. "What did you dream?"

"Did you learn anything?" Nick asked at almost the same time.

"Where are they?" Garrett asked.

"How can we free them?" Liam asked.

I didn't say anything, not right away. I was out of breath. Exhaustion apparently followed me between forms.

I looked across the room to draw their attention to the newcomer among us. "Kohana," I said quietly, and he inclined his head in silent acknowledgment.

Garrett yelped in surprise. Liam took a step back. The others gaped. I saw Jared's lips tighten. He dropped my hand as if it were nuclear waste and folded his arms across his chest.

Uh-oh.

"Are we sharing your dream?" Liam asked, looking between me and Kohana.

I almost laughed. I wasn't nearly that strong.

"No. This is Kohana," Isabelle said, as if it were perfectly obvious. "I've seen him before. Both Zoë and I dreamed of him. Simultaneously. In the tree." She eyed him. "Did you send that dream on purpose?"

He nodded. "I needed help. Zoë opened a conduit for me."

"He showed me the way home," I said. "He's a shifter, too. A Thunderbird."

"Here." Isabelle handed me a granola bar.

Kohana didn't appear to need the sugar hit. That could have made me feel like a serious amateur, but I was too bagged to care.

Besides, I *was* a serious amateur.

"I didn't know there were other shifters," Liam said.

Kohana smiled. "You thought we were just stories, maybe?"

Liam blushed.

"We need to save the older *Pyr*," I said. "They're in trouble. Kohana knows where and how we can free them."

"Not exactly," Kohana said to my surprise. "They're trapped at the red rock, and you should prepare yourself—they are injured." We exchanged concerned glances. "Also, I don't know what holds them there. It must be something specific to your kind."

"Something the Mages use against the *Pyr*?" Jared asked.

"But why?" Liam asked. "What did we ever do to them?"

"You exist." Kohana was grim.

I gave them a rundown of the Mage Plan for World Domination. Jared was quiet.

Kohana eyed him before he spoke. "Mages want to transcend the physical, but they need our abilities to do it. They take our strengths the crude way."

"They kill shifters," Isabelle guessed.

"They *eat* shifters," Kohana corrected, and we shuddered as one. "Right to the last shred and drop."

I swallowed, remembering how Adrian had become a lion in order to gnaw me to bits. I shivered and Jared took my hand again.

Wait a minute. Adrian had become a lion and a lion was a kind of cat.

Had Kohana lied to me about the four kinds of shifters left?

No. It had to have been a glamour, like his dragon form. Maybe I just hadn't noticed its instability because I wasn't a cat shifter.

"So they use tricks to lure us close enough that they can do it," Nick guessed.

Kohana nodded. "The red rock is a legendary place. My kind have always held it in reverence and treated it with dignity. We honor it for what it is and listen to its counsel."

"But the Mages twist the song of the Earth, subverting it to their own purposes." Jared's tone was thoughtful.

Kohana nodded. "They use it to fortify their spells, and to disguise them."

"And we don't expect to find any deceit in the Earth's songs, so they have an advantage over us," Garrett said. Kohana nodded agreement, his gaze lingering on Garrett. I wondered what he saw in our fledgling Smith, but there was no chance to ask.

"So we need to go to this red rock and save our dads." Nick nodded at Kohana. "Thanks for showing Zoë the way." Nick, being Nick, was ready to head out right away.

"It is not that simple," Kohana said.

There's always a catch, isn't there?

WE ALL LOOKED AT KOHANA. "You mean there are defensive spells?" Nick asked.

"You'll need a spellsinger, or you have no chance."

"We have one." I touched Jared's sleeve. "He already took down the Mage who was supposed to confine us."

Kohana looked skeptical. "There are many of them, and the spells are strong."

Jared straightened. "I'll give it a try."

Kohana's tone turned mocking. "I watched a spellsinger *die* giving it a try. Maybe you should have more of a plan."

"Like what?" Nick asked. "Do you have any suggestions to share?"

Kohana smiled. Evidently he had wanted to be asked. "They'll be in an uproar right now. They'll know that I escaped, but they won't be able to guess how. They'll assume I managed it on my own, that maybe they underestimated my powers. But the area will be swarming with them as they try to hunt me down."

Isabelle glanced up at the roof of the cabin.

Kohana must have noticed. "Yes, they might realize I've come here. Or they might have sensed Zoë's presence."

"Nice." Liam was grim.

"I don't believe that they will abandon their fresh prey just for me."

"Why not?" Garrett asked.

"They are too close to success."

This was not what any of us wanted to hear.

"I was an unexpected bonus for them. They aren't close to destroying my kind yet. But capturing all of you along with your fathers would put them very close to eliminating the *Pyr*."

If they had captured my dad and everyone who followed him, that would account for most of the *Pyr*. I didn't even want to think about losing them all.

"How do you know this?" Nick asked.

"It's what I overheard while I was hanging in the tree."

"But Zoë? They could follow her here," Isabelle said.

"No." Jared spoke with conviction before Kohana could reply. "They'll wait for her to come to them."

Once again he and Kohana stared at each other, the battle of wills between them growing stronger by the minute. What could Jared hear in Kohana's thoughts?

"For *us* to come to them," I corrected. "Our dads are the bait in the trap."

"When do we go, then?" Nick demanded, looking between us.

Kohana frowned. "Let's wait a few hours. Give them time to assume that I fled or that you're too afraid to attack."

"*Then* take them by surprise," Nick concluded.

"Get some sleep to ensure we're at our best," Liam said. "Can you tell us what we'll find at the red rock?"

Kohana dropped his gaze. "Little that's good. I believe that you will be in time to save most of them."

We couldn't even look at one another.

"This is a fight we can't afford to lose," Garrett said, then looked at me. "How far is it?"

"Not far. I think I could find it."

"I'll take you back there," Kohana said. "We'll go around and approach from the other side."

"Another surprise." Liam nodded.

"We can't leave Isabelle and Jared behind," Nick said. "I can carry Isabelle."

"I'll carry Jared," I offered, trying to be casual even though my heart was thumping. "I owe him a ride anyway."

He turned then, his warm smile giving me tingles that rivaled the blue shimmer. "Thanks, Zoë." He took my hand again and gave my fingers a tight squeeze.

I didn't complain.

But I did wish that I had the power to read minds. I would have given anything to know what Jared was thinking.

Of course, he smiled at me just as I had that thought.

Chapter 22

As the others kept talking and scheming, their excitement growing, I pulled out my rune stone and worried it between my fingers, feeling Kohana's gaze drop to it. He watched me, but didn't say anything. Maybe he felt he'd said enough.

Somehow I had to defend the *Pyr* against every possibility of a bad ending. I'd gotten us into this, after all. And I was supposed to be able to see the past, the present, and the future all at once.

It really would have been a kick-ass ability to have in my arsenal.

How were the Mages keeping the *Pyr* captive?

How badly were the *Pyr* hurt? All that blood in my dreams didn't bode well.

If we were going to succeed in saving our dads, we had to know what it was that held them in the Mages' custody. We *Pyr* had weaknesses, of course, but I needed to know which of them the Mages had exploited.

What weakness did we all share? Those *Pyr* with partners had a vulnerability in their human counterpart—who could be taken hostage or injured or whatever—but that didn't feel right.

"Did you say you talked to Alex?" I asked Jared. "And my mom?"

He nodded. "Yeah, why?"

"And they're okay?"

"Worried but okay."

So that wasn't it. And we kids were all here, together.

No, it had to be something else.

I didn't know what it was, but I realized there was a way to find out. "Your book says that the Wyvern could summon and share memories," I said to Jared. He nodded agreement. "Does it say any more on that?"

"Why?"

"I need to share my dad's memory from Saturday. That's how I'll know what happened to him, and what's holding him hostage."

Jared got the book from his bag. "Have at it."

I accepted the book, then paused. If you really want something, you might as well ask for it, right?

"You could give me this book," I said, giving him my best attempt at a seductive smile.

He laughed. He glanced at the others, who were still chattering, then hunkered down beside me. "And surrender the one thing that might make me interesting to a dragon girl?" His eyes glinted as he shook his head; then his voice dropped low enough to make me shiver. "I'm not that easy to ditch, Zoë."

Oh.

"You just want that ride," I teased, making a joke because everything in me was fluttering.

"That's not all I want," he said, mysterious and intriguing all over again.

I might have asked him what he meant, but he straightened and started to glare at Kohana again, all the way across the room. I had the sense that he was standing guard over me.

A girl could get used to that sort of attention.

THE BOOK, OF COURSE, WAS vague about the mechanics of dreaming.

Actually it was vague about anything important. I wondered whether this Sigmund Guthrie guy had really known anything, or whether he'd been making it up.

"Maybe he was hiding the truth," Jared suggested, doing that thought-listening thing when I was least expecting it.

"What?"

"Like a smoke screen. Medieval herbalists did that. You have one active ingredient, but you hide it in plain sight, in lots of ingredients that don't matter. Ideally, they might gross someone out, too."

"Eye of newt and toe of frog," I said.

"Exactly. Find what you needed?"

"No, and you probably know it."

"The book's not an instruction manual."

"Clearly. I could use one."

Jared smiled crookedly at me. "So you'll just have to give it a try. Trust your instincts."

"No pressure," I muttered, and he laughed again.

He leaned close. "*I* believe you can do it, Zoë."

I squared my shoulders. "Okay. So do I."

I closed my eyes and tried to summon a memory.

Well, you can probably guess what happened. Can't you? In hindsight, it shouldn't have been a huge surprise. I was feeling really good, like I was completely nailing this Wyvern thing. I'd saved Kohana in the dreaming world. I'd shifted fully to dragon form. I'd fought against a Mage—not well, but it had been my first fight as a dragon and I hadn't died. I was never going to be great at anything resembling gym class. I'd changed to a salamander, too. I had Jared looking at me as if I were It—apparently I was also mastering the Girl with a Bit of Something Special.

I was feeling confident and brave, sure that this dreaming trick couldn't be that tough. I was tired, but, hey, *I was the Wyvern!*

I reached out for my father's memory of Saturday, stretching my mind into the direction it went when I dreamed.

And I choked.

Nada.

I tried again, stretched farther.

Zip.

I tried the eye game.

Nope.

I summoned the blue shimmer, and even it was elusive, giving me a bit of a run for my money. When I finally coaxed the shimmer closer, I had a heartbeat to feel triumphant that I'd done something right, then *ooompht.*

Nothing.

Like sticking a pin in a balloon. I had nothing to share, nothing to offer, no clue and no idea where to find one. Worse, I was completely beat. Those cuts on my stomach started to throb and even the rune stone felt heavy to me.

I might have been evading the others and their expectations, but either way, I decided to go to bed. I fell asleep immediately.

It was divine.

Dreamless.

Deep.

Heaven.

THE MEMORY SLAPPED ME IN the mind so hard, I thought I might jolt awake and lose my hold on it.

I was on the roof of the loft in Chicago. I was listening to the distant hum of another *Pyr*, and smiling to myself that she was so clumsy in feeling my presence.

Right. I was an onyx and silver dragon deep in my *Pyr* heart, cool, composed, and worried about the kid.

I was in my dad's mind.

No. I was in his memory.

I didn't want to poke around too much there, certainly didn't want to learn things I'd rather not know about my parents—I mean, they must have had sex, right? At least once?—so I took a moment to get my bearings.

It looked like I was standing in a corridor, one lined with stainless steel filing cabinets. The floor was black, the walls were white, and the ceiling glowed, as if it provided some kind of ambient light source. I checked out the label on one drawer and saw that it had a date.

I shouldn't have been surprised that he was so ruthlessly organized.

I moved down the corridor with purpose, checking labels until I found the drawer that didn't have a closing date. It started earlier this year. I took a breath, pulled open the drawer.

The memory of him on the roof sharpened, becoming so clear that I could have been living it. It engulfed me.

I felt my dad listen to everything around him. The hum of traffic. The chatter of kids in the park. The sound of my mother's hunt-and-peck typing. The breath of the wind. His senses were incredibly keen, and I knew he'd worked to achieve this.

That gave me a new goal.

I felt him explore the world around him, stretching his awareness beyond his immediate vicinity. I felt him sense the presence of each *Pyr* in succession, checking on them like the superdad he is. I heard the murmur of old-speak from Donovan and from Rafferty, as familiar as my favorite homemade mac and cheese for supper.

I saw the blue shimmer on the edge of his talons, dancing there, just within reach.

And he was listening to me "feel" him for the first time.

I knew how he wanted to help me, understood that he knew that the best course was to let me master the trick myself. I felt his awareness of Monday's solar eclipse and the question in his mind as to whether it would influence my development.

Interesting. I'd never even anticipated that.

But important firestorms for the *Pyr* are triggered by lunar eclipses.

I'd worry about that later.

I supposed that for him this was like watching a kid learn to ride a bike. You might want to reach out and steady them, but it's better to let them wipe out a few times. They'll learn more from falling than from being saved from falling.

That wasn't my analogy.

It was my dad's. I heard him think it. It was how he kept himself from making it easy for me.

I heard our conversation and smiled to myself at the familiar sound of his old-speak. I heard him eavesdrop on my conversations with Donovan and Rafferty, heard him sigh and head back inside to bring my mom up-to-date.

And I heard the taunt.

It hurtled into his thoughts like a rock, one that shot orange sparks in every direction. It exploded into his mind like a bomb that he hadn't expected.

I felt him recoil.

I felt his anger at the intrusion.

And I sensed his outrage.

He was dared to save Quinn, the Smith, from certain death.

By a Mage, who had no right to do injury to a *Pyr* of any stature.

I didn't know how the Mage had hurt Quinn—the notion

pretty much shook my world—but I felt how livid the very prospect made my father. He demanded proof and I saw the image spill into his mind. It was awful. There was so much blood. I felt his anger boil and his need for justice light.

I knew he'd go.

So did the Mage.

Quinn was the Smith, the one of our kind who can heal our scales and repair our armor. A Smith is an imperative member of the *Pyr* team, especially when we fight—my father would have said that Quinn was more important than he was himself. He'd risked everything for Quinn before. Saving Quinn was quite literally the offer my dad couldn't refuse.

And he didn't.

He shifted and shot into the sky, zero hesitation. He didn't even tell my mother where he was going, as if he feared the chance would be lost if he didn't act immediately. He didn't leave her undefended— the loft is always encircled with a powerful boundary mark of dragonsmoke—and I'm sure he didn't think he'd be long.

He was wrong.

I saw him lured.

I saw him tricked.

They stole his *scales*.

And left him trapped on a ridge of red rock dusted with snow. My dad knelt down beside Quinn, checking that he was still alive. I felt his despair and didn't know what he'd discovered.

He'd always relied upon himself and upon the *Pyr* of his generation. This rescue was up to us.

It was one hell of a coming-of-age challenge.

We had to win—there was no choice.

I WOKE UP SUDDENLY, my mouth dry and my palms damp with sweat. All I could see was my dad, despondent. The sight shook me to my core.

The Mages had taken his scales. That wasn't even supposed to be possible. It must have been a new enchantment they had devised, one that caught every *Pyr* off guard because it had never been a variable before.

I opened my eyes again and tried to force the vision away. The cabin was almost completely dark, the fire down to glowing coals.

Kohana glanced up at my movement, or maybe he heard my agitation. Jared was still sitting beside me, and he was wide-awake. He slipped one arm around my shoulders, maybe thinking I was cold. I was glad to lean against him for a moment, although there was work to do.

I can't give you a ride, I thought, looking into his eyes. *Not today.*

He tilted his head slightly, inviting me to explain.

I took his book and opened it to the entry on clothes. There was a brief explanation there of how we *Pyr* fold our clothes away when we shift shape, yada, yada, yada.

Jared scanned the entry quickly and shrugged. I understood that this was old news to him.

It's backward, I thought, and his gaze brightened. *At least now. It's our* scales *we have to hide. The Mages made a spell to twist this. They've got our dads' scales and it's keeping them captive. That's how they snared them.*

He reached into his jacket, but he didn't seem to find what he was looking for. He rummaged in mine—well, Alex's—and pulled out that pad and paper. *Where?* he wrote.

Right.

That was the kicker.

I only had half the answer. The *Pyr* dads were at the red rock—but where were their scales? There'd been no sign of them in my dream. The Mages must have hidden the scales in a separate location.

When you can't solve a riddle, you might as well ask for help.

How can we find out where they've hidden the scales? I thought, meeting Jared's gaze.

He gave me that reckless smile, grabbed my hand, and led me quietly out of the cabin. We moved with as much silence as possible, but I saw the glint of Kohana's eyes.

He slept like my dad, except that the shine of his eyes was yellow.

Molten gold.

Once out in the snow, Jared scanned the sky. The stars were still out, but the sky was turning a lighter blue in the east. He walked up to where the bike and car were parked, then turned me to face him.

I didn't tell him that the guys would still be able to hear him.

"There was a place in Adrian's mind when I was fighting him. I don't know where it is, but I can tell you what it looks like."

"Can you show it to me?" I asked. "That might be good enough."

My reasoning was that if I could travel through space and manifest in other locations as Wyvern, then I should be able to direct where I went. If I knew what a place looked like or had a strong enough sense of where it was, maybe that was good enough.

Jared nodded. He framed my face in his hands and looked into my eyes. His fingers were warm. "I've never given anyone my thoughts before. But if you think it can work, it's worth a try."

"What do I need to do?"

"Relax. Don't blink. Just stare into my eyes and don't blink. I'll try to do all the work."

"Wait!" I opened Nick's car and dug in the bag that Isabelle had left behind. Just as I'd suspected, there were three granola bars. I shoved them into my pockets, then went back to Jared.

He looked confused but didn't ask. Instead, he put his hands on my face again and he opened his eyes wide. He began to hum and I noticed how long his eyelashes were. I looked at all the shades of green in his eyes, then looked straight into the darkness of his pupils. His chant grew a little louder, surrounding me with a sense of safety.

I felt something nudge against my thoughts, something that was not mine. Instinctively, I slammed a door.

But wait. Jared was trying to give me the key.

I needed his help.

I had shared my dad's memory. I could do this.

I had to trust him completely.

I looked deeply into Jared's eyes and let that mental door swing open. I surrendered to whatever he wanted to share with me, and, all of a sudden, it was there.

Someone else's thought in my own mind.

No, it was one of Adrian's memories.

This time I didn't see the organizational system of choice. I was flung right into the recollection itself.

I was standing alone in a cinder-block room. A basement. It could have been anywhere. It was damp and chilly, maybe because the floor was dirt. Cold, too. The window was barred and the door was steel. Probably locked. I couldn't hear anything or anyone above me.

As if the house or building above this cellar was empty.

But on the floor were piles of dragon scales. They were like suits of armor, more like chain mail, discarded in heaps.

It was a hoard of priceless treasure. I knew which belonged to whom by its color, by the talisman secured into the coat of scales by the mate of that *Pyr*. I recognized them all. Every single one.

The sight of them, dropped on the floor, shook me to my marrow. It was so wrong.

My dad's scales were onyx and silver; Donovan's were lapis lazuli and gold; Quinn's were sapphire and steel; Delaney's—they had Liam's dad, Delaney, too?—were copper and emerald;

Rafferty's were opal and gold. Thorolf's were moonstone and silver, and they were there, too.

I felt sick at the sight. All of these *Pyr*, captured. Helpless. Reliant upon us.

No pressure.

I could guess how it had happened, though. Somehow the Mages had gotten Quinn and all the other *Pyr* had tried to save him. They'd each been trapped.

Because the Mages had known our weakness, and had twisted it in a way that none of us would expect.

It was their first step in destroying us all.

Like I was going to stand back and let that happen.

I KNEW JARED COULD READ my thoughts, so I didn't waste time with explanations. I beckoned to the blue shimmer. I let it dance over my skin, flood through my veins, fill my body with its elusive starlight. I let it build and play; I coaxed it and made it stronger.

All the while, I studied details of the room Jared showed me, refining my sense of that place.

And my will to appear in that place.

The tide grew to a tsunami. The shimmer grew blindingly bright. I roared as I let it claim me.

I heard Jared swear.

But he was way behind me. I was hurtling through space. My stomach rolled as everything spun all around me. I was sure I'd retch this time and thought maybe I should have eaten for strength before getting the memory.

Then the whirlwind stopped as quickly as it had begun. The blue shimmer faded.

I opened my eyes.

There was a dirt floor beneath my hands.

And a sapphire and steel coat of dragon scales right beside me.

There was a lot of dried blood on the scales and under them, and it looked almost like rust. I wasn't going to think about that. I heard boots running as someone approached. I grabbed those scales right beside me. They rattled, making too much noise.

I wanted to take more than one set, but it was impossible. They were too large, too heavy for me to carry more than one at a time.

I wouldn't even think about making six trips.

Not yet.

Keys jingled outside the steel door. I could hear two guys arguing. Shit! I couldn't be discovered before I even started!

Maybe, somehow, they already knew I was there.

Terror made me falter. I fought against my panic, knowing I had to be calm to summon the shimmer.

Otherwise I would be caught there.

Trapped like the other *Pyr*.

I clutched the scales close, exhaled shakily, and forced myself to get calm. I called to the shimmer, and wished with all my heart to be at the red rock.

A key turned in the lock.

Okay, I prayed.

To every deity I'd ever heard of.

One of them must have listened.

Chapter 23

I kept my eyes squeezed shut, even when I felt snow under my hands. There was rock under the snow, and I was sure I could feel a curved shape cut into the rock face.

I exhaled in relief.

I had time to think that Jared would be impressed; then someone moaned close by me.

I opened my eyes cautiously. I was back on the red rock. Snow was swirling on all sides, obscuring everything beyond the rock itself. It was like being inside a tornado—or what I'd expect it to be like inside a tornado: dead calm, with that riotous storm just yards away.

The bizarre thing was that the rock was oblong in shape, the crest of a ridge. This particular tornado followed the shape of the rock, making an oval swirl.

Completely unnatural.

Quinn was right beside me—he was the one who had moaned. He looked more like a ghost than the robust Quinn I knew so well. There was a slick shadow beneath his body, a dark one that made me fear for him.

Then familiar old-speak rolled into my thoughts.

"*Fair enough,*" Quinn murmured, and I just about dissolved in relief. I moved closer to him, reached for his hand, and put it on the scales. I felt his hand tremble; then the scales vanished, hidden from view in an instant.

Quinn fell back, even the glimmer between his lids gone. I thought he'd maybe passed out from the effort. I hunkered close to him. He looked exhausted.

At least the scales were back in the custody of their rightful owner. I didn't need to know where Quinn had secreted them, just that he had them.

I would have answered him in old-speak, but he opened his eyes and I caught a flash of warning there. He'd probably guessed what I intended to do.

He shook his head minutely—which seemed to exhaust him—and I understood.

The Mages could hear old-speak.

Got it.

Just for the reconnaissance value—and because I needed to catch my breath—I played the eye game. Sure enough, the view through my left eye was different. That wall of swirling snow was filled with a network of orange flashes of light.

I didn't dare move and attract attention. I peered up and down the length of the rock and saw the *Pyr* I knew and loved in various poses.

There was Thorolf, shadowboxing, his disgust with his situation clear. There was a makeshift bandage on his thigh, and I liked that he hadn't gone down without a fight. Knowing Thorolf, he was working off his anger over getting caught. Probably healthier for everyone.

There was Delaney, drumming his fingers on the rock.

There was Donovan, murmuring to himself. Actually, I figured he was murmuring to the elements he controlled as Warrior, but his frustrated expression said it all—they weren't listening to him here. His gaze flicked to me and away, repeatedly, and I heard the rate of his breathing change.

Donovan wouldn't give me away.

There was Rafferty, lounging on the stone, utterly still except for the glint of his eyes. He seemed to be an outcropping of the rock itself, and about as flexible.

And there was my dad, on his feet, hands on his hips, glaring into the vivid maelstrom. He was deeply pissed off. I smiled at the sight of him. He might be trapped but he was okay.

They were all trapped, and saving them was up to me.

I had work to do. If Jared thought I wasn't trying, he'd soon learn differently. I was ready to push myself as far as necessary.

I reached into my pocket for a granola bar and scarfed down half of it fast enough that my mom would have told me to chew slowly. I scooped some snow into my mouth—closest available alternative to a drink of water—and reviewed the situation. Quinn had passed out or fallen asleep beside me.

I wanted to go back to that room, even though I knew there were Mage types there. I could picture the room. I could smell it. I wanted to get my dad's scales next. I recalled the layout of the room, and the position of the onyx and silver scales.

To avoid detection, I should arrive as a salamander.

Yes.

And I should manifest *under* the scales. I reviewed the room again, focused my intent, then touched Quinn's hand with my fingertips. His pulse was weak but still there. I had to hurry.

I met Donovan's gaze and nodded slightly. He pretended not to see me. I called to my shimmer and felt it tingle over my flesh.

Then the feel of Quinn's hand was gone.

No. *I* was gone.

"I TOLD YOU—THERE'S ONE SUIT of scales missing," a guy complained. It was Adrian. "You fucked up."

I smelled the musty aroma of a basement. I felt soil under my feet. I trembled from head to toe and closed my eyes against the tide of nausea. Salamanders don't have pockets, which meant my granola bars were inaccessible at this time.

Live and learn.

"I didn't do anything," another complained. There was something familiar about his voice, too. I couldn't quite place it. "The door's been locked all along."

"You can say what you want," Adrian argued. "I gave you one stupid job and you blew it."

I was busy keeping my salamander self from being mashed under the weight of the suit of scales on top of me. It was dark under there, so I couldn't confirm that I'd manifested under the right ones.

But really, I had to move them all eventually.

One down; five to go.

So long as the Mages didn't capture more *Pyr* while I was trying to save these. There was still Niall and Sloane and Brandt. . . . No. I wouldn't make that long list of possibilities just yet.

No pressure.

"It was your watch and your responsibility, and it'll be your butt for losing the scales," Adrian continued, his tone menacing. "If this is some kind of joke, you'd better put them back."

"I told you, I don't know what happened to them. The door was locked!" Why did I recognize his voice? I didn't know any Mages or Mage minions. But I couldn't deny that there was something familiar about it.

So, what should I do? Wait for them to leave? The blue shimmer would give me away—if they saw it (and as Mages, they'd have to notice it), the big mystery of the disappearing scales would be solved. Waiting seemed like the best idea, and it would give me time to recover.

As much as I *could* recover with my heart racing in terror.

"Then what happened to it? You can count, can't you?" I heard the chink of scales being kicked on the other side of the room. "One." Another kick of scales, this one closer to me. "Two."

Crap. Would I be revealed when they kicked the scales?

Or just mashed to oblivion?

My question was answered one second later. I heard a set of scales being picked up and dropped. "Three. And no extras underneath this set."

"I told you. I don't know what happened to them."

"Bullshit." Adrian was hostile. "You're hiding them, or studying them, or doing something to undermine this effort. You've never really been committed to becoming a Mage, have you?"

"I have! I am!"

"Tell me where they are."

"I don't know!"

A set of scales hit the far wall with a clatter, then slid to the floor.

"Four!" Adrian shouted. "And just one more. That makes *five*, not six." I heard the scales above me rattle as he grabbed for them. I saw his fingers sliding between the scales. I knew I didn't have a lot of time.

Unfortunately, I wasn't entirely positive that I could take them with me, not in my salamander form.

I could save myself. Maybe.

I wrapped my salamander tail around the scales, hung on tight, and wished as hard as I could. I called to the shimmer, telling it to get a move on.

"What the heck is that?" the second guy cried.

And I knew suddenly why I recognized his voice.

It was Trevor Wilson.

Yes, *the* Trevor Wilson. Suzanne's boyfriend. The guy who had asked me out, against all logic and expectation.

Because he was an apprentice Mage.

The shock nearly made me screw up.

But not quite.

Clearly, there is a Great Wyvern and she loves me.

So far.

I SKIDDED ACROSS THE RED rock face, spreading snow in every direction. It was somewhat less than an elegant entrance, and I skinned my newt cheek as well. The good news was that the scales had made it with me.

The bad news was that I didn't have my dad's scales, after all.

These were lapis lazuli and gold. I had one glimpse of them before they were gone, hidden from sight.

"*Nice,*" Donovan murmured in old-speak.

I was disappointed, though. I was doing my best, but things were not working out as planned. Not exactly. I mean, Quinn had his scales but was unconscious. Someone—probably multiple someones—would have to carry him to safety. This would seriously impact the *Pyr*'s ability to fight.

How many Mages were there to fight? How much time did I have before the guys attacked? How much did I have to do alone?

What if I failed?

Donovan leaned back, bracing himself on his hands, one of which was tented over my salamander form.

My dad moved in a flash, sitting down beside Donovan. He scooped me up in one smooth move and dropped me into the pocket of his shirt. I was right against his chest, and I could hear the sound of his heart beneath my scratched cheek. He cupped his hand over the pocket, holding me close. I heard that his pulse was racing, which I knew wasn't typical for him. He was worried sick.

I cried a little, overwhelmed. His thumb stroked my back, reassuring me. *"Stronger than you know,"* he said, and I shuddered, the tremor moving through me from nose to tail.

"Absolutely," Donovan agreed, covering for his comment. I remembered Quinn's warning that the Mages could hear old-speak. *"That spell is more powerful than any I've ever seen."*

Could I do this four more times? Successfully? I had serious doubts.

What had happened in the room after Adrian and Trevor saw my shimmer?

Would they move the scales away? Or lock them up some-where else? Maybe with a stronger spell protecting them? I didn't feel in primo shape, and there were plenty of challenges on my plate already. I knew I was shaking in my dad's pocket, and he had to have felt it, too.

This was hard.

What would Jared have told me to do? To believe in myself, definitely. To trust my instincts. To put it all on the line and hold nothing back.

Okay. I was good to go.

"Rafferty," my dad said softly, as if noticing that *Pyr* had moved.

"This is hard on him," Donovan said, covering again by pre-tending my dad meant something different.

But my dad was telling me to bring Rafferty's scales next. I wanted to argue with him; then I remembered something.

Isabelle knew that a *Pyr* needed sugar and water after travel-ing through space, because Rafferty could do it, too. He was the only one of the *Pyr* who had mastered that feat.

So he could help me.

It was a good idea, one that gave me new hope. Rafferty would probably be able to carry two sets of scales. He was really powerful. Which meant just two more trips for me, not four.

I thought I could do that.

I sure as heck was going to try.

Besides, I wanted to know whether I was right about Trevor Wilson. It seemed beyond belief that he could be a Mage apprentice. I had to know for sure.

I called that shimmer and got it in gear.

THE TWO GUYS WERE STILL in the basement room when I manifested there again. The air was crackling with tension as they argued and blamed each other. Fortunately, I'd nailed the salamander bit.

Unfortunately, I didn't manifest under any scales.

No one seemed to notice when I scurried under the closest set. My dad's.

Rafferty's were a good six feet away.

Crap!

Decision time.

"I told you," Adrian insisted. "I saw a blue light. Go ahead and show me that you've learned *something*. What does a blue light mean?"

"I don't know," the other guy said. He really did sound like Trevor Wilson. I crept to the edge of the pile of scales. "There are no spells that make blue light. Even the lowest initiate knows that."

"And you're lower than that, I guess. I'd give you a zero on that answer. Give me your explanation, then," Adrian said. "Where's the fifth set of scales, smart-ass?"

"Maybe you're hiding it. Maybe you're trying to make me look bad." The other guy snorted. "Or make yourself look good. That's a hobby of yours, isn't it?"

I crept out a little farther, my heart racing.

But I still couldn't see him clearly. I was going to have to go out into the open.

On the other hand, that was also the only way to get to Rafferty's scales.

Nothing ventured, nothing gained, right?

I took a breath and scooted across the floor. I rubbernecked on the way, then saw I'd miscalculated the distance. I accelerated, heart pounding, and slid beneath the opal and gold pile of scales.

It *was* Trevor.

"What was that?" Adrian demanded.

"I didn't see anything."

"I'll tell you what shimmers blue," Adrian said, his voice low. "The *Pyr* when they shift shape."

Crap.

Trevor fell silent, then started to stammer. "B-b-but they're huge. I mean, we'd notice a dragon in here."

"Not if he was in a different form," Adrian said. "Or *she* was."

Make that, *Shit.*

My heart was as loud as a brass band in my ears.

"Shouldn't we get one of the elders?" Trevor said. "Shouldn't we get help?"

"And lose the credit for trapping her?" Adrian asked, his tone oily again. "I don't think so."

He started to hum, and when the sound gave me gooseflesh I knew I had big trouble. He was making another spell.

Which meant I had just about nothing left to lose.

I seized the scales and called that fricking shimmer. With my left eye, I could see a net of orange sparks forming, encircling the pile of scales. I fought my panic and tried to concentrate on the slowly building shimmer of blue light.

In fact, I told it to move its glittery butt.

In the meantime, I thought I'd give Trevor a surprise.

I shifted to my human shape right in front of him. "Boo!"

He just about jumped out of his skin.

Okay, I enjoyed his astonishment.

Adrian cried out in shock, so surprised he forgot to hum. The orange sparks thinned.

"Bye!" I shouted, then mustered the shimmer and got the hell out of there.

Okay, that had been fun.

Chapter 24

I was back on the red rock, arriving in an inglorious splat that would have smashed a salamander to nothing. I barely had time to gasp before the scales were gone, snatched up and secured by Rafferty.

"*My thanks,*" he said, his old-speak a reassuring rumble. "*You should eat.*"

I remembered the granola bars in my pocket and inhaled another one. It was pretty smashed up—hey, just like me—but wow, did it ever help.

By the time my dad came to my side, I wasn't nearly so ready to heave. He caught me close in a tight hug. I leaned against him for a long moment, taking strength from him.

Then he pulled back, looking into my face. His eyes were all glittery, halfway to dragon, the way they got when he was really intense about something.

"So long as you try your best, you will never, ever disappoint me," he said. "Understand?"

I nodded and fought the urge to cry.

"I am so proud of you today."

Would Jared be proud of me, too? If this wasn't trying, I didn't know what the heck was.

"No matter what happens," Rafferty added, "you have exceeded all expectations, Zoë."

That was when I realized that they'd both spoken aloud. And they weren't trying to hide me. What had changed?

The captive *Pyr* were all on their feet, looking skyward. Quinn was leaning heavily on Donovan. My dad moved to support him on the other side. Otherwise, they were all as still as stones.

I stared into the swirling wall of snow, but it looked exactly the same.

Until I closed my right eye. Then I could see the orange network of light dimming. There were even a couple of places where it looked as though it were being torn to shreds. Soon holes would appear in the fabric it had woven to enclose the *Pyr*.

I wondered why, and then I knew.

I heard Jared singing.

Yes! The rescue party had arrived.

My dad and Rafferty were smiling. Rafferty offered me his hand, the hand with his black and white ring. I realized then that he never took it off—which meant that in dragon form, it somehow changed size to fit his talon.

"Shall we go?" he asked.

I looked at the ring. I looked at Rafferty. I smiled at my dad. I wished I could have seen Jared, but I had to content myself with the sound of his spellsong.

And the promise of seeing him later.

When we were triumphant.

I put my hand in Rafferty's. I saw the way he called to his

shimmer, so elegant and restrained, and tried to call mine the same way.

With mixed results.

The ring on Rafferty's hand began to spin around his finger. I stared at it, watching the black and white colors blur into each other.

"*You direct*," he said, his old-speak resonant and reassuring. "*I'll follow.*"

"*Deal.*" I imagined the room, saw the last three piles of scales. I could taste success and the near completion of the mission. I felt the confidence of having someone at my back. I heard Jared's song become louder and felt the fabric of the spell start to tear. The *Pyr* shouted all around us, and Donovan shifted shape to fight.

Just as the young *Pyr* started to come through the veil of sorcery to help. With most of the older *Pyr* in human form, Nick and Garrett and Liam had to take the brunt of the battle. It seemed as if there were Mages everywhere, and I feared for our side.

"*Be safe,*" my father said, his kiss brushing against my temple.

I had no time to say good-bye, because the shimmer claimed me, rolling through me with staggering force.

"Pyr," Rafferty advised in old-speak, in the same moment that the shimmer built to a crescendo.

I knew what he was going to do.

We were going to arrive in style.

Dragon style.

RAFFERTY'S GRIP WAS TIGHT ON my hand.

Then his claw held fast to mine.

The ring spun so fast that it was a blur of black and white. It rubbed against my talon, sparks flying from it as we left the red rock.

A heartbeat later, we exploded into that basement room. I'd done it! I'd led us both there.

I staggered a bit, even more shaken by the transition this time. Rafferty was like a rock, one I could cling to.

One that was breathing fire.

Sure enough, we weren't alone. Through the fiery flames of dragonfire that Rafferty exhaled, I could see Adrian and Trevor, as well as three other men.

They were chanting something in unison.

Spellcasting.

I followed Rafferty's cue and conjured up some fire of my own. The air was thick with orange bolts and raging dragonfire. There wasn't enough space in that room for the seven of us, especially with the flames and smoke. The Mages had backed into corners, and I guessed the three I'd never seen before were elders—they all appeared to be older than Adrian and Trevor. Also, each of them claimed a corner of his own. Adrian and Trevor were stuck in one corner together.

Maybe they thought we'd shift to smaller forms for lack of space, but Rafferty didn't give them an inch of room. He and I were back-to-back, breathing fire, standing guard over our precious hoard.

Three sets of dragon scales.

I breathed fire at Trevor and Adrian, enjoying how Adrian flinched. When I closed one eye, I could see that his spell wasn't coming together well, probably because of the pressure. I set his shirt on fire, just to mess with his game a bit more.

Then I turned my dragonfire on the elder on my side.

Maybe he needed to work on his tan. I exhaled slow and hot and even, roasting him so that he closed his eyes and turned away. He kept singing, though, his spell gathering form before him. It was a blob at first. Then it lengthened into a cylinder. It became brighter and brighter, then took on an inner light of brilliant orange.

I knew that color.

Suddenly it shredded itself, expanding abruptly into a net. He hurled it at me and I ducked it, slamming Rafferty down, too. The spell went right over the two of us and hit the far wall.

It slid down to the ground, its light extinguishing as it fell.

Dead.

I looked back and the Mage was gone.

There was a snake on the floor. I stepped on it, hard, and ground my heel down into the floor. I'm not such a skinny chick in dragon form. There was major mass on top of that snake.

His scream was very satisfying.

Trevor watched, his eyes widening in terror. I saw him lose control of his spell, heard him swear, and realized that Adrian was having some trouble with his spells, too. I guess having his shirt on fire distracted him. Poor boy. They weren't dangerous for the moment.

Meanwhile, Rafferty began to chant, humming the slow chorus I'd heard from him many times before. It was more guttural. Older. Less tuneful than the Mages' singing.

It felt honest to me. As old as stone. As strong as iron.

I felt a shudder roll through the floor, actually far beneath the floor.

Rafferty was summoning an earthquake.

Which worked for me. I felt my confidence increase with another *Pyr* at my side. I was already becoming strong enough to play on the team.

I caught a glimpse of movement and spun. A second Mage lifted his hands to toss a similar spell net at Rafferty. I had to have his back! I raged fire at the Mage, sending a scorching torrent of flames in his direction. It should have cooked him dead, but he shifted shape.

Next I saw the beetle on the floor.

I spit at it, miring it in dragon spittle.

The Mage changed to a snake, but he was easy to snatch up that way. He shifted to a bird in my grasp, but I pulled out a fistful of his feathers. He became a minotaur, but I had him by the horns. I slammed his body into the cinder-block wall, helping it to crumble.

He became a butterfly and flitted away before I could snatch him.

How many kinds of shape shifters had there been, once upon a time? Now just the partner species, the ones who couldn't shift, survived.

Thanks to the Mages.

Kohana said there were four varieties of shape shifters left. Just four.

I wasn't going to let that drop down to three, not so long as I could do anything about it.

The other Mage continued to sing, weaving a luminous barrier all around us. It was only halfway up the walls, glowing with that brilliant orange.

But the floor heaved and rippled as the earth answered Rafferty's song.

The walls cracked.

The ceiling fell, chunks of plaster and wood falling over our shoulders. It was a good moment to be in dragon form. I wondered whether this was what Godzilla felt like in those cheesy old movies.

The Mage wasn't so lucky. He stopped singing when a piece of concrete hit him in the skull. I saw his blood under the rubble, and couldn't feel a lot of regret.

The walls trembled one last time; then the building that was above the basement room started to collapse into rubble. Rafferty and I pushed aside the debris and freed ourselves from the ruins. There was more dust than I would have believed possible, but Rafferty reared up and spread his wings high. He sang with force and power, such force and power that it seemed he was one with the heaving earth.

It was certainly keeping time to his beat.

Trevor and Adrian climbed out of the wreckage and ran. I could have gone after Adrian, taken some justice out of his hide, but I had more important work to do.

Rafferty stopped singing, holding one long last note. Then he nodded at me.

It was time. I grabbed my dad's scales in my claws and Rafferty seized the other two sets. He had Thorolf's moonstone scales and Delaney's copper and emerald ones.

"We can fly back," he said. "Although I can move through space, it exhausts me to do it more than once."

I could relate to that. In fact, I was relieved not to have to do the manifestation tango again.

We were so out of there!

We had already launched ourselves into the air, triumphant with our victory, when I saw that there was a barrier forming around us.

A network of brilliant orange mesh.

"*Trap!*" I shouted in old-speak, and Rafferty shot skyward. He couldn't see the spell, but maybe he could sense it.

Or maybe he believed me.

Either way, we both flew straight up as hard and as fast as we could. That must have been why neither one of us saw the lightning bolt.

The brilliant yellow came right out of nowhere.

It struck Rafferty in the chest.

He was flung backward by the force of its impact.

And knocked unconscious. He dropped the two sets of scales and fell earthward. The orange mesh spell wall continued to climb high on either side, already curving in to close the top.

I could guess that there'd be no escape once it sealed itself.

I looked down at Rafferty, then at the scales in my grasp, then at the ever-diminishing hole overhead. I had to choose between helping Rafferty and keeping hold of my dad's scales.

With no confidence I could get out of this myself.

I had time to panic before I heard Kohana's laugh.

That was when I remembered who could throw lightning bolts. Yellow ones.

We'd been tricked.

THE RED TIDE OF RAGE rolled through me with savage power. It practically sparked from the tips of my claws. It gave me new power and strength unlike anything I'd ever felt before.

I'd helped Kohana. Even if his ploy had been a setup, I'd gone back to help him in good faith. He'd used my own nature against me.

And that was just evil.

I understood that Jared had sensed deceit in Kohana, that that was why he'd been so hostile. I knew Jared couldn't have seen the whole truth of it, because he would have warned me, but he'd sensed trouble.

I spun and saw Kohana. It wasn't a coincidence that I had to go back toward the ground to attack him, that retaliation would lead me deeper into the realm of the spell.

I didn't care.

"*Rafferty!*" I screamed in old-speak. To my relief, he stirred. He didn't manage it in time to keep from hitting the earth, but he didn't slam into it as hard as he might have. He managed to land on his feet, stumbling a bit, but still an improvement.

I could see that he was shaken. I swooped down toward him, dropping my dad's scales into his custody. I hovered beside him, simmering with anger.

"I'll be fine," he said, and coughed. He smiled. "Just not as young as I once was."

"He's mine," I said, eyeing the laughing Kohana. "He lied to me."

Rafferty considered the other shape shifter, then pulled that black and white ring from his talon. He pushed it onto mine. "You can do it, Zoë."

"Do what, exactly?"

Rafferty smiled. He settled atop his hoard of scales, giving them a pat. "Do what needs to be done. You *are* the Wyvern. Never doubt it."

He was sounding like Jared.

Okay. What needed to be done was that Kohana needed to be thumped.

And I'd won the job.

It was me and my inner dragon, kicking ass and taking names. Guess who had moved to the top of my Incinerate Now list?

I launched myself toward Kohana, letting that crimson rage fuel the blue shimmer. It was a strange feeling, like flying on the edge of a tornado. A dangerous balance. A precarious one. A single false move and I could be fried.

No, Kohana was the goose who'd get cooked.

"Why?" I shouted after him.

"You or us," he retorted. "Not much of a choice."

I was incredulous. "You made a deal with the Mages?"

Kohana's sneer was my only answer.

"But they want to eliminate all shifters. You had to know they'd betray you next."

"More time is always better than less time." And with that, he flung a lightning bolt at me.

I dodged it easily. I flew right past him, breathing dragonfire. I singed maybe the tip of one feather, but he moved quickly, dodging my assault. I snatched at him and missed. He was nimble, that was for sure.

He turned and I followed him.

He twisted and I went after him.

He flew in tight circles, but I was right on his butt, snatching for a piece of him and breathing fire.

Never mind gym class—this was contortionist class.

But I had motivation like never before.

His eyes flashed and heat lightning struck all around us, lighting the ground with blinding intensity. The spell shield sparked and glowed, seeming to respond to the lightning. He threw lightning bolts, never seeming to run out. I scratched him. I bit at him. I tossed in a little dragonsmoke, but he seemed unaffected. We wound an erratic pattern across the confined chunk of sky.

As soon as I got my chance, I seized him and flung him into the spell wall.

He went right through it.

He screamed and came back through it, his eyes blazing as he targeted me. I ducked; he missed; I zipped back and caught the end of his tail. One ebony feather tugged loose and he spun to cast a lightning bolt at me.

It caught me in the hip, burning, but I didn't let go. "Why?" I shouted at him again.

"*Wakiya* and *Unktehila* fought aeons ago, and we won this land for our kind." He threw another lightning bolt. It missed me. "You were supposed to stay in *your* lands."

"Where's that, exactly?"

"Over the water. Europe." His eyes flashed. "Your kind abandoned our treaty." He spun faster, twisting like a cyclone. Maybe he hoped I'd get dizzy and let go, but I was too angry for that.

"Or forgot it. We lost a ton of lore in the Middle Ages."

His disdain was clear. "No one with any dignity forgets the history of their kind."

"And that makes us disposable?"

"Better your kind than mine." His eyes gleamed. "Besides, you opened the door. You summoned me. Don't blame me for answering your call."

It wasn't my fault. He'd twisted things around, betrayed us, and used my inexperience against me. It wouldn't happen again.

At least we understood each other. We spun around and

around and around, faster and faster, black and white swirling together so that the colors were no longer distinct from each other.

A swirl of black and white.

I had a vision suddenly, a vision of a black dragon and a white one locked in an endless circle. I saw them spinning faster and faster and faster beneath a pulsing red light.

In time to Rafferty's song to the earth.

They disappeared, coalescing into a spiral that looked like liquid glass.

And when they were gone, a ring rolled across the stone floor. The vision faded abruptly.

That had been the ring that was now on my talon.

I knew it with complete conviction.

This ring was the product of a white dragon and a black dragon sacrificing themselves. In a flash, I guessed whom they had been.

Sophie and her *Pyr* lover.

And I had them right in my hand.

"Wyvern!" I roared in old-speak. *"Help me, Sophie!"*

Chapter 25

*S*ophie was there in a flash, as if she'd been waiting for me to invite her.

I recognized her from my dream.

But Sophie was transparent, not truly there. Fair and finely boned and truly beautiful, she had the most expressive eyes. A gentle demeanor. Maybe it was her ghost.

More important, there was a *Pyr* with her, as dark as she was pale. He was no more substantial than she.

"Never to be bound by sorcery again!" he roared, and slashed at Kohana.

Kohana didn't see the blow coming. Was I the only one who could see Sophie and her lover?

Kohana could feel them, that was for sure, because the *Pyr* beat the crap out of the *Wakiya*.

He was one mean fighting machine.

When he cast Kohana toward the earth, unconscious and bleeding, the *Pyr* spit after his falling body with disgust. "Liar," he said, making the word sound ominous. "Vermin. Oath breaker."

He turned to look at me, dark eyes glittering, and I had a moment of uncertainty. What did he want? What would he do? He hovered before me like an avenging angel with something to prove.

Sophie smiled at him with affection, which was encouraging.

"Wyvern present," he said, inclining his head formally. "I am Nikolas of Thebes, and I stand pledged to your service forever."

"Um. Thanks."

"You have loosed us to do your bidding. What else is your desire?"

So I had a magic genie in my ring. Bonus. Did I get three wishes or more? I decided to prioritize, just in case. "Can you break the spell so Rafferty and I can go free?"

Nikolas smiled. It was a slightly condescending smile, if you must know. Very dragonlike. "Of our kind, only the Wyvern can cast a spell," he said, then smiled at Sophie. His heart was in his eyes. I wanted a guy to look at me like that one day—and yes, I had a specific guy in mind. "Only her spell endures forever."

He offered his claw to Sophie.

Romeo and Juliet. Just like Isabelle had said.

Sophie met my gaze, then lifted a single talon, making a cutting gesture.

I blinked, not understanding. But she was finished with giving me clues, if that's what she had been doing. She turned away and flew to Nikolas's side. They were crazy in love with each other, these two ghosts. I'd have to be stupid to miss it. I wondered whether they were real at all, or some kind of vision.

I could see them only with my left eye. And even then, they were kind of hazy.

But he had thumped Kohana.

The pair started to spiral slowly before me, then spun faster and faster. They turned so that she held his tail in her mouth and he had hers in his. It was just like my vision. They spun in a circle that moved so fast, it seemed to cast sparks in every direction.

Red sparks.

They rose higher and higher in the sky, as if they would spin their way up to the stars. That circle spun furiously, faster and faster, so they were a brilliant blur.

And then there was just a ring falling through the sky toward me. I snatched it out of the air and shoved it back onto my talon. Funny—I didn't remember taking it off.

It glinted for a moment, seemingly filled with starlight, then looked like glass again. Just as it always had.

I looked down at Rafferty, who was watching me. He didn't look surprised, just interested. He probably couldn't play the eye game.

I looked at the ring with new appreciation. Sophie and Nikolas. They had sacrificed their lives for the good of the *Pyr* and the world. Maybe they had helped me because I'd been ready to make the same sacrifice.

Maybe I'd just gotten lucky.

I wanted to see Jared again, to tell him what I'd seen and to compare notes. I wanted to tell him about Sophie and Nikolas, because I was sure that wasn't in his book. It was a little addendum we could add to his collection of dragon lore.

And then . . . who knew?

His spellsong was so close. Tempting.

But I was trapped in this fiery spell prison.

That was when I realized that my talon—the one adorned with the ring—had a long, sharp edge.

Like a knife.

I guessed what Sophie had meant.

I HAD EXACTLY NOTHING to lose.

I flew to the top of the spell wall, reasoning that it might be weaker where it had been joined at the top. I took a deep breath, then shoved my talon into its glittering mesh.

I heard my nail pop through the barrier.

And the orange glitter dimmed around the hole I'd made. Encouraged, I slid my nail down, slicing the barrier formed by the spell. It cut like a knife through butter.

I let out a hoot of joy and cut faster, flying down toward Rafferty with incredible speed. I watched the light of the spell die, like an electrical grid going dark, on either side of the cut. It shredded beneath my nail more and more readily, tearing like rotten cloth.

I cut it all the way down to the ground, then flew in a little flourish. Rafferty was grinning at me. There's something about a dragon grin. It just makes you want to laugh out loud.

He tossed me my dad's scales, grabbed the other two sets, and we soared upward through that gap. There were stars on every side of us, glittering and magical, and I felt like I had conquered the world.

I knew exactly how I wanted to celebrate.

I owed a certain somebody a flight.

We heard Jared's song and saw the flash of dragonfire in the distance. The dads who had their scales were fighting alongside the young *Pyr*, battling Mages, even as they wrought new spells to replace the ones Jared destroyed. The dads on the red rock fought in human form, smashing Mages who became snakes, pummeling those who could be grabbed, and generally doing what damage they could. The guys defended Quinn, who was down on the rock again.

I had a bad feeling about that.

"The Wyvern returns triumphant!" Rafferty roared, first in

old-speak, then aloud. It seemed that the Earth herself took up his victorious cry.

As soon as the Mages heard that, they scattered.

Nick and the guys chased a few of them into the distance as we landed on the red rock. The last coats of scales disappeared in record time, secreted away by their rightful owners.

Thorolf spit after the Mages, his frustration clear. Then he bumped fists with Nick and Liam in congratulations for what they'd achieved. "Couldn't have done it without you."

"Guess you taught us something after all," Nick countered, and Thorolf grinned. The guys were looking pretty proud of themselves as the older *Pyr* congratulated them.

I shifted back to human form, immediately spotting Jared. He was kneeling beside Quinn with my dad, both of them focused on the fallen Smith.

Quinn wasn't the only one of the older *Pyr* who was wounded, but he was the only one who wasn't moving. He hadn't left the red rock, although he had managed to shift shape. Maybe the transformation had exhausted him. He was sprawled across the red rock as a massive sapphire and steel dragon, barely breathing.

Uh-oh.

We weren't out of the woods yet.

GARRETT KNELT BESIDE HIS DAD, his fingertips hovering over his injury. The scales on Quinn's back were blackened and shriveled, looking more like burned paper than burned armor. Even if he had been conscious, Quinn couldn't have reached the injury to repair it.

"He was cycling between forms before," Liam said.

"A sign of serious injury," Jared said.

Jared got to his feet and glanced at me. He was on the other side of the group, and I wished he'd been beside me. He looked exhausted, too—he was pale and there were shadows under his eyes. Our gazes held for a long moment, but there was nothing to celebrate yet.

"Is Quinn going to die?" Nick demanded, voicing the fear we all felt.

There was no old-speak, but we all knew the answer. As one, we turned to look at Garrett.

I saw that Garrett already understood that he'd have to fix his father's scales.

And that he was terrified.

"It's like a dragonsmoke wound," Donovan said, which didn't sound promising.

"But made with a spell," Jared said, sounding disgusted. "They've figured out how to replicate *Pyr* weaknesses."

A shudder ran through our entire group. The Mages weren't just alive and well and making trouble for us—they were really good at it. While the *Pyr* had been thinking everything was quiet, they'd been learning and refining new skills.

Now the Smith, our healer, had to be healed by a younger apprentice, one who had not learned all the necessary skills yet.

And there was no one who could help him out.

Or was there? I remembered Garrett's request. I tried to think of how I could fulfill it. Jared's head snapped up and he stared at me, new hope in his eyes.

Could I do it?

Jared held my gaze and nodded.

Meanwhile, my dad put his hand on Garrett's shoulder. "Your father used to cleanse a dragonsmoke wound with fire."

"Did it work?" Nick asked.

My dad shrugged, his features drawn with concern.

I'm sure I wasn't the only one who noticed that he had referred to Quinn in the past tense. I closed my right eye to look at him, and could see a slow spiral rising from his body. It looked like a waft of smoke, silvery and almost insubstantial.

A silvery cord that stretched into the sky. I stared upward but couldn't see where it went.

I could guess.

"There's a connection between him and the Mages," I said.

"It was how *Slayers* used to steal our life force, back before we eliminated them," Rafferty said. "That link has to be broken if Quinn's going to survive."

"Burn it!" Liam said. "Tell us where it is, Zoë."

"No," Jared said. "That won't work."

He knew more about spells than the rest of us, and I trusted him.

Rafferty flicked a look at him. "Never worked with dragon-smoke, either."

I put my hand on Garrett's shoulder. My heart stopped cold when I met his gaze. He was terrified, but no more than I was. His dad's survival depended upon his making a repair quickly and correctly.

With fire.

I wasn't sure I could give Garrett the connection he needed, but we had to try.

For Quinn's sake.

"Let's go for it," I said, and he didn't argue.

GARRETT AND I BENT OVER Quinn's body, both in dragon form. The other *Pyr* surrounded us in a circle, and we were beneath an umbrella of brilliant flames. The snow was melting away from the red rock in the heat, but I could watch only Garrett. He fussed over his lack of a forge, and frowned as he examined the wound. He lifted the damaged scales with care, blanching at the dark, festering cut.

I knew it was the worst injury he'd ever seen, and understood that he desperately wanted his dad's advice.

He'd said that Sophie had opened a connection to past Smiths for his dad. Well, she'd just helped us once. Maybe she'd help me again.

"*Sophie*," I murmured in old-speak, the single word sounding like an incantation. I turned the ring on my talon and murmured her name over and over again, a plea for her to listen.

Garrett closed his eyes and mustered his dragonfire. I saw him build it in his chest, coaxing it to burn higher, doing the best he could with what he knew. When his eyes opened, they were blazing, lit by an inner fire. And when the flames erupted from his mouth, they were so vivid a yellow that I couldn't look straight at them.

He bent over his dad, turning his dragonfire on the wound. The silver cord thickened then and seemed to burrow deeper beneath Quinn's skin, as if it understood that he meant to destroy it. Quinn shuddered and gasped and looked even more frail.

"No!" Delaney cried.

Garrett shook, but still he breathed his fire. I could see him fighting for control, wishing for more strength. I could see his knowledge that his power wasn't enough. The wound seemed to boil, some black stuff bubbling out of it.

I spun the ring on my talon, feeling when it took its own momentum. "*Sophie!*" I entreated, then tried old-speak. I felt my tears rise as Quinn shuddered again, as Garrett took a breath, as I feared Sophie had shared all the favors she would.

Or could.

I felt a hand on my shoulder and assumed it was my dad.

In the beginning, there was the fire, I heard Sophie say to me. I knew this passage as well as I knew my name.

I looked up at her, not understanding, and shook my head. This was no time for reciting old verses.

Sophie was beside me, as ethereal and beautiful as ever. I realized that no one else had noticed her—or could see her. She smiled. *The union of the four elements creates a power that can overcome anything.* I looked into her eyes, her enormous pupils defying belief. I saw the guys and thought it was a reflection; then the pieces of the puzzle snapped into place.

"We have to do this together!" I shouted. "Nick, you're earth. And Liam, you're water. I'm air. Garrett is fire. Come on!"

They came and we made a circle around Quinn's fallen form, holding claws so that we made an unbroken ring. As soon as Nick took my left claw and the circle was complete, I felt a shiver run through me. I saw Quinn's body quiver, as well.

"Breathe fire on the wound," I instructed them, running on instinct. "Bring your element to bear." Then I leaned toward Garrett, opening my thoughts to whatever Sophie had to offer.

I felt a dizzying rush in my mind. I was surrounded by stars, or falling snowflakes, something brilliant and glittery that swirled around us. Sophie's claw was light on my back, anchoring me in the onslaught.

I held Garrett's gaze, and I saw him gasp. I saw him nod and swallow back a tear. "*Oui, Grandpère,*" he murmured in old-speak. I'd forgotten that Quinn's family was French. "*Oui. Je comprends maintenant.*" He swallowed. "*Merci mille fois.*"

And when he turned his dragonfire upon Quinn's wound, it burned white and hot and was filled with sparkles. The silvery conduit sizzled, spewing orange sparks, then abruptly snapped. Black venom boiled out of the wound. Quinn's skin lost its pale hue, and the sapphire and steel scales began to regain their proper shape.

I watched in awe, marveling at what he could do.

Lock the portal, Sophie murmured in my thoughts, and I paid attention as she secured that door in my mind. There was my connection to the wisdom of the ages, but I sensed it was something that should be sampled in moderation.

We stood as one, all breathing fire simultaneously, as Quinn grew more substantial again. He was taking power from his son's dragonfire, recovering before our very eyes. His scales bright-ened and shone. I saw his claws flex and there was power in his grip once more. I felt the older *Pyr* draw closer, felt my dad's hand on my shoulder. I couldn't even look at Jared, I was so excited by what he would say.

He couldn't accuse me of not trying, not anymore.

Maybe we could share a celebratory kiss.

When Quinn sighed with relief, I knew it was going to be okay. He rolled over, and we stopped the onslaught of dragonfire.

He shifted shape and smiled crookedly at Garrett, who was still pale and shaking. His gaze was bright and assessing as he surveyed his son.

"Fair enough. We have a new Smith," he said, his voice the low rumble we all knew so well. "His apprenticeship is complete." Quinn stood and hugged Garrett tightly, while all the *Pyr* cheered.

Then I looked for Jared. I had lots of ideas of how we could celebrate—another kiss, or maybe that ride I owed him—but I heard the revving of a motorcycle engine.

Fading into the distance.

Which pretty much said it all.

I am the Wyvern. I'm not some clingy chick. So I wasn't go-ing to hang around pining for some biker rock-star rebel who couldn't even be bothered to say good-bye to me. I had become what I was destined to be—or at least I'd made some big steps in that direction.

I had better things to do than whine.

This was cool. This was a triumph. And if Jared was too proud or stuck-up to enjoy the moment with us, well, that was his loss.

No. I didn't really believe it, either. But it sounded good.

I was hugged by most of the *Pyr*, kissed by a few, had my hand shaken so many times that I thought my arm might fall off. I could feel how proud my dad was, especially when he put his arm across my shoulders and tugged me closer.

"You must be exhausted," he said, while the *Pyr* continued to talk.

"Pretty much. But I have a question."

"Ask away."

"What happened to the last Wyvern, to Sophie and Nikolas?"

My dad looked down at me. "You know their names?"

"I saw their ghosts." I gestured, and I noticed how his gaze locked on the black and white ring. "They helped us. He said that the *Pyr* should never be enchanted again."

"Nikolas was one of Drake's Dragon's Teeth Warriors. They were cursed for thousands of years, until first Nikolas was freed and then the rest." My father frowned. "And Nikolas loved Sophie as soon as he saw her. He adored her."

"Sounds like that was a problem."

"It is forbidden for us to mate with our own kind."

"Mates are always women."

"Human," my father corrected. "And I can only assume that it will be so with you."

"You're not sure?"

"I've never known a Wyvern well, Zoë. They have been elusive creatures in my time."

"Do we even get firestorms?"

He shrugged.

Great. I was getting used to the less-information package. "But what about Sophie and Nikolas?"

"They loved each other. I don't know exactly what happened between them—"

"But you can guess."

My father chose his words with care. "Something happened that persuaded Sophie that they couldn't be together, after all. It wasn't that she didn't care for him."

"You think they did it."

My father inclined his head, too diplomatic to speculate on anyone else's sexual relations. "Whatever happened, I believe she lost her Wyvern powers over her choice."

Wait a minute. . . .

He continued, not waiting at all. "And so she chose the greater good. They destroyed the academy together, dying for a good cause."

But she lost her powers with her virginity. This sounded like a very bad deal to me. Was it because she lost her virginity at all, or because she lost it to the wrong guy? I was pretty interested in the nitpickity details. I was already fond of my powers, such as they were, but not excited by the prospect of lifelong celibacy just to ensure that I kept them.

It seemed unfair to have to choose one option or the other without getting to try both first.

It seemed unreasonable not to know absolutely, for sure, in advance.

Jared, though, was human. Theoretically that shouldn't be an issue. . . .

Have you noticed that there's not a really good way to ask your dad about sex? It would take me a while to formulate *that* question.

My dad and I left the red rock to walk through the prairie that surrounded it. I could hear the snow melting, a little trickle of water coming from all sides, and the snow didn't seem as deep. The sky was perfectly clear above us—it was a brilliant, clear midday blue.

I was thinking about my dream when my vision of Sophie morphed into Isabelle. "Can I ask you something else?"

My dad smiled.

"This is going to sound weird, but do you think people can be reincarnated?"

I thought he would laugh. Instead he turned and looked back

at the group of *Pyr* still on the rock, his expression thoughtful. "Sophie and Nikolas died during my firestorm with your mother."

I knew that was why they'd assumed I was a Wyvern when I'd been born a girl, so I didn't interrupt him.

I was glad I didn't, because his next words surprised me.

"Donovan had a bond with Nikolas, as Nikolas had been freed from enchantment during his firestorm. Alex was pregnant with Donovan's child when Sophie and Nikolas died, and when that son was born, Donovan was struck by how much the boy reminded him of Nikolas." My father met my gaze. "That's why they named him Nick. It wasn't just to honor a lost comrade. Donovan believed that Nick *was* Nikolas reborn."

"But why?"

"A romantic would say that he'd come back to find his Sophie."

I looked at the celebrating group and spotted Isabelle with Nick. *The present is where the future shakes hands with the past.*

And I knew then why she and Sophie had merged into each other in my dream. I knew why Rafferty had ended up adopting a human daughter, and I knew that I had the power to help the former Wyvern win her heart's desire in this life.

And maybe get a good friend in the bargain. I smiled at Isabelle and she smiled back at me.

I still wanted her boots. Just so you know.

"Should we fly home?" My dad bumped my shoulder with his. "Your mom will be worried sick."

I nodded and my dad shifted in a brilliant shimmer of blue, a jubilant shimmer. He was magnificent. Then he gestured to me and I shifted right after him, loving the feel of that change racing through my body. We leapt into the sky together and flew straight toward the sun. There was no one to fight.

Just Dragon Air, under my own speed.

And it was every bit as fabulous as I'd always expected it to be.

Even if I couldn't share it with my human of choice.

FIVE THINGS I WILL TELL MEAGAN ABOUT
MY SPRING BREAK

1. I met an extremely hot guy who is a musician, and I found his band's music online.
2. I've listened to the eleven songs available for download on their site 943 times already.
3. I have in my possession the newest, shiniest, most fabulous messenger ever, even though it doesn't ship to the rest of the world until Christmas. It incidentally has amazing sound and lets me take those eleven songs everywhere I go. I can hear Jared as clearly as if he were singing just for me. He's not and I know it. But still.
4. I stole an insulated pizza carrier to keep our pizza hot, the closest thing to breaking the law I've ever done. I took it back later to make sure the guy didn't get fired over it. My life of crime is officially over.
5. I had my first kiss and it was with an extremely hot guy. Who has a band. And a vintage Ducati motorcycle. And the greenest eyes I've ever seen.

PHOTO BY MICHELE ROWEN

DEBORAH COOKE has always been fascinated by dragons, although she has never understood why they have to be the bad guys. She has an honors degree in history with a focus on medieval studies, and is an avid reader of medieval vernacular literature, fairy tales, and fantasy novels. Since 1992, Deborah has written more than thirty romance novels under the names Claire Cross and Claire Delacroix.

Deborah makes her home in Canada with her husband. When she isn't writing, she can be found knitting, sewing, or hunting for vintage patterns. To learn more about Deborah and her dragon shape shifter's, please visit her Web sites at www.deborahcooke.com and www.thedragondiaries.com. Her blog, Alive & Knitting, is at www.delacroix.net/blog.

Read on for a peak at the next
exciting installment in the
DRAGON DIARIES series by Deborah Cooke,

Winging It

Coming from New American Library in December 2011

*T*he black envelope fell out of my locker when I unlocked the door before lunch. It was three weeks after the eclipse, and I was worn to a frazzle. I wasn't sleeping well, probably because I kept waiting for someone to make a move. For the Mages to embark on their plan. They were far too quiet for me to rest easy.

Everything was too quiet. It spooked me.

I let the envelope fall.

Why would someone shove an envelope into my locker, instead of just talking to me? I couldn't think of one good reason.

I'm not *that* scary.

And if I am, courtesy of my ability to shift into a dragon at will, no one at school knows it. I'm all about managing information these days. Keeper of the Covenant—that's me.

Which doesn't do much for friendships, in case you weren't sure.

The envelope landed right-side up, my name printed on the front in sparkly gold ink. Not a mistake, then. I lifted it with the toe of my boot, still skeptical. It didn't look thick enough to hold a practical joke.

Suspicious—me? You bet. Ever since we'd fought the Mages—and won—I'd been expecting them to take another shot. Treaty or not. Their plan was to eliminate shifters one species at a time by assuming the powers of each kind of shifter as they were moved to the extinction list. We knew that the *Pyr* were in the hot seat, so to speak.

Just because we'd foiled one plan didn't convince me that it was over. Just because we had a treaty didn't persuade me that they would forget the whole thing.

Never mind that Trevor Wilson, the hottest guy in my school, was one of them. He was an apprentice Mage, although I didn't know what their education process was, much less how close he was to graduation. I'd been watching him so carefully this fall that my best friend, Meagan, was convinced that I was sweet on him.

That couldn't be further from the truth.

It also compounded the friendship problem because *she* was sweet on him.

I'd spent all summer in intensive training with my dad, learning to shift more quickly. He'd timed me and pushed me and made me fly laps around the city at night to build my speed. On the upside, I was getting good at the basic dragon drill.

On the downside, there was a chill between my parents, and it was because of me. My mother didn't agree with my dad's decision to train me, and she made her feelings clear. The loft where we lived was about as cozy and homey as a meat locker these days.

Oh, and when I'd finally worked up my nerve to contact the hot motorcycle-riding rebel rocker Jared, he'd sent me only a short reply. Then silence.

Like he was ducking me.

Even after that kiss.

I told myself I didn't care about that, that my only interest in him was that he had the one copy of the only book about the *Pyr* that I knew existed.

Even I knew that was a lie.

And then there was the dynamic between Meagan and me. Not good. She had a best friend's sense of when she wasn't being told the whole story, and she knew something had happened last spring break. More important, she knew that I wasn't telling her about it.

I couldn't, not without breaking the Covenant that my dad, leader of the *Pyr*, made all the dragon shifters swear to.

I picked up the envelope just as Meagan appeared beside me. Her timing was perfect.

Perfectly awful, that is.

"What's that?"

"I don't know."

She tilted her head to look at it. "Then maybe you should open it and find out. It looks like an invitation."

I smiled at the very idea. No one ever invited me to anything. I wasn't a brilliant student like Meagan, although I aced art every year. I was different, though, and people smelled it on me. Meagan had been my only pal since kindergarten. Until now, I'd liked that just fine. Now it just made me feel more alone.

Which reminded me of another issue I wanted to avoid with Meagan. My birthday was coming up in two weeks, my sixteenth, and my dad wanted to invite all of the *Pyr*. That meant my human friends—specifically, my very best friend, Meagan—couldn't be invited, so she couldn't see something that she shouldn't.

Having secrets from Meagan sucked, but I could see no way around it.

I hadn't yet figured out how I'd tell her about the party she wasn't invited to attend.

I ripped open the envelope, avoiding the inevitable.

"It *is* an invitation," Meagan said, reading over my shoulder. "To Trevor Wilson's Halloween party!" She was amazed and impressed. "It's like a dream come true."

Uh, no. In fact, there was a shiver of dread running down my spine. Trevor's party was the last place I'd be on October 31. It had to be a trick or a trap, and I wasn't going to walk right into it—like the heroine in a scary movie, who goes down to the basement by herself to check out the strange noise, despite the creepy organ music.

Funny that I'd been waiting for something to happen and now that it *was* happening, I wanted it to stop.

Meagan poked me with one finger. "You must have known!"

"I didn't."

"Oh, come on. You've been talking to him, haven't you? He doesn't invite just anybody."

"No, I haven't talked to him at all. You're the one who tutors him in math."

Meagan opened her own locker. No envelope fell out.

She rummaged a little, then gave me a look. "I thought we were friends. Forever." Her voice was quiet and I knew she was hurt.

And I'd done the hurting. Inadvertently, but still. "We are."

"So why don't you tell me what's going on?"

"There's nothing going on that you don't know about."

Have I mentioned that I'm the world's worst liar? Well, I am, and Meagan has my number. That's a hazard of having known someone most of your life.

She leaned in really close and said a word I never thought I'd hear cross her lips. "Bullshit."

I blinked.

"Something happened in Minnesota, and you've been holding out on me ever since. You never even told me what you said to scare Suzanne so much. Something's changed. Don't think I don't know it. Don't think it doesn't hurt my feelings that you won't tell me." She took a deep breath, and I saw a shimmer of tears on her lashes. Her next words were in a clipped tone. "If you don't want to be friends anymore, maybe because you suddenly know all kinds of cool people, then at least have the guts to say so."

"That's not true."

Her lips tightened. "Okay, then. Promise me that you've told me everything."

Trust the math queen to have put me in a logical corner. "Well, I haven't and you know it, but that's because I can't, not because I don't want to."

"Why can't you?"

"Because I promised not to tell anyone."

"Promised who?"

I fidgeted. There was no way to make this better. "I can't tell you that."

"Sounds like the same excuse to me." She folded her arms across her chest and leaned against the lockers beside mine. "You think I didn't notice that you haven't mentioned your birthday party?"

I grimaced. "My dad wants me to have a family party."

"For your sixteenth? I don't believe it. Your dad isn't a jerk."

I chose not to argue that. "Well, he's determined this time."

"Your mom would never put up with it. If he wanted you to have a family party, she'd let you have another one with your friends." Meagan was on a roll and it wasn't one that made me look good. "You know what I think? I think you're having a party and you're just not inviting me."

She stared at me, daring me to correct her.

And I couldn't hold her gaze.

Because she was right.

"Nice, Zoë," she said, her tone more bitter than I'd ever heard it. Meagan is not a bitch—that I'd made her sound this way said more about me than about her. "Really nice. Here's hoping that your new friends are more worth keeping than your old ones." She started to walk away.

"But Meagan, it's not like that. . . ."

She paused to look back at me. "You can tell me anytime how it is," she said, her gaze hard. "But I know already that you won't."

I looked down at the stupid invitation, wishing I'd never gotten it. As much as I liked my new *Pyr* powers, it really sucked to have to keep everything secret from my best friend.

"Have fun at Trevor's party," Meagan added. "And don't worry about me. I've got a new friend of my own."

She slung her pack over one shoulder and marched down the hall, and I knew I couldn't change her mind. I watched as she stopped beside the locker of the new girl, the one who had moved to our school this year.

The one I really didn't like, although I couldn't have said why.

Jessica has dark hair and dark eyes. She's slim and pretty and quiet. She's another math whiz, so she and Meagan bonded in the land where calculating derivatives is as easy as pie. (Or pi, maybe. As in recalling the first hundred digits of. So not my territory. Never mind citizenship; I don't even have a visitor's visa to that place.) The thing is, I should have liked Jessica; there was no reason I shouldn't.

But she gave me the creeps.

Big-time.

I always felt like she was hiding something. It wasn't just that she wore really baggy clothes—like she'd raided her brother's closet—or even that she kept a baseball hat jammed over her head all the time.

She smiled at Meagan and hugged her, then over Meagan's

shoulder smiled at me. There was something hungry about that smile, something completely untrustworthy.

Like she had a big secret. As someone who has a pretty hefty secret herself, I think I know something about it.

That smile sent a shudder right down my spine.

And gave me the worst feeling I've ever had in my life.

Then it was gone. As if I had imagined it.

Was Meagan in danger? Or was I just seeing things that weren't there because I was lonely and jealous? It didn't much matter either way—Meagan wasn't going to listen to any advice I might give her.

I kicked my locker shut, jammed the invitation into my pack, and headed home.

Alone.

I had no idea how to fix this, and no one to ask.

An older sibling, even one who found me annoying and tedious, could have been helpful.

It was almost my sixteenth birthday and there were three things I wanted:

1. A grudge match against Kohana, the Thunderbird shifter who'd lied to me, and worked with the Mages to nearly wipe me and the dragons off the map.
2. A tattoo.
3. A chance to see Jared again, if only to find out that I was never going to see him again.

Of the above, I had only a remote chance of achieving number three. Even with it being my birthday. I knew what my dad thought about me risking my health in a fight, and I knew what my mom thought of tattoos. But they both knew Jared, and they knew I knew him. And his band was playing a concert in town, on a Saturday (thus not a school night), at a co-op club downtown that didn't serve alcohol.

The way I saw it, Jared had chosen the venue because he *expected* me to come.

Or he was daring me.

He's like that. Irreverent. Daring.

Hot.

Whether it was to deliver the flight on Dragon Air I owed him, to snag another kiss—just to verify that the first one had, in fact, been amazing—or to barter for another peek at the book he had on my kind, didn't really matter.

I wanted to go.

All I needed to do was persuade my mom that going was a good idea. And do it without beguiling her.

Uh-huh.

And no, even being irritated with my dad didn't make me think that sneaking out of the loft to go to the concert without approval would end well for yours truly.

Even to see Jared.

My dad would never go for it. I *had* to convince my mom.

And I was running out of time.